FORGIVE ME, SISTER

PATRICK HAMILTON WALSH

Patrick's disclaimer

Please don't do anything silly that would harm you or others. It would make us
both less happy. Consult someone with lots of letters after their name, such as a
lawyer, doctor or even a common-sense specialist before taking any ideas from this
story. Enjoy the book, but most of all, be cool, respect others and play nice.

Trafford rev. 05/31/2019

 www.trafford.com

North America & international
toll-free: 1 888 232 4444 (USA & Canada)
fax: 812 355 4082

Such power.
Visible to the heart.
Its essence. That colour.
She can make it happen.
Knowing in her core, is all.
She is of this world,
… not from it.
Without thinking, she feels.
It is there.
Re-remembering.

Thanks, Go raibh maith agat, Bedankt,
Danke, Благодаря ти, Merci, Tack

Therese Clarke
Eva Cremers
Daniel Dotterer
Greg Downey
Mary Hamilton
Dominic Hoben
Atma Gian Kaur
Emma Kearney
Esther Liet
Maria Modig
Ida Norrby
Julia Oehler
Elaina O'Shea
Stewart Pearce
Luke Richmond
Irene Rompa
Jullietta Stoencheva
Camille Tuutti
Catherine Walsh
Tracey Walsh
Johanna Walsh

My friends and family

… and the women of Ireland.

Without you, this book would not be possible. I truly
appreciate your insight, patience, wisdom and love.

Patrick Hamilton Walsh
Co-Creator

Contents

I

Boys Will Be Boys

Thirty-Nine Seconds

"*Is she pissing herself? Look, bru, she's pissing herself.*"

The snarl came from a soldier with a strong South African accent. He was a white Afrikaner, who joined the army after release from juvenile prison. As a teenager, he witnessed his mother being raped and murdered on the front porch of their farm. He watched the events unfold hiding in an adjoining outhouse. As the gang left his house, he shot one dead. He went to prison for his crime as the ransackers went free. It made him bitter.

"*She is, bru. Bitch's causing a mess,*" responded another soldier, kicking the bars of her cage in disgust.

He was a "Coloured" struggling to find a place within the new South Africa following the fall of the rigid hierarchy of apartheid.

Neither black nor white, South Africa's Coloureds derived from intermarriages between white settlers, African natives and Asian slaves brought from the Dutch colonies. Caught in the political battle between the newly powerful "Blacks" under the ruling ANC party and the "Whites" fighting to maintain their way of life, the Coloureds increasingly faced discrimination.

"Zap her again, bru. Turn it right up. Give her a good blasting. She must learn she can't just come in here and mess the place up."

The Coloured soldier, who had his combat fatigues around his ankles, reached down and pulled a Taser out from the holster on his belt. He stepped back from the cage containing the girl and fired the military-grade weapon at her.

Cramped into a cage, the prongs pierced through the skin of her naked body. One embedded into her neck with the other dug into her upper thigh.

As 60,000 volts of electricity passed through her body, she went rigid, her muscles cramped. Ten seconds had passed.

The girl was silent. Her eyes rolled back in her head. She burned and contracted. She suffocated, all simultaneously.

The drunken soldier kept his finger on the trigger as the other watched with a smirk. Twenty seconds had passed.

Her muscles tore as the electricity burned through her skin. She was pushed up against the bars of her cage as her body convulsed. Thirty seconds had passed.

Finally, the soldier released the trigger. Her body immediately turned to jelly as she slouched onto the urine and semen-covered floor of the cage. Thirty-nine seconds had passed.

Without hesitation, the Afrikaans soldier, still smirking, said:

"Where are the towels? I'm taking her from behind this time."

"You get the towels, I will get the beers," responded the Coloured soldier.

They both shuffled out of the small storage room pulling up their combat fatigues as they went.

A few minutes later, the Coloured soldier returned to the room with a bucket of beer. The Afrikaans soldier was already there. He had laid the towels on the ground and reached into the cage. He slapped the woman on the cheek.

"What's up, bru?" the Coloured soldier asked, gently placing the beers on a chair.

"No response. Seems she couldn't handle a little zapping. Think she's gone, bru," responded the Afrikaner.

"*She's gone? You kidding me? That's shit, bru. The boys won't be happy,*" said the Coloured soldier, hunkering down as he ripped open the girl's eyelids, searching for a sign of life.

Pushing the girl's eyelids closed, the Afrikaner turned around and sat back on the ground.

Reaching for a beer from the chair, he paused for a moment. Shaking his head, he looked up and said:

"*They won't be happy at all. Turn off the camera, bru. You just broke our only entertainment. You're gonna have to go out and get us another one.*"

Cure for Cancer

Almost three years later, deep in the Amazon rainforest, a new group of men had settled into the camp. The soldiers left the area believing they had wiped out the native tribe. Just following orders.

"Is the electricity gonna be reconnected tonight?" Mickey spat over the radio as he cut down another tree.

The tree was just one of hundreds they would cut and process that day. He did not realise the trees were the last of their kind. Neither was he aware their sap contained a cancer-curing compound.

"The engineers are working on it all day. My laptop is drained. Everyone's phone is dead," responded another logger over the crackling radio.

"I'm sick of those filthy savages. Especially the women. They are the ringleaders of this whole thing. Running around here half naked, throwing things and cutting our cables. They should be in one of those cages," Mickey ranted to no one in particular.

The "savages" he referred to were the remaining members of the Myayama tribe, native people of the Amazon rainforest.

Once numbering approximately 36,900, the matriarchal tribe had been virtually wiped out because of the continued encroachment onto their lands by loggers and ranchers.

For 120 years, almost all their land had been gradually pilfered from them to meet the increasing expansion of cattle ranches. Now only numbering a few dozen, the tribe's female warriors regularly battled with the invaders.

Like all indigenous peoples, the Myayama tribe cultivated detailed knowledge of the plants and animals and had a deep spiritual connection to the land. They derived their knowledge by elevating to the spirit world where they would connect with their ancestors and the spirits of the forest.

To acquire knowledge, the Shaman would drink ayahuasca, a brew made from the caapi vine, and journey to the home of the spirits to receive insight during ceremonial sessions.

The Myayama elders claimed the area was precious and needed protection as it contained plant life that held cures to all the world's illnesses, including cancer.

The tribe had been fighting Western companies who came in to clear the trees for animal agriculture. The logging in that area was primarily done for cattle ranching, to meet the growing demand for beef burgers in fast food restaurants around the world.

Three years prior to the loggers entering that area, representatives and scientists from Vertunia, the world's biggest drug company, came to meet the tribe and ask for the cures the rainforest held.

The tribe had known about their arrival in advance. The Shaman leader of the tribe had foreseen this during an ayahuasca ceremony.

Mother Ayahuasca had informed the Shaman during a ceremonial session the world was in a state of disease. It was time to share the secrets of the rainforest with the Western world.

The sickness that had spread from the mind of Western men was now affecting the entire planet, including Mother Earth herself. Humanity needed access to the cures.

When the scientists arrived, they were warmly welcomed by the tribe and invited into its settlement. The tribe graciously shared the healing properties of the various plants, vines and roots that thrived throughout the rainforest.

The scientists brought the latest technology. Using their mobile laboratories, they quickly proved the plants and roots of the area possessed properties that could, in fact, cure cancer.

Test after test, the scientists obtained results confirming what the female Shaman had told them about the healing properties of the plants. For each confirmation, the Vertunia representatives clapped and cheered.

The tribe gave the scientists plants and roots to take back and grow in a simulated environment. The understanding was they would be used to eliminate disease and suffering worldwide.

When the scientists left the rainforest with all the required samples, the tribe rejoiced. It held a celebration in honour of Mother Ayahuasca for allowing the tribe to be the carriers of knowledge that would ease the suffering of millions of people.

The tribe also celebrated the assurances it received from the Vertunia representatives the area would now be protected. These assurances came in the form of a verbal agreement the shaman made before providing the samples.

However, within weeks the tribe learned in the most violent of ways this was not the case. The Shaman had foreseen a great fire in her vision, but not knowing about modern military capabilities, she had interpreted it to mean a great celebration.

At the stroke of midnight, as the Myayama tribe slept, soldiers entered the area to eliminate the tribe members. They were not government soldiers, but private military sent in from South Africa, with a reputation for brutality.

First, they came in with helicopters and firebombed the area. Using heat-sensing technology, they pinpointed the settlement and dropped firebombs on the sleeping tribe.

Screams filled the air as the skin of the tribal members burned. The soldiers then swept the area in formation, shooting everything that moved.

All men they encountered were shot dead on sight. The soldiers captured six female members of the Myayama tribe and kept them as "*spoils of war.*" They considered the girls to be "*jungle bunnies*"—animals. Less than human.

The soldiers were ordered to remain stationed at the site for weeks after the attack to ensure the area was secured. For entertainment, they recorded themselves raping the girls of the tribe—the videos were widely available online.

The girls were kept in cages and brought out when a soldier needed *"some release."* Within days, the men had broken the girls' spirit in the most inhuman manner. Through burning and being tasered, the soldiers had trained the girls to perform sex acts through the bars of the cage, to the soldiers' laughter and applause.

The loggers who later came to the area to clear the precious trees had downloaded the videos shared online by the soldiers. Mickey and the other loggers watched these videos on a nightly basis as the foreman provided a running commentary whilst the others drunkenly cheered along.

Eye Smile

In that immeasurable moment when two souls fall in love, a cosmic explosion takes place. They are given the opportunity to simultaneously look through the lens of the other's eyes and into the depths of the universe.

There, they find their cosmic self. They see birth and they see death. They understand we come from the darkness and we return to the darkness. From dust to dust.

There is a realisation life is merely a flicker of light in the timelessness of emotion.

Our time experiencing this planet is the apocryphal match flaring all too briefly in a sandwich of eternal darkness. In that hole, beauty is whole. It is all-encompassing. Love is everywhere. It is everything. It is all there is, and all that we need.

To love in life is to simply take another by the hand and go home together, to the darkness. Love is life. Love is death. What bigger privilege is there than to hold our lover's hand and walk her or him home?

Richard's pondering mind was brought crashing back to the physical reality of chopping carrots, as a crackling interrupted his train of thought:

"Hey, Poofter. Poofter? Can you hear me? Tonight, you had better have some of that sauce ready. You know the one?" A voice shouted across the crackling radio. *"This shift ends in exactly twenty-seven minutes and it better be ready when I get there!"*

He was shouting at Richard. There was no answer.

As well as being the on-site EMT first responder, Richard's job was in the kitchen. He helped with the provision of food and the clean up after each sitting. That usually meant going beyond the confines of the dining hall in search of plates, glasses and cutlery, which the loggers spread around the living quarters without consideration.

Richard often listened to audiobooks as he prepared the food in the kitchen. His mind swept away on a line or phrase sparking his imagination.

He was connected to the loggers by radio, but he usually turned it down to almost mute. He did not want to listen to the relentless misogynistic conversations.

Whilst working, the loggers openly discussed details of the women they had sex with and the sports or porn they had watched the previous night. Usually, their conversations did not get much deeper than that.

During his shift, when he was not listening to audiobooks, Richard tuned into a very specific selection of music. He believed music and personality should not mix. He liked to listen to music new *to him* without receiving it through the filter of the musician's personal life.

Thus, every few months, he would have a friend load ninety-nine new songs on to his MP3 player. He would choose a different friend each time, with the only rule being he could not be told the artists name. He would then plug into the selection and listen to music for music's sake.

The music would often be a selection of tunes from around the world, spanning many decades. It was unusual his friends would include anything from modern popular artists.

Richard could express himself best when consumed by music or silence.

Light informs, sound transforms.

He avoided all social media whilst in the rainforest. He enjoyed being completely disconnected from the outside world for those few weeks. The only exception Richard made was on the twelfth evening of his twenty-one days stint on site, when he quickly checked in with Anne via video chat.

They had been seeing each other on and off for nine months. At first, they were just friends with benefits.

As time progressed, it developed into more than *"just sex"* as both began showing increased commitment and contact.

Anne had become more devoted to Richard and was now in a position where she was not sleeping with anyone else. Despite this, she still casually chatted with various people via dating applications. He knew this, but was happy to maintain an unofficial open relationship. He had always been very comfortable with girls and slept around until he met Anne.

The fact that Richard worked in the rainforest for three weeks at a time suited Anne. She was in the final stages of her master's degree and worked hard to ensure its completion.

He was happy to give her space, as he really liked her and knew she would change once she was done.

The stresses and strains would be removed and the energy focused on writing a paper no one, apart from her lecturer, would ever read, would then be set free. Her energy would search for a new way in which to expend itself.

Because of her studies and his being in the rainforest, they did not have much to talk about during the calls. They usually just spent thirty minutes looking at each other on the screen and laughing at the various face filters that distorted their features in quirky ways.

Their screen time was something a casual observer would consider weird, but it was enlightening for both as it brought many belly laughs. It was very much needed.

He was fond of Anne. He was soft towards her—more so than with any other girl. She was the strong, silent type. She let her actions speak louder than her words, operating from a heart level, not from the mind. Words were precious to her. As a result, when she did speak, it meant more. People listened and followed her.

Anne more than accounted for her sparse use of words, with what she showed in her actions towards those close to her. She loved to cook for her friends as a way of unwinding from her studies. When together, she would use Richard as a testing ground for new dishes, as he was open to eating anything vegan. When he was gone, she was regularly looking for new music to send him.

In return, Richard was very attentive towards Anne, when they were together. He would fix the blanket on her as she slept. He would put the toothpaste on her toothbrush in the morning.

They smiled with unadulterated happiness as they walked down the street holding hands.

One big turnoff for Richard was girls who had their "personal PR routine" down to a fine art—self-promotion experts. When they talked, it appeared as if they ticked every box on the *"have-it-all"* list. They had all the qualifications and were great at their job. They were experts in Bikram yoga or whatever the newest fad was. They were always involved in the latest "save the world" project popular on social media.

They had it all. They were it all. They said it all. They really made sure everyone knew about it all. He knew too many girls like that, and generally, when he scratched below the surface, oftentimes, their feet could not keep up with their mouth.

What was attractive to Richard was a girl with a smile. A real smile. One that came from the heart showed in the eyes and lit up her face. Such a smile could light up the room, and his world.

He wanted a girl who was happy with whom she was. Anne had that— it was magnetic to him. Dress size, bank account, qualification, job title, follower count—none of that mattered to Richard.

The Straight Poofter

Richard was known on the site as *"Poofter," "Bitch," "Faggot"* and every other derogatory and homophobic term the loggers thought of. These nicknames derived, bizarrely, from his choice to journal and listen to music or audiobooks in the evenings when the others watched sports or porn and drank beer.

Only one person on the site called Richard by his name: Mickey, his father.

Mickey was one of the most senior guys on site and one of the most vulgar. He was the reason why Richard had gotten the job in the rainforest.

Mickey's wife, Angel, had died of cancer, leaving him with a set of twins.

The twins, Richard and his sister Kate, were twelve when their mother died. Mickey was left to bring them up on his own, as they did not have much of a support network.

Growing up in a warm and loving home, Richard and Kate had been sheltered from poverty by their mother. Their father provided for all the family needs, but not their wants. They did not have a lot, but they had enough. In their neighbourhood everyone was poor, so no one felt poor. They were all on the same level in that neighbourhood. It brought a sense of parity.

Standing by the graveside as his mother was buried, Richard lost some of his innocence. As those around him wept, he stared into the grave as the clay dropped on his mother's coffin.

He had watched as his mother got increasingly weaker by the day. Despite this, he never understood the finality of death until they arrived home the evening following the funeral. As the front door closed behind Mickey with a thud, their once warm home now felt like a house: wood, concrete and mortar. A roof held up by walls. With *stuff* inside.

When their mother died, the twins lost their safety blanket. They became more exposed to the world. The luxury of staying home with their mum was gone as they were required to travel across town with their father as he attended meetings. This exposed them to wealthier neighbourhoods and the realisation they were impoverished.

In their mixed suburb of Washington, D.C. gun crime increasingly became an issue. With their mother gone, the gunshots seemed closer and louder. The police were confronted with aggression. Drug dealing was the only means of income for some people as the rot set deeper into the neighbourhood by the year.

Following Angel's death, Richard was determined to become a doctor. He would say he *"didn't want anyone else's mum to die."* However, with a sense of exposure, obtaining safety for his twin sister was a long-term goal. It is what fuelled him.

He never really grieved or talked about the impact his mother's death had on him. He buried it deep inside and used school as his crutch. He focused on his homework. His mother had always valued their performance in exams, and he wanted to make her proud.

As he began high school, he studied hard and excelled in sports. He got into medical school and, taking everything in his stride, he achieved his qualification in medicine, coming second in the year, overall.

However, during his medical placements, he learned the Western medical establishment focused more on treating the symptoms than eliminating the cause of sickness and disease. He became dissatisfied and frustrated with the politics and corruption within medicine.

In addition, he was exasperated by the insecure, substance dependant doctors with the big egos and a thirst for power.

Twelve months after qualifying, whilst working as a general practitioner in a disadvantaged area, he quit his position and went backpacking. He needed a break from the frustration and the restrictions. He planned to take one year out. Everyone told him he was crazy, that he was jeopardising his career, throwing it all away.

To pacify them, he expressed his desire to work with tribal communities during his travels before committing to a speciality upon his return.

He was true to his word. As he travelled, he worked with people in villages across Africa and South America. But he soon realised the tribal people were generally healthier than those in the so-called wealthy nations. Both in body and mind.

It was this freeing of his own mind whilst travelling that helped him decide he would not return to the rigid, corrupt and uncaring profession of Western medicine.

Now, he knew what he *did not* want to do, he had to find out what he *did* want to do. So, he continued to travel and do odd jobs until his father recommended to him the dual role as EMT first responder and cook in the rainforest.

"There are two main reasons why people change significantly. Either their hearts have been broken or their minds have been opened," Mickey would say. When not vulgar, he had an enlightened mind.

The latter had contributed to Richard's change. The reason for Mickey's significant change was obviously the former. It was not a positive change.

He believed Richard had grown soft following the heartbreak of his mother's death: he spent a lot of time in the company of females, including his twin sister and her friends. Mickey had hoped that bringing Richard into the rainforest, surrounded by *"real men,"* would toughen him up.

It did not have the desired effect. The experience pushed Richard further away from his father as he witnessed first-hand Mickey's behaviour and his general attitude towards women.

Richard's motivation for accepting the job was he planned to backpack around the world for a year with Anne when she graduated. The money in the rainforest was exceptionally good considering the low skill set required.

In fact, his earnings were better than what he received as a doctor in general practice. Thus, the money made him less reluctant in accepting a twelve-month contract with the logging company.

The company would fly them on and off the site where they had twenty-one days on and nine days off. Being surrounded by people he viewed as sexist homophobes was not easy, but it gave him a chance to listen to audiobooks, journal and research his future backpacking locations.

Early in the mornings before starting work, Richard went into the trees to bathe in the silence. He often watched as the tribeswomen worked in teams to mend the smaller, more flexible trees damaged by the machinery, but not cut down.

He was fascinated by the care they put into re-harmonising the environment.

To rebalance a damaged tree, they had a very specific technique of bending it the opposite way beyond its normal upstanding position. Then, using entwined vines, they tied it into place, in the overexaggerated position.

When they untied the tree a week or so later, it would then spring back up into its original upstanding position, as it was before the damage. The tree forced out of alignment was now perfectly balanced again and could grow in a more harmonious manner.

The tribeswomen were completely aware of Richard's proximity, as he watched them with a soft gaze. They never once threatened attack or showed displeasure at his presence. They were conscious he was sympathetic to their plight.

Away from the forest, Richard was a popular guy. Men and women respected him because of his open mind and common-sense approach to life. As well as spending a lot of time with his female friends, he was also a fanatical football fan, which kept him connected to a large array of male friends.

Richard was paradoxical in how he lived. He liked people, but he valued his alone time. He loved to go out, dance and party, but he also liked to disappear for a while to recharge and replenish. Working in the rainforest allowed him ample alone time.

When his grandmother was alive, she used to say he had two big strengths that made him different from most people.

Firstly, she would compliment him on being *"a good listener."* He would listen to absorb what he was being told, as opposed to listening for his turn to talk. Following careful consideration, he would then respond with a balanced contribution to the conversation. His strong opinions were loosely held.

Secondly, she used to say he *"was energetically well balanced."* He had as much femininity as he did masculinity. Around the age of nine, his mother's friend, who was an empath, told him his *"soul was half boy and half girl."*

Despite her simplifying it, Richard had no idea what she was talking about at the time. Regardless of his ignorance on this matter, the result was females felt understood by him and they were comfortable in his presence.

However, following puberty and entering adulthood, this was a problem for those who were hypermasculine. They did not understand how a straight man could be so in touch with his femininity. They were suspicious of him. Their usual conclusion was that he was gay. They needed to attach a label to him. Thus, pigeonholing him as being homosexual was an all-too-common and lazy label to place on Richard.

Despite this small-minded minority acting in this way, men generally respected him. When Richard walked into a room, he was confident. Not in a way where he felt he was better than anyone else, but in a way where he did not need to compare himself to others. He was just comfortable in his skin. He was comfortable with the man he was and did not feel a need to explain or complain.

In a way, he never got involved in the subtle and silent battle on the spectrum of the male dominance hierarchy. As opposed to being an alpha or beta male, he was simply an observer.

Although overly macho men were suspicious of him initially, they respected him once they understood he was not vying for dominance and was not a threat to their fragile hierarchical position.

The loggers, individually or collectively, did not put in effort to spend any time with Richard, so they never gained an understanding of him. They maintained a groupthink mentality. It did not help Richard that his father had kept a distance from him since his arrival. His fathers' public behaviour towards Richard led the loggers to believe it was acceptable to treat him disrespectfully.

Mickey thought this extreme approach would eventually spark a reaction from Richard. He thought wrong.

Painful Jokes

During dinner, the electricity cables were reconnected and the lights came on to cheers. As the Wi-Fi was connected, the loggers lifted their plates and ran to their quarters to charge their electronic devices.

After dinner, the loggers sat around drinking beer. Some played cards and others scrolled through their phones and tablets.

The large television, when no live sports were available, streamed porn. Letting it autoplay from one video to the next, the loggers showed little consideration to what came on next.

Richard walked around the social room collecting the dinner dishes.

When gathering cups and plates from around the logger's feet, he noticed a familiar voice coming from the TV, above Stig's commentary.

He paused. The TV was directly behind him.

He turned around and saw his friend Emma on the screen. Pure coincidence. She faced the camera and grimaced as a man attempted to insert his penis in to her anus. She appealed for him not to.

Richard froze. He stared at the screen for a few seconds to ensure he was not mistaken. The footage was from a few years ago, when she was about twenty-one years old, but it was definitely Emma.

"Just let me try it," the man said. *"Relax. You will love it, baby."* Her face contorted with pain.

Richard remembered the guy as her first boyfriend she met at college and was suspicious of him from the beginning. The guy had spent months chasing her and asking her out. Emma was not interested initially, but he was relentless, trying every cheesy trick in the book, until she conceded.

What Richard did not know was that from their first date the guy was pressuring Emma to have sex. He was determined to take her virginity after learning from a mutual acquaintance she was sexually inexperienced.

They dated for five months in total. After three months, she had sex with him for the first time—he recorded it on his phone despite her pleading for him not to.

Within two months of taking her virginity, he had anal sex with her for the first time. He also recorded that. The next day he dumped her. He simply changed his relationship status to *single* on Facebook, without ever contacting her again. He also blocked her from all his social media. She had not been in a relationship since.

The guy sold the videos of Emma to a website specialised in "revenge porn." These websites had grown exponentially because of the increasing global demand for sexually explicit content that did not have consent from one or both subjects.

The loggers had become so desensitised by porn, they generally watched it more for entertainment than arousal. Stig considered himself a funny guy and despite being the senior foreman on the site, was usually at the centre of the jokes and horseplay.

On this occasion, he thought it would be hilarious to run sports commentary over the video of Emma with her boyfriend.

"He comes around the back. He goes in for the tackle. Ohh, what a manoeuvre from her, as she swerves him. He hasn't given in. With a look of

determination on his face, he goes after her again." Stig continued in this vein, as they watched this most delicate of footage unfold.

Richard stood frozen behind them, his mind raced, trying to grasp what was unfolding. It was surreal.

"With a swivel of his hips, he cuts past her defence. Now one-on-one with the last defender. Oohhh, my Lord, did you see that? He pushed the ball between her legs and now he is in on goal." Stig, thinking he was hilarious, went on with the commentary.

"He looks up ... he lines up his shot.

He shoots ... aaaaaaand ... he scooores."

With the loggers cheering and laughing with Stig as the guy finally squeezed his penis into Emma's anus, a rage swept over Richard.

He stomped to the screen, barging past Stig, and ripped the power cord out of the wall. The TV screen went black.

Instantly, the men stood up and confronted Richard.

"Who the hell do you think you are, bitch?" growled one of the men.

"I thought that would be your thing? Faggot," sneered another.

Stig stared directly at Richard but did not say a word.

He calmly walked over to him.

Despite the others abusing him from his left side, Richard's full attention was on Stig, as he edged closer.

Stig, being the smaller man, came right over to Richard and looked up into his eyes. Richard gulped.

Just as Richard was about to explain that Emma was a close friend, Stig, with all his force, punched him in the stomach.

He had always disliked Richard. He thought he was an embarrassment to his friend Mickey, whom he had worked with for many years.

Crumpled over and searching for a breath, Richard dropped to his knees.

"Boys, it's long overdue that we did Mickey a favour and toughened up his faggot son," Stig said.

The others yelled in agreement.

With that, he then kneed Richard in the face, with all his power, knocking him back against the television stand.

As Stig was the senior foreman on the site, the junior men did not hesitate for a second. They began attacking Richard with their fists and boots. He was on the ground in the foetal position, arms up over his head as he attempted to cover his face.

As he squirmed on the floor in defence, kicks and punches from the mob rained down on him.

The last thing Richard remembered of the beating was a big dirty boot coming between his arms and connecting with his nose. He blacked out after that.

In the early hours of the morning, Richard came around.

He quickly realised he was in the first aid tent. He was alone.

On the bed beside him was a folder with an accident report form and a pen. It had few words on it. He read the words aloud, slurring through his swollen lips:

"I was drunk on the job and I slipped in the kitchen. I take full responsibility for my injuries."

His nose was broken, two side teeth missing, and his right arm had a hairline fracture. There was bruising all over his body.

Someone had placed an 'X' beside where he should sign.

Under the accident report form was a discharge sheet. His contract had been terminated.

The termination hurt more than the beating. He really needed this job. Backpacking and travelling were his passion. He thrived on meeting new people, hearing their story and learning about their environment. It was the thought of backpacking that motivated him to keep going whilst working on site.

Richard was disappointed it had ended like this. It made him sick to his stomach, but he had to do the right thing for Emma. The footage was upsetting. He could not stand back and allow these men to treat his friend like that.

He dropped the folder on the floor and allowed his head to crash back onto the over-used flat pillow. Looking to the roof of the tent, he let out a sigh and muttered, *"This is perfect."*

A few hours later, as the sun rose over the trees, Mickey entered the first aid tent. He stood there for a moment staring at his son. Shaking his head.

He then reached over, grabbed a multi-coloured rosary from the metal lamp above Richard's head and placed it in the back pocket of his cargo shorts. Mickey always carried it with him or wore it around his neck. Richard had not noticed it hanging there, but he recognised it as his mother's.

"Come on, our lift is here." Cold and detached, he tossed Richard's work boots towards the flimsy camp bed where Richard lay. He never checked to see how his son was feeling.

As their transport crept along the track, Richard wondered why his father was travelling with him.

Whilst arranging for Anne to pick him up from the airport, Richard contemplated whether his dad was finally showing some compassion, ensuring his son got to the landing strip without issue, considering his fragile condition.

However, he soon understood Mickey was also being sent home.

Friend of a Friend

Mickey had walked in as the loggers watched the remainder of Emma's video. He saw his son lying unconscious and bloodied in front of the TV with empty cans and cigarette butts on him. In a rage, he started swinging his fists at whoever was close. He grabbed John and started head-butting him repeatedly.

John, the smallest man on the site, was outside streaming a call from his girlfriend when they beat Richard. He walked in when he heard the commotion but was not involved in the attack in any way.

Despite this, both Mickey and John were suspended for a week and ordered to fly back to the city with Richard.

Mickey and John sat tightly together as the little twelve-seat propeller airplane lifted from the dirt track landing strip, deep in the rainforest. The two men were already halfway through a large bottle of Irish whiskey the company had provided, almost apologetically, for suspending them.

"Another tour done and we still haven't captured one of those tribal bitches for the cage," Mickey laughed, as he half-filled John's plastic cup with another whiskey.

"That will be a laugh when it happens. Can you imagine?" John responded, trailing off in his imagination.

Mickey looked across at Richard to ensure he was not eavesdropping.

John then declared:

"You do know that we can do that in downtown D.C., right? There are girls there who love being locked in cages. There's one place I have been. It's a basement where this guy keeps girls in cages. It's invite-only, but once you get there, it's actually quite reasonable. You can do whatever you want with the girls and just pay by the hour. They don't speak English; I don't know where they are from. Probably Eastern Europe or some shit like that. It's a Russian friend of mine who does the door, so I can get you in if you want?"

"Yeah, sounds like fun. Get me an invite. Who is the guy that runs it?" Mickey asked, lowering his voice.

"It's a friend of a friend," John said. *"He and his wife are doctors and they keep the girls in the basement below their practice. Patients come and go through the front door all day long not realising what goes on downstairs. It's awesome, man. Can get quite busy though, so we must book ahead. Many bigwigs visit the place. Politicians. Loads of politicians. Even seen a female politician in there."*

"Female politicians?" Mickey queried in a high-pitched tone.

"Absolutely," John said. *"One very prominent. If I told you her name, you'd be shocked. One time I was sitting at home watching TV and she was on there preaching for women's rights, equality and all that other shit. Then later that evening, I walk into the basement and there she is with a big purple strap-on, getting stuck in. Sweat dripping down her chin, she is calling this tiny girl every name under the sun."*

Mickey burst into laughter at the thought of what John was saying.

"I know. I know, man. She was a complete animal. You couldn't make this shit up," John said.

"Well, those politicians are well used to screwing the helpless," Mickey added, with a nod.

As John continued to paint a mental picture of the goings-on under the prestigious medical practice, Mickey listened intently trying to limit his response, as he knew Richard was within earshot.

"I bet the girls are just happy to have escaped their shithole country. They don't mind being kept in cages. It is better than what they had back home," Mickey contributed, attempting to play down what he was hearing, whilst trying to justify it to himself.

Richard was lost deep in an audiobook, with his headphones plugged in. He was in so much pain from the beating he was trying to zone out from the turbulent ride on the small plane.

Despite his bravado, the reality was John had not been to the cellar in eighteen months. He was actively working on his sex addiction, as he was deeply in love with his girl and wanted to become a better man for her. He wanted to heal.

John could go with his friends to strip clubs, but he had stopped visiting prostitutes and watching porn. It was the real reason why he was "coincidently" out of the room on a call when the men were watching the porn, the previous night.

He was the oldest of six children to Irish immigrant parents. At twelve years old, his mother sent the kids to stay with her best friend as she went to the hospital to have her youngest child. Whilst there, John was raped by his mother's friend after she insisted on separating John from his siblings and putting him up in her own bedroom.

Although not blood related, he considered her an aunt. It was the first of many rapes he suffered over a three-year period. It had really messed him up, sexually.

"Sorry for the attack, bro," Mickey said to John during a pause in the conversation about girls in cages. *"A rage went through me when I saw my boy like that. I know you weren't the instigator, so I apologise."*

"Aww, no worries, bro. You can buy me a beer in the club tomorrow night," John said.

"I'll even get you a lap dance, bro. With that little Asian slut you like. How about that?" Mickey offered.

"Deal," John reluctantly accepted with a fake smile, extending his hand to Mickey, avoiding eye contact.

"What about that girl who was sending you the nudes during the year? Have you dumped her now?" Mickey asked.

"Nah, I haven't dumped her, Mickey. She has really been putting on the pressure the past few months. She wants to have a baby," John said. Again, all bravado. In truth, he was slightly offended at Mickey's question, as he really liked the girl.

"Is she actually that stupid, bro? You need a new broad, man," Mickey spluttered in a burst of laughter.

Wiping his chin, gaining composure and lowering his voice, he continued:

"Forget it, bro. Having a kid sucks. I had twins and it was relentless. I had to give up my life. I would never wish that on anyone. Anyway, there is no rush. That girl is only about twenty-eight. She has loads of time. Make the most out of that body while you still can, because once she has kids, it'll all go south and you won't want to touch her again."

Unbeknown to Mickey, the lady was John's girlfriend of two years and had recently celebrated her thirty-sixth birthday. Despite this, John thought it was acceptable to share with his co-workers the intimate photographs she sent him. He did it to gain attention from the boys and feel part of the gang for a few minutes.

His girlfriend was indeed encouraging John to have a baby. It had always been her dream to be a mother and start a family. It was only now, after coming through a tough few years that she was rediscovering her self-confidence and felt ready for children.

She had worked hard in finance until age thirty-one—putting in countless hours to prove herself to her male peers. Eventually, she burnt out and had a nervous breakdown—she pushed it too hard.

It was during her recovery, whilst working part-time in a coffee shop visited by labourers, that she met John. He came in for lunch and she agreed to go on a date, after he complimented her breasts. It was the first time anyone had noticed her since the breakdown. A tall, blonde, pretty girl, from a good family, she was highly educated and well spoken. But she lost her sparkle with the breakdown.

John was not a man she would ever consider going out with before the breakdown. Now, she was just happy with the company and fell into a routine with him. He was not around that often, as he was in the rainforest on contract, *"logging the shit out of that place,"* as he described it.

"Nah, she is a great girl. She seems to know something about everything and always teaches me new things. She's so smart, man. And great to be around," John said, becoming protective.

In fact, he had considered getting a new job for a while to get away from the macho and sexualised environment the loggers operated in. It had already begun to wear on him. But the beating from Mickey was the final straw.

He was going home to get a job closer to his girlfriend so he could help her achieve her dream of becoming a mother and be around to support her during the pregnancy and the raising of their child.

The money in the rainforest was good, but no amount of money was worth the challenges he continually confronted as a recovering sex addict.

"It's great to be going home to the city again. I couldn't wait to leave that jungle. There is nothing there," Mickey said, changing the subject, and refusing to acknowledge John's kind insight into his girlfriend.

He wanted to return to his fifteen-square-metre flat in downtown Washington, D.C.—back to his box life where everything was concrete and square.

"I love my box life. It suits my mind. And I've also missed being on the dating apps. As soon as this plane touches down, I'll be swiping right on every bimbo on there. These bitches just want straight sex—no talking. They come in through the door, they don't even say hello, they walk to the bed, pull up their skirts and bend over."

For Mickey, sex was always *doggy style*. He did not want to see their faces. The girls reminded him too much of his daughter, who at twenty-eight was older than most of the girls he had sex with.

"The girls I go for are all between nineteen and twenty-three. They all have 'daddy issues' so they love visiting an old-timer like me on their lunch break, or before they go meet their pussy boyfriends. I give them the good seeing-to that they need. The young guys these days, they have it too good. I don't understand them at all," Mickey said to John, motioning towards Richard, with a nod.

The conversation between John and Mickey continued in this vein throughout the flight, lasting for hours until they arrived at the International Airport in Suriname. In fact, this was how the conversation between the loggers unfolded all day, every day, when they were on-site. The level of verbal abuse aimed towards women was as extreme as it was relentless.

During a quick stopover in Suriname, Richard called Kate. He told her he had *quit* his job and would be returning early from the rainforest. He did not want to worry her. She was extremely protective of him.

Believing that he had finally decided to leave an unfulfilling job, she was supportive. Having met some of her father's workmates over the years, Kate was aware he would not fit in with the loggers. However, she was unaware of the level of abuse he received.

Her support meant a lot to him, as they talked. It soothed the sense of disappointed his father radiated following the beating.

Respecting a final call over the public announcement system, Mickey and John finished their beer and Richard ended his call with Kate. The three men then boarded a larger aircraft for their onward flight to Washington National Airport.

Sleeping the remainder of the journey, Mickey and John drunkenly snored loudly, disrupting the other passengers.

II

Everything Inverted

Actions Speak Louder

Getting off the plane, Anne was waiting to bring Richard home and care for him.

When they arrived at her apartment, she helped him settle on the sofa. She had already prepared a blanket and some extra pillows.

She gave him some medicine followed by a completely oversized cup of his favourite tea, which he always relished.

Once he was settled, she then carefully cuddled up beside him. She had already chosen a classic movie for them to stream: *Darby O'Gill and the Little People.*

However, within minutes of it beginning, he was fast asleep.

Just twenty-four hours before, he had been in the rainforest with six guys kicking him unconscious. Richard was exhausted. He completely blacked out for the night.

He woke for a few moments just after 6 a.m. with Anne taking his clothes from his bag and putting them into the washing machine. He could not keep his eyes open for more than a few seconds and fell back asleep.

He awoke again just after 9 a.m. to Anne kissing him on the forehead. Breakfast was ready.

She was happy to have him there, but despite her cheery act, she looked tired and worn. Richard had an enhanced sense of intuition. He was very good at reading people and tapping into their true feelings.

Still under the blanket, he inquisitively asked her if everything was okay, eating his breakfast at one side of his mouth, to avoid the gap where his missing teeth once resided.

Anne's eyes welled up.

"Richard, I'm sorry. I know you've been working so hard to save money for the trip. I'm sorry. My dad won't let me go backpacking with you after I'm done with school."

Without saying anything, he reached over and pulled her close, giving her a cuddle.

In truth, upon hearing this news, he needed the cuddle more than Anne did.

Under the Midnight Sun

Anne's father was a dominant man who micromanaged the lives of his wife and daughters.

"He says I have to do a Ph.D. He doesn't want me getting a job before completing a doctorate. His co-worker's daughter just finished her Ph.D. and he wants me to do the same. He says any self-respecting woman should be able to hold her own position in the office. So, it's best if I get as many qualifications as possible."

Richard held her left hand in both of his, as she talked:

"My dad thinks starting a family isn't a priority. That we already have enough children running around and we don't need any more." Anne had tears flowing down her face. *"In his opinion, I should focus on my education and my career and forget about my stupid ideas of backpacking. He was going on and on."*

Her father, the CEO of the company he founded, had promised a cash prize if she completed her master's and came top of the class. She was close to achieving that, using the backpacking as motivation.

More than the backpacking trip, Anne was excited it was with Richard. She knew he was popular with women. However, despite her best intentions, she found herself falling for him.

She believed backpacking together would provide an opportunity to solidify their relationship. Once her formal education was done, she wanted to open herself to Richard, without the interference of her studies.

Her studies had been a distraction since they met and she wanted to reveal her playful side to him—her inner child. She knew she could trust him with that most vulnerable side of her.

When she had revealed it to him in flickers, it really lit him up. He laughed so loud from deep in his stomach during those revelations. Anne increasingly trusted him as a result. It was what made her develop strong feelings for him.

When they were together, they never got involved in any chit chat. Richard did not really know what she was studying. He did not know what her father did for a living, or the names of her friends.

What he did know was how she felt when a particular event happened or a certain person entered a room. They talked about the big things, whilst relaxing to each other's music. Discussing ideas, they shared their thoughts on the unseen.

Each listened intently as the other revealed the memories triggered by smells, sounds and sights. When she was thinking about him deep in her heart, he could feel it in his heart.

When they first met, Richard had just returned from a backpacking trip where he had travelled primarily by train from the Arctic to the Equator. He began that trip in Lapland, northern Norway, sitting under the midnight sun. He completed it in Singapore watching the city's fantastic *Light and Water Show* at sunset, three months later.

During that trip, Richard passed through Mongolia and the Gobi Desert on his way into China and South-East Asia. That region had fascinated Anne ever since she watched a documentary on Genghis Khan and his armies, as a child.

Introduced by mutual friends, she had wanted to know how Richard could go on such magnificent adventures. As her friends asked the usual questions about backpacking, Anne stood at the back, listening to his words and how he phrased them.

Then, she asked a single question:

"So, what do I need to do to make such a trip possible?"

Richard looked directly at her, taking a moment to respond. He knew she was there, but he had not fully engaged her. Now, he was captivated. Time slowed down during a moment of deep eye contact.

He then snapped out of it, regained his composure and nonchalantly responded:

"To be a backpacker, you need access to two things: time and money," he said. *"When you're younger, you'll probably have more time than money. When you're older, you'll probably have more money than time. So, for men, as long as they don't have children, the optimum time for backpacking is between the ages of twenty-seven and thirty-six. For women, the best time to travel is between the ages of twenty-four and thirty-three. That's generally speaking, of course."*

"Yeah, but what about the money you need for travelling?" enquired the smallest of the girls.

"Everyone always thinks that backpacking is all about money. Just let me be clear about this: going on holiday is all about money. Going backpacking is all about attitude. A smile and a positive attitude are the best assets and protection you can have on the road. For sure, you will need money to get started, but not as much as you would imagine, as you can make money along the way."

Richard quickly glanced at Anne, before continuing to explain:

"But to get to the specifics of what I recommend. Usually it's best to complete your education and have a few years' experience in the workplace, topping up your CV. Y' know, that'll allow you to save more money and have something to fall back on when you return. But more than anything, it'll allow you to know more about yourself and who you are before you go out into the world as a backpacker. Because all travel is ultimately a journey within ourselves."

With the girls standing around Richard slowly nodding along in silence, he added:

"That being said, the average age of a backpacker in hostels is now forty-two."

"Forty-two? Really?" asked one of the girls in surprise.

"Yeah, people are always surprised at that," he said. *"It's because the people who have their kids young, usually end up going backpacking when their kids move out or when they retire.*

By then, they are sick of pretending to fit into the rat race world. So, they then go out and explore the world. Both inner and outer."

His well-thought-out and carefully explained answer fascinated Anne. Many backpackers offered a throwaway response when she asked that question—trying to make themselves look cool, or hint that backpacking was some sort of elite club for the *"woke"* kids.

Richard believed backpacking was for everyone, and should be a rite of passage, no matter if the person was eighteen or eighty years old.

Anne's motivation to study came from the cash bonus her father offered her. Now, he moved the goalposts so she would not get the money until after her doctorate was completed.

Instead, he offered Anne a token amount of the bonus, but it was only a fraction of what he had promised. It would certainly not be enough for backpacking.

The truth was her father often moved the goalposts. He dangled the proverbial carrot in front of his wife and daughters. But when they reached the goal he set, he then moved the goal. He was the one who controlled all the spending in the home and only allowed his girls to buy things he approved of.

Richard met Anne's parents once at a family occasion when Anne brought him along as a friend. Richard was very fond of Anne's mother—she was a gentle and kind lady, with a thunderous laugh, and that same heart-melting smile as Anne.

Her father, on the other hand, was quite different. After meeting Richard, he spent fifteen minutes asking direct questions. He enquired about his upbringing, the school he attended, his job and other subjects along that vein.

After his interrogation, Anne's father suddenly turned and walked away. He did not approve of Richard, despite his medical qualification. He certainly did not want his *"favourite daughter going backpacking with a guy from that side of town,"* as he continually reminded her.

The Pendulum Swings

As Richard lay on Anne's sofa, he felt broken. His head was physically sore from the kicks he had received, but his heart hurt most.

To lose his job for protecting the decency of his friend, Emma. To be beaten up by his work colleagues. For his father to be disappointed in him for not fighting back. This all made him question his place in the world as a man.

But what hurt most was the realisation he could not afford to go backpacking—and that his lover had been forbidden from going with him, anyway.

He was sad about the past and worried about the uncertainty of the future. These thoughts were weighing increasingly on his mind.

Richard spent his time at Anne's apartment lying on the sofa. He was mostly sleeping or just staring at the wall. Sometimes he would listen to audiobooks. He usually listened to audiobooks at double speed, as his brain still absorbed the information and he could get through them twice as fast.

However, as he lay on the sofa, he did not notice what he was listening to or that it was playing at normal speed, which usually frustrated him. He was completely out of balance.

By the third day, he was in a daze. He overthought everything.

Like a pendulum, he swung between two opposites. One moment he was disinterested and detached from everything: not caring.

An hour later, his mind raced, making checklists for everything he had to do once he healed: over-caring.

This led to him becoming overwhelmed, allowing the pendulum to swing back towards being uncaring and disinterested.

His worrying about the past made him depressed. Worrying about the future made him anxious. He knew the only way to have peace of mind was to live in the present. To fully utilise the *"power of now."*

But it was not easy.

As he lay on Anne's sofa, it appeared as if the walls were slowly moving. They were inching closer towards him, moment by moment.

He felt like a big dog forced to shelter in a small kennel because of the rain outside. His increasing discomfort forced him to twist and turn within an ever-tightening box.

Each twist and turn exhausted him—and it was not only because of the beating. Richard had a bone-deep weariness that went beyond feeling tired. Each thought weighed ever heavy on his scattered mind.

Anne had a ticking clock in the kitchen. The sound was faint from the sofa. But he could still hear it. He could hear it clearly.

Each *tick* was a hammer crashing against the side of his temple. Every *tock* was a rumble of thunder—approaching, but never arriving.

Audiobooks helped dull the sound of the clock. But they also irritated him—they could make him feel like he was sitting in a dentist's waiting room sandwiched between a couple bickering over whether the toilet seat should have been left up or down. Each giving their ever-increasing in-depth never-ending rationale for why they were right, while the dentist's drill screeched out in the background. He felt extremely stressed.

The recorded voice of the audiobook would eventually sound whiny and scatter his brain, so he ripped out his headphones in frustration.

Sleep was his only sanctuary.

But sleep brought nightmares. A recurring nightmare found him sitting in an unlocked car slowly filling up with water, with him unable to get out.

It was difficult to fall asleep.

Lying waiting to sleep, it felt more like he was falling apart than falling asleep.

He only realised he had been sleeping when he dramatically woke up in a panic, completely covered in sweat. His t-shirt stuck to him, beads of sweat formed on his brow and his blanket had a heavy dampness.

For his soul, these were long, dark nights.

Anne invited him to stay at her place for as long as he needed. She liked having him around and being accessible, despite her lack of time at home. She was mostly in the library, but prepared breakfast and lunch for him before leaving.

When she got home, they would sit down to have dinner. Neither of them had much to say. Anne was so immersed in her study and the completion of her master's degree that nothing else noteworthy went on in her world.

As a result, conversation between them dried up. He wanted to talk to Anne about how he felt. Yet it was impossible for him to explain what was going on in his head when he could not understand himself.

Victim Mentality

They had sex only once since Richard got back from the rainforest. He was in a lot of pain, but the main reason for the lack of intimacy was Richard's state of downheartedness. He wanted to be alone and was slowly developing a victim mentality.

Following his sixth night at Anne's, she rose early as usual. She left breakfast on the table for Richard, put some lunch in the fridge for him and prepared to leave for a hard day of focused study at the library. Just before Anne left, she came into the bedroom.

Richard pretended to sleep, when she softly leaned over, kissed him gently on the head and warmly whispered:

"I love you, Richard. Get strong again."

She tucked the blanket in around him ensuring he was warm and went off with her laptop and books to the library.

Feeling her kindness and love towards him, during a time of great stress for her, triggered a distinct memory of his mother's unending support.

No matter how upset or stressed she was, Angel always took a moment to tuck him into bed at night with a kiss on his head.

Anne's act forced him to take account of his current state. It made him realise he needed to get his life together. However, the thing that resonated deepest with him was her saying the word "*again.*"

"*Get strong again.*"

She did not say, "*get well,*" but rather "*get strong.*" It was evocative. He was strong once. Anne knew him and was aware of how much inner strength and belief he had. He was strong. He knew he needed to show it. Importantly, he needed to show it to himself.

He understood it was necessary for him to be stronger. No one was going to knock on his door and offer to put things right for him. Sitting around feeling sorry for his circumstances was not going to help.

This was not who he was. He knew he was better than that. No one else could fix him. If his mother were there to see him, she would have been disappointed. And he never wanted to disappoint his mother.

As a child, Richard had grown up on the edge of Southeast D.C., an undesirable part of town. A suburban area of Washington, D.C., it was not exactly a ghetto at that time, but an area of disadvantage, nonetheless.

Despite his father coming from a more affluent part of town, they stayed in that neighbourhood because it was where Angel was from. She wanted to be close to her parents, to take care of them. Mickey was a supportive and loving husband who contributed a lot, to their marriage and the raising of the twins.

When Richard was fifteen, he recognised the biggest problem where he lived was not the unemployment or the alcoholism, but the *victim mentality* that simmered in the people. They had a habit of blaming others when they failed to get what they wanted.

In the area, it was common to blame the government, the unions, the rain or anything else—it was never the *fault* of the individual when "*life didn't work out.*"

As a child, Richard vowed to Angel to never allow himself to become a victim of anything. He had a mantra:

"*I am not the victim of anything. I am responsible for everything that happens in my life.*

If things go wrong, then I will take the blame. If things go right, then I will take the credit."

He learned that from his mother. She once firmly told Richard and Kate:

"If you allow yourself to be the victim, you will lose your power. Always take responsibility for everything that life throws at you. No matter how bad or unfair it may be. Take ownership of the situation, and then you can build yourself back up from there."

Angel was well named. She was a high achiever despite her tough upbringing. She was the youngest sister of three girls and six boys. The siblings watched their father beat their mother every time his football team lost a game. Even sometimes when his team won. He did not have to be drunk to do this.

Although she was never sexually abused, she suspected her older sisters were. The girls left home after finishing school, moving to other cities. Both of Angel's sisters had suffered from mental health issues and lived as recovering alcoholics. As neither was on social media, they had very little contact with Richard and Kate.

Despite her strength and desire to better herself, Angel lacked the power to overcome the biggest obstacle of all: cancer.

She was diagnosed with breast cancer during a routine check-up.

Twelve weeks later, she was dead.

Some people die when they are twenty-four but are not buried until they are eighty-four—they give up and simply exist.

Angel was not one of those people. She was so passionate and energetic. Her friends would often say, *"she squeezed two lives into one,"* before the cancer took control.

The cancer was aggressive. It spread through her body rapidly, leaving her in increasing pain by the day. It was cruelly ironic it was her husband, Mickey, who would be responsible for cutting down the last tree containing the cure in its sap.

Now, that specimen of tree was extinct, that particular cure was gone from nature for good. At least until Vertunia, the drug company that visited the rainforest, decided to release the cure. Unfortunately, that would only happen when their accountants calculated it would be more profitable to cure people with cancer, than to treat them for it.

Lying in his bed and thinking about all that had happened to him over the past months, Richard knew he was indirectly responsible for all the negative things in his life. Like every other soul that chose to come to this planet, he had free will.

He resolved that he had been compliant in everything that had gone wrong. He understood that he was completely responsible for the beating he received. This realisation empowered him. He had gotten his motivation back. Just as his mother always said:

"Take ownership of the problem so you can take control of the solution."

He knew he needed to take dominion of his situation. One way of changing a situation is to change the environment. Getting away from everything for a while and starting afresh would help him recuperate and rejuvenate.

He had enough cash to survive for a month or two if he was careful with spending.

Energised by this plan, Richard jumped out of bed and had a shower. The cold water running over him felt invigorating. He put on the freshly washed clothes and searched for flights leaving that week.

Destination: anywhere.

Anywhere but his hometown.

Scrolling down the page, there was nothing at an affordable price that appealed to him. He clicked to the next page. Doubts crept in. Maybe it was not such a good idea.

Then, third from the top he saw a direct flight to Ireland. It was departing that night at midnight for an unbeatable low price, on an airline he had never heard of.

It just felt right.

"Everything is perfect," Richard muttered.

He booked it.

He wrote Anne a note.

When she came home that night, she was surprised he was gone. He had washed and folded all the sheets and towels he used and tidied the kitchen, living room and bathroom.

The apartment gave off a wonderful aroma. On a table, in a vase, he had left a big bunch of wild flowers. Her favourite. At the base of the vase was a note. Anne picked it up and whispered it aloud. It read:

Hey amazing A

Thank you so much for your kindness and care over the past few days. As always, you are a complete sweetheart. I need to go and get my life together. I need to breathe new air, feel new energy and see new horizons.

Ireland is the place that can provide me with this right now. I have just booked a one-way flight, so I will be on the Atlantic coast of Ireland for a while to re-energise my body, mind and soul.

I am going to be off the grid for the next few weeks, so I can look inside and focus on healing myself. I must go and work on myself, for myself, by myself.

Sending you a lot of love and energy in the completion of your master's. I will call you when I get my head together.

Luv, hugs and kisses.
God bless.
Richard XX

"That's my boy," Anne whispered, placing the note back beside the flowers.

She felt a tinge of sadness, as she really wanted to go with him. Anne would miss him, but she knew he needed to do this to find himself and *"get strong"* once again.

She lifted the flowers to her face and breathed deeply through her nose, savouring the raw aroma with a smile as her eyes welled up.

The Matriarchal Island

Despite being well travelled, Richard had never been to Ireland. In his mind, it was a mystical, magical island that held great energy and a fascinating past.

It did not have a globally iconic landmark like the Eiffel Tower or Statue of Liberty the country could use to market itself.

Nevertheless, what came out of Ireland were stories of the people and the energy of the land. It had something intangible that could not be captured on camera or sold with a cheesy tagline dreamt up by a team of marketing interns.

As he had a tight budget, Dublin would be a mere pit stop. Besides, capital cities never truly represented the essence of the country they claim to lead, Richard believed.

He would travel to the west to really feel the magic of the countryside. It would offer him a purer experience more reflective of the *real* Ireland, whilst allowing him to stretch out his limited budget more effectively.

Therese was a friend he had met at university. She moved to Ireland the year before to work for one of the many large technology companies that operated out of Dublin.

Richard messaged her whilst travelling to the airport. Therese responded in excitement, inviting him to stay with her in Dublin, for a night, before he went to Galway.

Therese was living in Smithfield, on the edge of the city centre. The area was dominated by a large market square recently regenerated. However, the subtlety of the development helped maintain the working-class essence of the area, despite the gentrification.

An Irish pub stood at the top of the large market square, which the tourists could never seem to locate. It was hidden in plain sight. As a result, it maintained the spirit of a *real* Irish pub. Every night, locals came along with their various instruments to join in on a "*trad session.*" This was a strong part of Irish culture.

When Richard enquired into what this was, Therese explained:

"*A 'trad session' is this, like, informal sporadic gathering of traditional musicians. It's for nothing more than the purpose of celebrating a mutual love for music. These folk just come together and casually play their instruments in a relaxed setting. So, with this being Ireland, the casual setting is usually the corner of a local pub.*"

"*Of course,*" Richard joked.

"*But, OMG. They create this beautiful once-off melody that glides through the air. As a busker, you will love it, Richard.*"

After arriving in Dublin late on Tuesday evening, he went to the pub with Therese. She had sworn the pub offered one of the best pints of Guinness in Dublin. Walking in, the first thing that stood out for Richard was the popularity of the pub on a Tuesday evening.

As a trad session filled the air, from the back corner of the pub, he was struck by how busy it was.

At the bar, an older man stood reading a newspaper with a perpetual smile on his face. Beside him sat two hipsters discussing something that was on one of their phones. A gang of rockers dressed in black sat in one corner. In another corner was a group of girls with full makeup on their way to a concert, kitted out in colourful short dresses and high heels. Everyone had a drink in front of them.

Richard captured a photo on his phone and sent it to Kate, without any text.

She instantly text back:

Nooooo waaaaaay

Are u in Ireland?

Maybe...
;)

No way

Hahaha
Is it really that obvious from one photo?

U said we would go together?

We will. Next time

I'll hold u to that

I know you will

Why are u in Ireland?

You would love it here
Therese says hi

I'd love to be there with u.
Maybe u will meet some of our cousins?

Anything is possible here.
The people are as wild as the wind

OK gotta run
Love to you and Terry

Tell her I said hi
Love u. Call me soon

Putting his phone away, one other thing that stood out for Richard were the different types of people of all ages who squeezed into the bar. Pubs in Ireland appeared as if they were like the third living room—a place where anyone could go to hang out and have a chat and a pint, or even a quiet cup of tea and some dinner.

Behind the bar was a small-in-stature, but strong-in-mind landlady, as evident by how she patrolled the bar area.

Richard's grandmother used to tell him Ireland was a genuinely matriarchal society. It was a small island where women were the true leaders.

The woman behind the bar was the kind of woman he imagined when his grandmother regaled him with stories of Ireland. Richard's grandmother emigrated from there as a teenager in search of a better life, on the East Coast of America.

Her first stop was to join her cousin in Boston. But after a few years, she had clawed her way up sufficiently to be offered a role as an office administrator by an old Irish neighbour in, D.C. It was at this job she met a second-generation Irish immigrant who became her husband.

As she regaled her tales and insights, his grandmother always seemed to be knitting. She always sat in the same chair close to the fireplace. After school, as Kate played with friends, Richard would usually sit with his grandmother as she knitted whatever clothing was needed for the family at that time.

Once she knitted him a bright red woollen hat, which he still used and brought with him everywhere. Following her death, it was his connection to her.

As a kid, the hat was oversized and as he grew the hat seemed to have grown with him, as it was still too big. He cherished that hat, because his mother complimented him on how nice he looked when he wore it.

As Richard's grandmother knitted and talked, he always listened attentively. She would say things such as:

"In Ireland, they say it takes a village to raise a child. They're right to say that, because over there it's true. The kids are brought up not just by their mother, but also by their aunts, grandmother, neighbours and all their female friends. All the women contribute to the rearing of a child in some way. Children get to a stage where they become oblivious to what

their parents are saying. It is always good to have different female voices contributing to a child with the wisdom they will need during their life."

As Richard paid close attention to her words, listening with his eyes, she would continue:

"In Ireland, the men are all full of talk and bravado when they're out on the street with the boys. But once they go home, they give their salary over to—who they call 'the boss'—the woman of the house. In Ireland, all the men are mummy's boys—big softies at heart. That's why they're so good with the women. They understand femininity. It's where they get the 'gift of that gab'—it doesn't come from kissing a stone. They grow up surrounded by women. Respecting women. Ireland is the last great matriarchal society in the Western world."

In the pub, Richard talked to about thirty new people who came and went during the evening. They wanted to know who this new face was. It was nothing to do with suspicion, but it came from the natural inquisitiveness of the Irish.

Even though he did not drink alcohol anymore, some offered to buy him a pint. Others asked him to buy them a pint. The girls were strong and feisty, yet open and humorous. The result was a night of *"craic,"* consisting of laughter, music, storytelling and new friendship.

It seemed as if every second person was Bono's cousin. Richard was in his element as his Irish roots shone through.

The following morning, Therese, still in her nightdress, waved him off from the window of her apartment as he walked the three hundred metres to the quayside. There, he hopped on a bus for Galway City.

He had arranged to do some couchsurfing the first week until he got his feet on the ground.

In addition, he planned to do some actual surfing on the world-class waves at the small coastal village of Fanore in the early mornings.

After all, salt water, whether it comes from tears, sweat or the ocean, can remedy all. He hoped the cold Atlantic would help heal his aches and pains, as well as revitalise his spirit.

In the evenings, he would return to Galway City to earn some money from busking on the streets. Busking was a popular pastime sown into the fabric of the city.

He had been practicing the guitar since Mickey gave him one for his ninth birthday. He was not formally trained. He had become a busker by chance, when his mother gave out to him for making a racket on his guitar whilst talking with her friend on the telephone.

This made him go practice at the edge of the local park and with his guitar case sitting on the ground beside him, a passer-by tossed in a few coins.

From that day forth, he always practised outside when the weather permitted. His mother was supportive. However, not all passers-by were.

In his early years, he was often verbally abused when practising a new song. It toughened him up, when it came to name-calling and "*feedback*." This non-constructive criticism also helped him to develop his musical skills with urgency.

Galway was a vibrant and energetic city filled with music and character. Around every corner was a busker and wafting out of every pub was the sound of laughter and *craic*.

It really felt like a young-at-heart-person's town, with people from all around the world setting up camp there for the surfing or the music. Richard instantly felt at home.

The people of the city made him feel part of the local tribe.

His only issue was the other buskers. He was not completely stuck for money, but he needed to cover his day-to-day costs of staying in Galway and travelling to Fanore. His problem was when he returned from surfing each afternoon, all the best busking spots were taken.

In addition, it seemed friends would hold spots and slots for each other in the best busking locations. That made it difficult for him to earn some proper money. He always found himself busking away from the main thoroughfare, meaning he only earned a fraction of what the others made.

Come Saturday night, he was again busking in an out-of-the-way position with low footfall. He hardly made any money. He was hungry, tired and becoming demotivated so he packed up to leave.

With the sun setting, the temperature along the Atlantic coast had dropped, so he pulled on the now-severely worn red woollen hat his grandmother had knitted for him all those years ago. Making his way up the main drag with his guitar swung over his shoulder, he noticed one of the buskers had packed up and was walking away.

A stroke of luck.

He walked quickly to the spot, pulled out his guitar, hastily threw the cover in front of him and started playing.

The city was exceptionally busy as it was a Saturday night and many stag and hen parties came to the city each weekend from across the United Kingdom and Ireland.

In one hour in the new location, he made more money than in the previous three days combined.

Boisterous groups came along and requested songs. They then danced along in the middle of the street, pulling other groups in with them.

On the streets, a real party atmosphere filled the air and revellers would leave a few euros each—he could earn up to twenty euros for one song. Especially if a stag party was trying to impress a group of women on a hen party.

Pussy Hat

Time flew by. He was in the midst of the true Irish party culture, and he thrived. It was the best he had felt in months. About three hours into his session on the main thoroughfare, he realised mid-song the guitar case he had laid down was full of coins. There were even a few five-euro notes in the mix. He was grateful for the stroke of luck.

He considered it wise to pack away the money for safekeeping when he finished the song. However, his thoughts were distracted when a guy walked up beside him shouting a song request.

"Play 'Beautiful Day' *by* U2. *Ye know* 'Beautiful Day'?"

He shouted it repeatedly, disrupting Richard.

With Richard distracted, another guy walked by and quickly scooped up two handfuls of cash—most of what he had earned that evening.

Before Richard could react, the guy darted into the crowd, as coins trickled through the fingers of his clasped hands, and disappeared. It happened so fast.

"Thief! Thief!" he shouted. *"Police! Police! Someone call the police? Thief! I've been robbed."*

As events unfolded, two drunk guys who witnessed what happened stood laughing at him.

One of them said:

"Ah mate, come on. What are the police gonna do? Those guys will have that money spent long before the police catch up with 'em. If yer stupid enough to leave that amount of money lying out there, then yer stupid enough to be robbed. You deserve all ye get."

"Dammit!" Richard shouted again, stamping his right foot in frustration.

"Everything was going well for... as usual, something happens. It's the story of my year," Richard whined incoherently.

Defeated, he sank onto the ground. He pulled his red hat over his face, put his elbows on his knees and head in his hands.

"Just can't catch a break at the moment," he snarled aloud through gritted teeth.

With that, he was alerted to some girls shouting at him:

"Hey, you. You. Hey. Who do you think ye are?"

He pulled his hat up from over his eyes to see what is going on. Three girls stood over him.

"Who do you think you are, wearing that hat here? Men have no right to wear that hat," insisted one of them.

As she said that, another of the girls stepped in from the side and attempted to grab the hat from his head. Richard instinctively put his hand out and grabbed his hat. A struggle took place.

Richard, jumping to his feet, found himself in a tug-of-war with a drunken woman for his hat.

"That's a Pussyhat—give me that. No man is allowed to wear that. It's a symbol of our rights. Only for women. Take it off ye, ya little prick," the woman slurred.

"Hey! Stop! What are you doing? My grandmother made me that hat," Richard protested.

"Well, she shouldn't have." the girl snapped.

Richard, now really annoyed at her response, yanked the hat out of her hand.

As this unfolded, the girl who stood directly in front of Richard, looked him right in his face and screeched:

"If you like pussy so much, then here you go."

Hunkering over his guitar case, she pulled up her tight, short skirt and began urinating on the last few coins that remained. She was not wearing underwear.

Richard's mouth dropped open and his eyes bulged. She looked him directly in the eye whilst gushing urine across his guitar case and cash with a grin on her face.

As she did this, the other two girls laughed so much they doubled over.

Some drunken passers-by cheered her on.

When finished, she stood up and shouted some slurred profanities at Richard. Then, without pulling her tight pink dress back down, the three girls staggered up the street laughing and high-fiving.

Richard sat back down against the wall. He inspected his hat. It was not torn, but the baggy hat was now even more stretched.

He had had enough. He flicked the urine and cash off his guitar case, grabbed his guitar and wandered off back towards the apartment where he was couchsurfing.

Penniless after a day of busking, his head was bowed, the guitar case dragged along behind him. He just could not catch a break.

Thankfully, no one else was home when he arrived. It allowed him to shower his guitar case without the embarrassment of having to explain what happened.

Having put up with all the sexist remarks in the rainforest from men, he now faced even more extreme actions from women.

"Is this what feminism has led to? Is this the equality women wanted? Women becoming equally as vulgar and sexist as men?" he ranted as he showered down his guitar case.

During the night, he did not sleep a wink. His body was still sore from the beating in the rainforest. Now, he was extremely frustrated and humiliated from being robbed and having the girl urinate on his gear.

"I'm so sick of people right now. I need to clear my head. Get away from everyone for a while. I need to get back into nature," he mumbled as he tossed and turned during the night.

He needed to spend some time bathed in the silence of nature. Whenever Richard required time for reflection, he practiced "forest bathing."

Being around trees, the air just felt fresher and cleaner. The *chi* was more potent. Just being with the trees energised him. It improved his overall wellbeing. With the silence derived from the trees, he thought more clearly.

However, it went further than that. Although he had never discussed this with his friends, Richard believed the trees were alive and could communicate with him at a deeper level. He could obtain great insight by being with the trees. Although most of his friends were fairly open-minded, he doubted few of them were open to communicating with trees.

Being in Ireland, known globally as the *Emerald Isle* because of the abundance of nature and greenery, he needed to leave the city and go deeper into the countryside for some *"green air."*

One place he wanted to visit was the Hill of Tara—an ancient Neolithic Age site deemed one of Ireland's historic treasures, bathed in Celtic mythology.

Centred on the island of Ireland, the Hill of Tara was surrounded by fields for as far as the eye could see. It was exactly what he needed.

Richard quickly searched on his phone and found a bus leaving 5:40 a.m. that would take him close to the ancient grounds. It was 5:19 a.m. He had enough time to get up, shower and get over to the bus station before departure. *"Everything is perfect,"* he muttered.

Stepping out of the apartment, into the cold morning on the Atlantic Coast, a heavy black darkness smothered the streets of Galway.

The darkest hour sits before the turning of dawn.

3

An Untrod Purpose

Push-Button Locks
Loved and Listened To
Guide Lady
Less is More
She's Not Dead Yet
International Women's Day

Push-Button Locks

The sun glimpsed over the horizon as the early morning bus dropped off Richard at the side of the main road. From there, he walked a kilometre up gently sloping ground towards the Hill of Tara. The site encompassed a wider area of grassy fields and several mounds.

The landscape of this ancient valley was not spectacular by Irish standards. But this fertile region, with its rich soils and rolling hills, had been fought over and occupied for millennia.

As a result, the Hill of Tara shared the valley with the world's oldest standing buildings, leaving the Egyptian pyramids and Stonehenge looking like newly builds. The sense of history and importance was palpable.

Arriving at the site, he stopped outside the wooden gate. Inside, a few stragglers aimlessly scouted despite it being only 7:50 a.m. on an overcast Sunday.

He came to a standstill. *"What am I doing here?"* he muttered aloud. There was a deep hesitancy about entering the site, as a strange pull swept through his battered body and jaded mind.

"To travel this distance at this time of the morning is just stupid," he sighed, as he looked back down the slope he had just climbed.

His breathing was high in his chest.

Glancing to the ground, a small grass snake caught his eye as it slithered under the hedgerow. It startled him, as he believed Ireland was not home to any reptiles.

His doubtful thoughts were interrupted by a message coming through on his phone:

> Richard, I know it must be early there, but just got the urge to send you some love. I'm so proud of you and the journey that you're on. Your bravery always inspires me. Also I hope that 'the old country' is living up to all the stories from Grandma? Love you. K x

It was from Kate. A simple message of support. Perfect.

It provided the encouragement that he needed. It also snapped him out of any thoughts of turning around and going back to wait for the next bus.

He sheepishly pushed through the gate at the entrance.

Inside, he dragged his feet through the dewy grass and, as the others appeared to be doing, aimlessly wandered around, gradually making his way up the hill towards the centre.

Arriving at the summit, he noticed a standing stone that indicated the centre of the site. As he stood looking over half of the counties of Ireland, taking in the beauty that unfolded, he felt no joy. He was empty. He felt shattered.

His body was broken from the beating. His mind was frazzled as he felt he had come to the end of a cul-de-sac in life. His heart was heavy because he felt lonely and vulnerable.

All were feelings very alien to him. Normally, he had an objective in life—something to progress towards.

Now, there was nothing.

With his hands on the Standing Stone, he dropped down on one knee. Emotion swept over him.

He began to cry.

It felt like he had been handed a bunch of Yale Keys before being pushed into a room with many doors, only to find that when the door slammed shut behind him, all the doors had push-button locks.

His mind wandered to new territory.

"Do I deserve to see the future?" he pondered.

Big thoughts. Heavy thoughts.

His sniffling turned to wailing, as he was overcome by the desolation of everything. Catching himself, he looked up. The entire site was empty. He put his head back on the standing stone but again, he was consumed by emotion. His wailing turned to bawling.

Although a grown man, it was in times like these he most missed his mother. He wished she was beside him to tell him everything was going to be okay, to run her hands through his hair. That always soothed him.

After a few minutes, he turned around and sat on the dewy morning grass with his back to the Standing Stone.

Loved and Listened To

Lost in time, he stared out into the nothingness, despite Mother Nature's masterpiece unfurled in front of him.

Tears trickled over his high cheekbones.

After some time, he heard a soft warm voice speak to him:

"Better out than in."

In shock, Richard looked up. His grandmother used to say that phrase. But she would quietly say it after breaking wind.

"There is nothing as beautiful as seeing a grown man cry. Taking ownership of his emotions ... dealing with the anger in a positive way."

"Anger? I'm not angry. I've nothing to be—"

"Relax. There is nothing wrong with Anger," Interrupted the voice. *"Anger gets a bad rap. It's a valid emotion. Like all the others, it has its place. If used correctly, with control, in the right circumstances it can be a very powerful and rewarding emotion."*

Richard did not respond.

He closed his eyes. He allowed his tongue to rest heavy on the floor of his mouth.

A silence descended over the hill for a few minutes. Not awkward. Peaceful.

With the sun quickly rising above the horizon, it found a gap in the clouds and spat its ruby rays across the site. Hitting Richard on the side of his face with warmth and light, he opened his eyes.

"This hill we're on is known as Ráith na Ríogh—*meaning the* Fort of the Kings, *in Gaelic."*

Without prompting, the voice continued to talk:

"The most prominent earthwork within this entire enclosure was known as the Forradh, *or* The Royal Seat. *And right in the middle of the* Forradh, *is the Standing Stone. That is believed to be the* Lia Fáil, *which translates to* the Stone of Destiny—*it served as the coronation stone for the High Kings of Ireland. So, if you need me to be any clearer on that, James, then that stone that you're leaning against is the* 'King's Stone,' *as we say locally. And you look very comfortable against it, I might add."*

Richard, now curious, turned around to see a lady. Wearing a long dark cardigan, she appeared to be in her sixties, but had a soft look about her face, which held a constant smile.

What stood out most were her distinct eyes. Unusually, her left eye was a bright green and her right eye was a deep blue. Each eye sparkled like a freshly polished diamond under the overcast Irish sky.

"Did you just call me James? Um, I think you may have ... mistaken me for someone else. My name is Richard," he said, correcting the lady.

"Oh, I know who ye are. Whatever ye wanna call yourself is your business."

The woman then giggled and turned away from him.

"Come on. Let me show ye around." She had a warmth in her voice as she spun and walked from *the Stone.*

Richard jumped to his feet. In a state of confusion, he followed the lady. As a backpacker, he had vast experience of meeting new people in peculiar circumstances. He intuitively felt whether a person could be trusted. It was rare for him to meet someone who wanted to harm him and when he did meet those people, it was usually when alcohol was being served.

"So, are ye feeling better after the good cry that ye had?" she asked.

Feeling slightly embarrassed, Richard said:

"Yeah, much better, thanks."

"Good. Because you'll need to stop feeling sorry for yourself. You've a lot of work to do in the next few years. But before any of that happens, ye need to work on yourself. Ye have strayed from your path. That's why you're feeling depleted and broken," she said in a firm voice. *"That's what happens when ye swim upstream against a river that ye shouldn't be going up. It's time that ye stepped back from everything for a while and listened to your inner child."*

Richard looked at her wondering what was going on. Who was she?

Dressed from head to toe in various shades of black, with a set of violet beads hanging outside her oversized cardigan, this tiny woman had the posture of someone who had spent a lifetime leaning into a sink. Her slightly swollen reddish hands knew what a hard day's work was, but the softness of her face glowed as if she was looking at a smartphone in the dark.

Nevertheless, everything she said was correct. Despite her getting his name wrong, everything else applied to him fully. He was feeling depleted and broken. He sensed he was going against the tide, without really knowing where or why.

"What do you mean when you say, 'listen to my inner child?'" Richard asked, in desperation, discarding the whole name thing for the moment.

He was trying to gain a sense of insight into healing the pain he felt.

The woman responded:

"Well, your inner child is the guardian of your heart and your true connection to the other side. *He is fuelled by love and fulfilled by creativity. Like every child, it is his desire that ye be happy. This comes through play, exploration, inventiveness and all those other things the stern adults frown upon."*

She quickly glanced up at Richard to ensure he was on board with her message, whilst she talked. He was staring directly at her and listening with intensity.

"But when ye were about nine years old, ye became very angry with your inner child. Ye didn't want to be playful and soft and open. Ye felt exposed and lonely. Being open to the world in your child-state brought ye, what I can best describe as a perceived ungainliness. Ye felt it didn't serve ye to be soft in a hard world, as that made ye stand out too much. It made ye different from everyone else."

Richard got it. It felt true and real. He listened carefully to her words as they floated towards him.

"During this unprovoked suffering, ye chastised your inner child and told him to go away. Banishing him to the darkest corner of your soul where he has been hiding ever since ... in silence ... afraid to connect or communicate."

Then pointing directly at Richard's core with her red swollen index finger, she changed her tone, saying:

"But your inner child is still with ye. He hasn't abandoned ye. He never will. The inner child will always be there, hoping for your attention. Your inner child will wait to be invited back into your life for as long as ye are alive. So, running away from him will never end the pain you feel; it will only prolong it."

Interrupting the lady, Richard asked:

"Sorry for butting in, but can you please explain that point about running from the pain?"

"Of course I can," she said. *"There is no need to apologise, lad. The simplest explanation is that there is a level of pain that comes with all healing. To heal, we must go through that pain barrier. Many run from the healing process, as they don't want to face the pain. But that only makes it worse. Do you understand what I am saying now?"*

"I understand that part, one-hundred per cent." he responded, rubbing his hand along his ribcage.

She continued:

"Your inner child wants to help ye through the pain barrier so ye can heal. But to avoid the pain, ye will do anything but listen to your inner child. So, ye always attempt to keep yourself entertained—ye will watch movies, read, hang out with friends, party or sleep. Or the big one today is scrolling through the phone—because ye will do anything to

avoid the conversation ye need to have with yourself—ye don't want to go through that suffering all over again, because, as I said, long-term healing requires short-term pain."

Rubbing her hands together in the fresh morning air, she continued:

"The inner child only wants to be acknowledged and loved and listened to. But ye do the opposite. Ye run away because yer afraid of being faced with yer true self. So, the first step before ye listen to him is ye need to go and find him and invite him back."

"Find him and invite him back?" Richard asked.

"Exactly."

"Well, how am I going to do that?"

"To reconnect with your inner child, we need ye to go on a trip. In every sense of the word. Ye need to go on a sacred journey."

"A sacred journey?" Richard asked in surprise, almost sniggering.

"In a few weeks, there will be a secret retreat in the south of the Netherlands. That will be the beginning of your sacred journey. Ye need to go there."

"Okay?" he responded in disbelief.

"Go on that Interweb thing and ye will find it. But ye need time to cleanse and detoxify your body and mind before ye can even think about going there."

"What do I have to do when I get there?" Richard asked, not taking her words fully seriously.

"All that, ye will find out when ye arrive. If I were to tell ye everything now, then it wouldn't be a secret retreat, would it?" she said with a smile.

"Any hints at all?" Richard asked, slightly sarcastically.

She paused and looked at him for a moment. He was not getting it. She took a big inhalation and softened her voice:

"Okay, in plain terms, the secret retreat is where ye will retrieve your inner child." Now, she had Richard's close attention. *"Once there, ye will complete exercises designed to help ye achieve this."*

"Such as?" he asked.

"Such as chanting and meditating, stretching, connecting and cleansing. Ye may also be forced to purge your body and soul to get to the next level, if that's what ye require."

Then, pausing to scan his body, looking him up and down, she said:

"Ye will certainly need to purge your body."

Starting to walk again, the woman continued:

"Most importantly, when ye are there, ye will have your first conversations with Mother Ayahuasca since ye were a child. She will provide the building blocks ye need for the next stage of your journey."

"Building blocks?" Richard asked. He was so desperate for guidance. He wanted to ensure he was hearing the woman right. He was more serious now.

"Yeah, ye will receive very precise insights that are specifically for you. The information ye receive will derive from what ye need to know at that time and what ye can handle at this stage of your development," the woman detailed.

Staring straight ahead but listening intently, Richard asked:

"Why do I need to do this?" He had discarded the fact she got his name wrong. This information was for him. He could *feel* it.

"Because it is your calling. Because now we need ye," she responded. *"We need men to communicate our message to men. Men understand men. Men listen to men. Ye are a man with a strong feminine essence running through ye. Ye understand women and femininity. Generally, ye have maintained a perfect balance between your masculine and feminine energy."*

It was quite a big statement to throw at Richard, but he had heard that before as a child, although not as forcefully.

"Time is running out. Men have controlled and run this planet with their machine minds for the last few millennia. The mechanical nature of their minds has caused them to become uncaring, systematic and detached from the damage arising from their actions. Their mechanized approach has caused havoc and destruction across the planet."

He did not balk at this information and allowed the lady to continue to talk uninterrupted.

"Mother Earth is sick and she is calling out for our help. Her rainforests are being eliminated. Her water is being poisoned. Her air is unfit to breathe. The short-term, profit-minded approach of men to the planet has left us in a position where the planet will be uninhabitable if

we continue. Souls will be forced to find a new planet for their education. With the dawning of the Age of Aquarius, the reign of man has now come to an end."

Then, coming to a halt, she stopped walking, turned and looked firmly at Richard, saying:

"It is now time for women to reclaim their rightful place, as the leaders and rulers of this beautiful planet. The feminine energy must rise if we are to save our Earth from destruction."

Guide Lady

He was not completely aligned with what was unfolding, but the woman's declarations felt real. Deep in his heart, he recognised it was the truth.

With the lady still staring deep into his eyes, he wanted to say something, so he asked:

"Are you sure you have the right guy?"

Without answering, she turned and walked away.

He followed her.

"If it's time for women to rule the world again, why are you telling this to me, a twenty-eight-year-old man?" Richard asked.

Stopping in her tracks and spinning around, she looked Richard dead in the eye as she said:

"Because of that. Because you are a twenty-eight-year-old man."

The soft look had dropped from her face, as she scolded Richard.

Grasping the seriousness of the moment, he quickly followed her and asked for more insight. It was all a bit much for him to take in.

The woman ambled to a set of fairy trees to the side of the site, but very much in the open. Richard's grandmother had told him about the fairy trees of Ireland, and how they were highly protected and held sacred as gateways to the underground world of the *faeries*.

Getting to the twin fairy trees, she sat down, motioning Richard to sit beside her. With their backs to one tree each, she opened her bag and pulled out a bunch of long thin green leaves, which she called "*rushes*."

Folding the rushes into each other, one by one, making a pattern, the woman started to talk in a more composed manner:

"*Women are beautiful and pure. They have an aura about them and an inner warmth that can light up a room. The power of a feminine woman is one of the strongest powers we have on this planet. We have all witnessed this. No matter the man, his title, his wealth, his access, when a beautiful feminine woman walks across his path he will be brought to a standstill, forced to swallow. He will need to gulp down the lump in his throat as he admires her strength and power. Like a lioness strutting across the plains, all life within vision will know the direction of her movement and admire her as she purrs and strides towards her destination.*"

As a red-blooded male, with a high sexual appetite, Richard completely understood.

The lady continued to paint the picture:

"*The beauty of a woman is that inner beauty. It is a deep resonating power that is channelled from the core of the Earth and oozes up through the soles of her feet and out of every pore, creating that simple smile and those sparkling eyes. No amount of makeup, dressing up or jewellery can recreate that beauty. It can't be faked or copied. It can't be controlled or caged. This is the definition of power and all can feel it.*

The knees on show, the straight back, the bottom and breasts perked out, head held high, lips slightly apart with a cheeky smile and long hair falling down her slightly arched back."

Richard did not really know where the woman was going with this, but he listened intently, watching her weather-beaten hands as she moved the rushes through them.

As she talked, she continued to grab for one rush at a time and fold them into formation.

"Our Mother, the Earth, needs women to obtain and reclaim their femininity. Men with their machine minds have diminished it over generations."

Richard noticed a very distinct pattern appeared in the rushes as she folded them.

"These machine minds are destroying our Earth, as they search for the next profit from their short-term goals. Their short-termism is leading to the long-term death and destruction of our planet and all its animal, plant, human and other inhabitants."

The rushes were loosely forming into a square-like pattern as she continued folding whilst talking.

"A woman is a feeling creature. She understands the long-term impact of decisions. She considers the children and the environment that will be left for them. She values long-term health and safety over short-term profits. Her family, her surroundings and their health and safety are her focus. Their protection is her natural instinct."

Focusing on her hands as she talked, she continued to reach for rushes from her bag and weave them together.

"As a result, the great Mother, our Earth, has called to the feminine power of women to protect her. She is creaking and depleted. She is sick and tired. She needs protection from man. The only thing that can neutralise masculinity is femininity. Mother Earth is now calling on her soul sisters to come to her aid."

As the woman said that, she stopped what she was doing and glanced towards Richard. He was absorbing every word.

"I'm with you. I get it," he said, sensing her looking at him.

She continued, softening her tone to a more calming voice:

"Mankind as a race must now elevate the feminine woman into all positions of power, in all industries. In politics, in government, in law, in health and in finance. All over the world. The patriarchy and its short-sighted focus on profits and the feeding of their greed at the expense of everything else, is leading to the ruin of this planet. Starvation, poverty, dis-ease, war, division, mutilation and deforestation. These have all fed the machine of men and provided them with the profits they so desperately crave."

"But no more," she continued. *"As far as the destruction of the planet is concerned, we are now in the endgame. Feminine women must look within themselves and say: 'Stop! No more. You are destroying my home—the home of my children. Now, it is time to think bigger, wider and more sustainably. Now, I must take control. My Mother has called me to return.'"*

Richard was distracted for a moment as two young boys ran past, with their mother hurriedly following, with an anxious look on her face. The old lady scanned the scene intently, without missing a breath as she continued to talk whilst weaving the rushes.

He wanted to say something to show his compassion for the mother, but he did not want the lady to think he was changing the subject or not interested in her message.

Too often, his silence was mistaken for disinterest. In fact, it was his silence as she talked that indicated his level of concentration and focus.

"This time, we must take Mother Earth and hold her to our bosom, as we protect, nourish, feed, clothe and sustain her. As she has done for us, for millennia. Now, we must make the decisions that will preserve life on this planet.

The matriarchy is on the rise based on true feminine power—the deep power that comes from the core of the planet. Men love their mothers like no one else. They respect and respond to her. Now, it is time to step back and take orders and direction from their mothers again."

Richard nodded along and simply muttered, *"Yes. We do."*

He deeply missed his mother. He carried a profound love and protection for his mother that could not be matched. He was now fully in tune with the words of the woman.

With an increasing assertiveness in her tone, the woman continued:

"The fun is over. Playtime is done. A mess has been made. As usual, these silly little boys must turn to their mothers to re-order the havoc they have created.

Once again, the loving mother looks to her silly and short-sighted son with her caring nature and unending patience and she will gladly tidy up after him. It is for the greater good. It is also for him.

The feminine mother understands that boys will be boys, but she knows never to let him out of her watchful gaze. There must be a short leash on the boy with the machine mind. The shorter the leash, the less trouble he can cause. Now is time to reign in that leash.

Call the boy to his mother and put him behind her—back in his rightful place. Mother will take the lead now. It is time for bed, boys. Playtime is over. Mother needs to save our Earth before it is too late."

Richard had never heard someone talk in these terms before, using such words and phrases. Yet, he got it. He understood the essence of what the woman was saying.

His thoughts went back to the death and destruction caused during his time in the rainforest. He pondered on the words and actions of the men there.

How detached they were from the Earth. How they had considered the tribeswomen as objects to be captured and held for their entertainment.

As a collective, modern man possessed a machine mind, Richard believed. They had a short-term approach to life. The result of this approach was a detachment from the long-term, more holistic picture.

Richard understood fully. The woman was right.

He watched as she wrapped a final strand of rush around the four tips of her creation. It looked like she had created a sun wheel. As she solidified the fourth and final tip with a rush, she pulled a penknife from her pocket and tidied the ends into a neat stump.

She then handed it to Richard and said:

"There ye go. It's a cross. A Saint Brigid's Cross, to be more precise. She is the female patron saint of this island. Brigid was a woman of power, in touch with her femininity. Here in Ireland, we use her and her cross to protect us from fire and evil. Stick it in your bag, James," the woman motioned, *"you might need a bit of feminine protection along your journey."*

The woman got up, turned to the fairy tree she had been sitting against and whispered, *"Thank you"* as she gave it a hug.

Then, she wandered down the field away from the entrance. She did not look back.

Watching her go off into the distance, he wondered again why she called him James, when he had already told her Richard was his name. He observed the woman until she disappeared into a hedgerow, out of the site and out of sight.

Richard continued to sit against the fairy tree for the best part of an hour, twirling the Saint Brigid's Cross around in his hands, pondering all she had told him.

Eventually, he stood up and copying what the woman had done, he awkwardly patted the fairy tree and said, *"Thank you,"* hoping no one was watching him.

He then walked to the top of the site again. He was drawn back to the *Stone of Destiny*, as the old lady had called it. Putting his hand on the Standing Stone and taking a moment in silence, he felt a sense of gratitude. He felt he had found his path. And a purpose.

"Everything is always perfect," he silently concluded.

He looked upon the stone for a moment and felt comfortable in its presence. With his left hand on it, he circled around the stone several times as he considered the other hands laid on this *Stone of Destiny* over the centuries.

What great women and men had been here before him, he wondered.

Turning back towards the exit, to return to the bus stop, he felt himself stand tall and proud.

With his shoulders back, his chin up and a longer stride, he walked down the hill from the *Lia Fáil* with a new sense of pride as the morning sun shone on his face.

He certainly felt like the High King of Ireland as he went back through the gate of the site.

Less is More

On his way back to Galway, the words of the old lady continued to echo through his mind. He was sitting upright, with his back barely touching the bus seat.

Watching the Irish countryside zoom past, he felt energised and determined.

As he considered what the woman had told him about obtaining the *"building blocks"* for the next stage of his journey, he pulled out his phone and used the free Wi-Fi on the bus, to search for:

> Southern Holland femininity retreat secret journey

Strangely, the search engine gave only one result. He clicked it and despite the basic website, it was exactly what the woman had described.

Reading through the requirements, he would have to begin preparing his body and mind straightaway. A very strict diet was necessary to completely detoxify his body for three weeks before the retreat. He had no problem with that. He understood and welcomed the benefits of self-discipline.

He emailed the listed contact, enquiring if they had any places available. He also asked for more details on the required preparation. *"It couldn't be so strict, could it?"* he mumbled.

Then, he searched for flights. As Richard had more time than money, he was willing to book flights to the Netherlands with stopovers. The journey time would be longer but cost a lot less.

From the results of his search, he learned the flights could be very cheap. The cheapest flight required a six-hour stopover in Kiev on the way to Amsterdam and a short stopover in Stockholm on the way back to Dublin.

Whilst searching for flights, he received a response to his email.

They had accepted him to join the retreat. The mail stated the retreat had been full for months but unusually, someone had cancelled just minutes before they received his email. A stroke of luck.

However, it was not going to be as simple as he expected.

The email listed a more detailed criterion before and during the retreat. As the retreat included an ayahuasca ceremony, they informed him the guidelines were quite strict and should be taken seriously.

For three weeks before arriving, he would have to partake in a strict detox, cleansing his body. He would have to remove sugar, alcohol, black tea and coffee from his diet.

He would be required to drink a glass of purified water containing a slice of lemon and a teaspoon of pure sodium bicarbonate baking soda every morning. This would help to detox his body at a rapid pace.

In addition, he would have to go full vegan and the food he consumed would mostly have to be in soup format. None of that was a problem for Richard, as he had been a vegetarian for many years and was already living a healthy lifestyle as a vegan. A few simple adjustments would see him meet the criteria.

In preparing for the retreat, the stricter he was in relation to his diet, the more powerful the outcome. The more he put in, the more he would get out. Discipline was never an issue for Richard. It was why he was so successful with his studies and profession before he quit to go backpacking.

The big challenge for Richard came at the end of the email. It confirmed in no uncertain terms that for three weeks prior to the retreat, he should not have any peak orgasms. He re-read the last line aloud:

"'No clitoral orgasm for women and no ejaculation for men.' Are they for real?"

He was only eighteen days away from leaving for the retreat, meaning he would not get the chance to have sex again until after the retreat was over.

"Anne will be happy to hear that," he smiled.

As he read further down the mail, it explained how refraining from orgasm would help heighten the energy levels in his body and therefore enhance the healing power of ayahuasca on a much deeper level.

Doing this, he would conserve this potent energy and allow it to spread and circulate internally through his body instead of it being released externally.

"Perfect," he muttered. Now, he felt a lot more motivated.

The flight was departing eighteen days from then, which was just less than the suggested time he needed to prepare for the ayahuasca ceremony, as it would leave him in Amsterdam the night before the retreat began.

He booked the flight to Amsterdam, via Kiev and sent a mail to the retreat confirming his attendance.

It was all done.

Richard settled into his seat for some catch-up sleep, as the bus sped along the motorway to Galway.

She's Not Dead Yet

Less than three weeks later, Richard was on-board an early morning flight taking off from Dublin airport, en-route to Amsterdam, with a stop-over in Kiev.

The flight offered only snacks and sandwiches, with tea, coffee and soft drinks. As he was now on a liquid food diet, he had his own food confiscated when coming through airport security.

His stomach was rumbling when the plane touched down on Ukrainian soil.

Arriving in Boryspil Airport in Kiev, he went to the restaurant to refuel on some food during his stopover. The only vegetarian item on the menu was vegetable borscht, a delicious local soup. Served in a disposable plastic plate, the flavours exploded in his hungry mouth as he devoured it in record time.

As he was sitting there in the glow of a fulfilling meal, a Danish man close by introduced himself and his lady friend.

"Hey, how are you?" the Dane asked, nodding towards Richard.

"I'm good, thanks. And you?" he responded.

"Did you find anything you liked when you were here?" the Danish man queried.

"I'm on a stopover in the airport. On my way to Amsterdam. Unfortunately, I didn't get a chance to explore the city," Richard responded.

"Oh, I thought you were here in search of something nice, as well?" the Danish man asked. *"I just found my new wife here. She is eighteen. A real little hottie."*

As he talked, he pulled out some documentation and flashed it towards Richard to prove her age, without being prompted.

To Richard, the girl looked more like a sixteen-year-old.

She did not speak any English or Danish. The man had found her online via an agency selling young brides to Western men.

They looked like an odd couple. He was overweight and balding and could have been in his early forties but looked like he was heading for his early fifties.

The girl, on the other hand, wore high heels, a white miniskirt, a tight-fitting pink vest with possibly a push-up bra underneath, making her already prominent breasts even more noticeable. Her blonde hair was in pigtails and she was wearing an abundance of makeup to go with her strawberry red lipstick.

She seemed at ease with the circumstances as she took *selfies* on her basic smartphone. Her parents instilled in her and her younger sisters that it would be best for the family if they moved to the E.U. or U.S.A. and got married there.

A move would make it easier for her parents to obtain residency visas in the *"free world."* Her older brother was guaranteed to inherit the family farm, following family tradition.

Richard and the Dane spent the next hour chit chatting about nothing in particular, basically killing time until boarding. Richard was unsure if the guy had been drinking or taking drugs, but one thing was for sure, he was extremely happy with his *"new purchase,"* as he once let slip when describing the girl.

As the conversation continued, Richard asked, *"So, did you get married in the Ukraine?"*

"No, we are only engaged, but she will be my wife soon. I call her my wife because it makes me happy to think I will be married to such a cute little thing. My wife in Copenhagen is still alive. So, legally we can't get married until she dies," the Danish man added, in monotone.

He appeared to be a man of wealth, but his social skills left a lot to be desired. He had no filter in discussing personal matters.

At this point, Richard was confused and shocked, to say the least.

"So, you are still married ... and your wife ... is alive?" he asked confused.

Without dropping the smile, the Dane casually replied: *"Yes. My wife has been sick with cancer for the past twelve months. The doctor said she has a maximum of six months left to live. It has been a terrible sickness for her. So, I have been trying to run the house myself ... meet all the demands of our home. And trying to fend for myself. I've had to do all the cooking, as well."*

"Really sorry to hear that," Richard said. *"It must be so tough?"*

Still smiling, the Danish man said:

"Yeah, it has been very tough. I never recognised how much work went into cooking and cleaning. I have had to bring in a little Asian girl to help me with it. She is such an ugly girl, but she is a great cook. So, that is good. And the place is kept clean now. Much better than when my wife had that job, actually."

"That's, erm, good," Richard stuttered *"but I was saying it must be really tough that your wife is dying from cancer?"* he attempted to clarify and not sound insensitive.

"Not really. We've been married for fifteen years. We haven't really been having sex for the last five or six years anyway," the Danish man stated bluntly.

"When we met she was a really happy girl. And very horny. We had a fantastic sex life. But over the years, she just dried up in every way. She became no fun. So, I was paying a lot of money to young prostitutes from Eastern Europe to meet my needs."

Not wanting to judge, Richard awkwardly said, *"It's uumm, cool that you have a relationship where she allows you to, erm, sleep with ... prostitutes."*

"Oh, no," the Dane interjected *"She didn't let me. She wouldn't allow it. I had to sneak around behind her back. It was really selfish of her, actually."*

"But now, she is okay with ... you bringing home your new fiancée?" Richard asked incredulously.

"Oh, no. She won't ever know about her," the Dane said confidently. *"It won't be a problem. Women are quite stupid anyway.*

She won't even notice. We have quite a large house and I have brought in a private helper to care for her now. I have been researching my new wife for the past few months. I planned ahead and moved my old wife up to the small room on the top floor. It is warmer for her up there."

"I have totally revamped the master bedroom," the man continued. *"It is downstairs overlooking the lake. So, this sexy little thing will move into the master bedroom with me. She will stay downstairs. She won't be allowed to go upstairs or anywhere near my sick wife. It'll be fantastic. I have it all planned out."* He beamed with pride.

Richard felt sick.

With an awkward smile, he barely nodded along, as the beaming Dane shared the details of how he was managing the issue of his critically ill wife. He was almost boasting.

"The only problem I have with this one is getting her through immigration at Copenhagen. To avoid any problems, we will fly to Stockholm and drive down from there. The Swedes will let anyone enter the country," he declared.

"Part of the deal with the agency is they provide lookalike European Union passports," he added. *"These allow the girls to enter the E.U. So, as we both have the same name on our passports, the immigration officers will probably think she is my daughter. Then, they will just wave us through."*

"Or they may think she's your granddaughter," Richard cut in sarcastically, with an overly fake smile.

The Danish man exploded in laughter, at the thought of immigration officers thinking the girl could be his granddaughter. Not getting the sarcasm, he slapped Richard on the back in glee.

"Yeah, my granddaughter!" he roared. *"This is going to be so much fun. I can't wait to get her home. I have already picked out her new wardrobe. I've been ordering clothes online and having them delivered. The agency gave me all her details. Dress size and everything, so I could begin purchasing the clothes and lingerie I want her to wear. I can't wait to put them on her. She is so excited."*

Then turning to Richard, the Dane said:

"You are a good guy. What is your name?" He reached into his pocket.

"I'm Richard." He stretched out his hand towards the Dane, despite being repulsed by him. *"What is your name?"*

Without responding, the Danish man brought out his phone and opened the photo gallery. He leaned towards Richard and said:

"Here, James, have a look at this."

That name James again. Why did people continue to do that? It was a mistake people had made since he was a child. The names Richard and James did not even sound remotely similar.

The photo on his phone was of the girl wearing lingerie in a very seductive pose, taken in a professional setting.

Richard recoiled, *"No, no, no. They are for your eyes only."* he said, as he sat back and looked away.

At that point, the Danish man let out a big laugh and turned to his new fiancée. Patting her on the head, he said in a creepy baby-esque voice:

"It won't be long until I get you home." The girl glanced at him for a split second, before turning her eyes back to her smartphone.

Looking at the Dane with a blank stare and trying to comprehend what he was hearing, Richard made excuses to go to the bathroom.

Despite the conversation starting in a weird place, it seemed to get sicker and more bizarre by the minute, and he had heard enough. This was not the ideal preparation leading up to an ayahuasca ceremony, he thought.

He went to the bathroom and washed his face and hands. He almost felt dirty, rerunning in his mind some of what that guy had said. All of that unfolded as the young girl sat beside him with a blank look on her face, having no idea what she was in for.

Richard walked to the listed gate, put on an audiobook and zoned out until he boarded the plane to Amsterdam.

International Women's Day

Arriving in Amsterdam, Richard had three hours before his train departed for Venlo in the south east of the country, so he joined the evening walking tour of the city.

During the tour, the group crossed the canals, found the once-forbidden, hidden Catholic churches and learned how the city had controlled up to forty-five per cent of the worlds cash via The Dutch East India Company. The guide relayed many other titbits of information as they walked, until the tour inevitably led into the infamous Red Light District of Amsterdam.

Even though Richard had known about this infamous area, he was quite taken aback when he came across a girl standing in a window.

She was in her underwear. She was for sale. She was looking him in the eye, beckoning him to come forth.

Indeed, he wanted to go to her. Deep in his core, he felt as if he wanted to protect her and remove her from that environment and into safety. It just seemed unnatural.

The guide spun the situation as being favourable to the girls, explaining how they had many employment rights and wanted to be there. He said they had travelled from around the world to work in those windows, being paid for sex.

In fact, each day, they had to provide their passport to obtain the keys to the window for their shift. This was a way of proving they had not been trafficked nor controlled by gangs. It was all sold as being rather family friendly and cuddly.

However, the look on the girls' faces and that missing spark in their eyes told a different story.

Most of the girls appeared to be of Asian and Eastern European descent. Maybe the guide was right: They had travelled from around the world to work in those windows. But to Richard, it appeared it was more by force than by choice.

It seemed more than likely that many of the girls had been trafficked by criminal gangs, despite the authorities safeguards.

As they walked, Richard overheard a girl on the walking tour say human trafficking had become more profitable than drug trafficking, globally.

The reason was when criminals sold a drug, it could only be consumed once. When a girl or a child was sold for sex, they could be used and abused by multiple consumers twenty-four hours a day, for years on end. The money made from people trafficking was substantial and the profits increased every year, the girl explained.

Richard had seen enough. He slipped out of the tour and into a restaurant to have his last meal before going to the retreat. He devoured a small bowl of tomato soup and a bottle of water. Eating in the Red Light District tourist area, it cost €12.

A healthy diet is costlier, but Richard did not mind. As he handed over his credit card, he reasoned it was better to pay a little more now for good food than to pay a lot more on health care in later life.

After his basic meal, he made his way to Amsterdam Centraal Station and boarded a train to Venlo. On the train, his already strange day was about to take a bizarre twist. Making sure he was on the correct train, he asked a couple sitting across from him if the train was indeed going to Venlo. They turned out to be siblings.

"It is," the sister said. *"It stops in Eindhoven, my brother will get off there and I will continue onto Venlo, so just stay with me."*

The three of them chit chatted as the train sped through the majestic Dutch countryside. When asked, Richard told the siblings he was going to a retreat involving an ayahuasca ceremony. The sister sparked up. She became very attentive, sitting up and leaning forward to hear what Richard was saying.

When her brother went to find the bathroom, she asked immediately about the ayahuasca ceremony.

Richard did not really know how the retreat would unfold, and he did not fancy telling her the reason for him attending was because an old lady he met on a hilltop in rural Ireland had told him to. So, he turned the question around, asking the girl what she knew about ayahuasca.

She told him how one of her friends had attended a retreat a few years earlier and following it, she decided to quit her job, sell everything she had and move to Morocco.

When the brother returned from the bathroom, they were still talking about ayahuasca. To invite him into the conversation, Richard asked him if it was something he would be interested in. His response was quizzical:

"Everyone likes to think they are open-minded. The reality is, we're only open-minded about the minute number of subjects we are open-minded about. I am open-minded enough to understand that I am not open-minded enough to go down that rabbit-hole."

Richard looked directly at him in silence for a moment, trying to comprehend what he had just said.

As Richard replayed his words in his mind, the sister broke the silence.

She began to explain how they had recently lost their mother and had just been at her home clearing out all her possessions. It had been a tough few months for the family since the mother became sick. Richard could sympathise as his mother's sickness had also spread quickly.

The sister then explained how her mother had been euthanized just two weeks before.

"Wait, what? She had been euthanized? Is that legal in the Netherlands?" Richard asked in disbelief.

"Yes," the girl said in a thick Dutch accent. *"It has been legal here for quite a while. It is very normal."*

"What happened to your mother? Did she have no other option? Was she sick for a long time?" Richard was spitting questions at the girl.

"No. She took sick just a few months ago and with her boyfriend they decided, because of the pain, she should be euthanized."

The girl looked up at Richard and *surprise* was written all over his face. His eyes bulged and his mouth hung open. She continued:

"Okay, it is not that surprising, hey? She went through all the various loopholes with her boyfriend. They consulted two independent doctors before everything was signed off. It's quite popular here. I was recently reading an article that said, last year, euthanasia accounted for four-point-four per cent of deaths in the Netherlands. It's not such a big deal to Dutch people."

Looking at the girl, who appeared to be in her early twenties, Richard enquired about the age of their mother.

"She would have celebrated her forty-eighth birthday in three weeks," the girl said.

Doing the maths in his head he roughly calculated that around one in twenty-two people in the Netherlands were dying as a result of being euthanized.

Not for the first time that day, Richard was shocked. As he sat with a sympathetic smile trying to show compassion for these siblings dealing with the recent loss of her mother, he could not believe how strong they were. Thinking back to when his own mother died and the impact it had on him, he could not believe how casual they were about their situation.

"What about your father? Is he holding up okay?" Richard asked.

"He left when we were both children. My mother brought us up on her own, so we don't really have any contact with him. He didn't turn up for the funeral, either," the girl said.

"But at least she had a boyfriend to comfort her in her last days?" enquired Richard.

"Yeah, she did. I guess." The girl trailed off in her thoughts.

"Today he came to my mother's home as we were sorting through her things and he brought his new "friend" with him," chirped in the brother, initiating air quotes with his fingers.

"It seemed like he's had a very special friend for quite a while, hey? I just hope my mother did not know about her," the girl said, turning away.

As she looked out the window, with the train speeding through the heart of the Netherlands, Richard observed the silence until the girl was ready to talk again.

Whilst sitting quietly on the train, Richards phone began to vibrate. It was a call from his father. He probably wanted him to sign something regarding his contract termination, assumed Richard.

He let it ring out. Whatever it was he did not want to have to deal with him at that time. He placed the phone back in his pocket.

When the train arrived at Eindhoven, the siblings quietly embraced before the brother departed.

Richard did not put his headphones on, out of respect. He wanted to show he was open to talking if she was.

She did not say another word until the train pulled up at Venlo station.

Then, in a way he had seen his female friends do many times, the girl cheerfully turned around and seeming to have buried the pain deep within her, she said:

"This is our stop." She reached for her bag and took out her phone.

"Can you please give me the details for the ayahuasca ceremony?" she asked, handing Richard her phone.

"Of course," Richard said. *"I'll add you on Facebook, so we can stay in touch. I can send you some feedback following the ceremony, if that would be better?"*

"I'd appreciate that," she responded. They both walked off the train.

Handing back her phone, they came to the corner of the street, where both would be going in different directions. As he always did, Richard widened his arms and motioned the girl to come in for a hug. She went straight in and held on tight as Richard squeezed back.

Richard did not want to be the first person to let go, so he held the girl until she loosened her grip. The hug lasted for nine seconds. A long time for a hug with a stranger.

"You are really awesome. Stay in touch. God bless," he said, as he walked away, towards the direction of the farmhouse where the secret retreat would take place.

He looked at the map on his phone. Twelve minutes by bus. Thirty-three minutes walking. Richard decided to walk; he needed to clear his head before arriving at the location of the meeting place.

Based on everything he had learned, witnessed and heard this day, Richard reflected: We buy young brides. We put girls in shop windows for sale. We encourage euthanasia as an option when girlfriends show signs of ill health.

"Is this really how we treat women?" he spouted, aloud.

He was being a bit dramatic, but it reflected what he had experienced that day. His heart was heavy as he made his way through the town.

As he continued walking, at the edge of the town, before entering the countryside, he noticed a sign on the window of a small boutique that read:

HAPPY INTERNATIONAL WOMEN'S DAY
TO ALL OUR CUSTOMERS

IV

Lifting the Veil

Vine of the Soul

Walking along the country roads outside the town, each turn seemed to take Richard down a road smaller, darker and less inviting than the previous. He wondered whether he had taken a wrong turn, until he came to the entrance of a small Dutch farmhouse.

The gate was shut. Yet, beyond it lay a narrow dirt track with large trees in perfect formation lining the track. It created a dark and almost eerie feeling.

"This can't be the right place," he muttered, looking around to see where he should go next, hands on top of his head with fingers interlocked.

Then, directly behind him, a voice said:

"Go ahead."

Richard jumped in shock and spun around.

"Try the gate. It will open for you."

Standing against a tree was what looked like an old farmer. Upon closer inspection, it was a young boy of school age. Bizarrely, he was wearing clothing more suitable to a stereotypical determined-never-to-retire farmer.

Without saying a word, yet still looking at the boy, Richard traipsed backwards until he reached the gate. As the boy suggested, he turned the handle and the gate opened.

He awkwardly thanked the boy and crept inside, as the gate creaked closed behind him. He turned around and began to walk towards the old farmhouse.

It felt like a light had been turned on, as the path now felt airy and well lit. It seemed a lot more inviting from inside the gate than it did from the outside.

Richard gingerly ambled to the front door of the farmhouse and rattled the large knocker three times. From the outside, no one appeared to be home. Yet, almost instantly, the door opened and a warm smiling face greeted him.

The girl, who appeared to be in her early twenties, was dressed in a long airy white gown. She had a healthy glow and sparkling brown eyes to go with her flowing brown hair. Waving her hand to invite Richard in, she said:

"Welcome, Richard. We've been expecting you."

Stepping inside, he was struck by how deceptively large the house was. There were approximately thirty people spread across the room. All dressed in white, looking up at him with warm welcoming smiles on their soft faces.

The room consisted mostly of white walls and ceiling, broken only by massive brown wooden beams. In the corner, a gentle fire crackled, as a splashing of candles flickered across the array of surfaces.

The scent of firewood mixed with the burning of exotic oils nibbled lightly on the nostrils. All blended naturally, creating a homely and warming environment.

With an awkward smile, whilst removing his shoes, Richard nodded at the people, to greet them. Inside, his mind was working overtime, as he said to himself:

"I didn't really think this through."

Richard had no expectation of what he would find when he arrived at *"the secret retreat,"* as the old lady had called it.

Before boarding the plane, he had spent the best part of three weeks focused on himself. Detoxing and cleansing his body and mind. Preparing his energy for what may lie ahead. Not once did he envision he would be confronted by this sight upon walking in the door.

"My name is Zeni," said the girl closing the door behind him. *"I will be your guardian during your stay."*

She reached out and gave Richard a big hug. It felt soft and natural, warm and protective.

"Come. Let me show you to your dorm room." She walked down a few steps, and across the large room of people lounging, with Richard in tow.

An older man, sitting in the corner, gently taught a girl half his age to play the hang drum as they walked by.

Richard's room was quite basic with three beds and a door to a simple en-suite bathroom. He would be sharing with two other girls. On his bed lay a bundle of neatly folded, white clothing he had to wear throughout his stay.

"Everything is always perfect," Richard said, looking around as he tossed his bag on the bed.

Richard changed into the soft white clothing and returned to mingle and have food with the others. On the menu were vegetable soup, rice crackers and green tea. The jugs of freshly squeezed fruit juices were already empty.

Everyone was welcoming and seemed genuinely pleased to have Richard in their company. As they chatted, Richard tentatively told the story of what had happened in the weeks leading up to his arrival at the retreat.

To his astonishment, no one thought it strange an old lady on a hill in Ireland had been responsible for him coming to the Netherlands.

Listening to everyone talk, Richard noticed the stories they shared were quite similar at their core. In addition, they all shared similar motivations for being there. They all wanted more from life and they were searching for a greater purpose. Each of them had long realised there was more to life than: Eat. Sleep. Work. Repeat.

Each reason given for turning up at this farmhouse, at a remote location in the Netherlands, was as vague and mysterious as Richard's. These people came from all over the world and from every walk of life. The only common denominator was they had all listened to their heart's desire and it had led them to the old Dutch farmhouse at that time.

As the others drifted off to bed, eventually only Richard and Zeni remained on a beanbag in the corner. Richard was still not fully aware of what the days ahead would consist of. He did not know much about ayahuasca.

He explained to Zeni how he had turned up on blind faith, following his heart, simply because it resonated with him after meeting the old lady in Ireland.

Letting out a giggle, Zeni sat up on the beanbag and turning to face Richard, she said:

"Okay, when most people are going to reconnect with Mother Ayahuasca for the first time, they seem to be quite nervous. But you seem, like, so chilled. It was, like, so awesome to listen to your story and hear how you've followed the messages from nature to get here, despite the whole name thing."

"Yeah, I don't have any nerves around what will unfold, but I'm still not sure what to expect," Richard said.

"So, let me, like, try explaining to you what ayahuasca is, from my experience."

Zeni then continued to explain, in a Dutch accent with a Cali' West Coast twang.

"So, the word 'ayahuasca' means 'vine of the soul' or 'vine with a soul'—depending on whom you ask—and it is basically a plant mixture from the Amazon. What is unique about ayahuasca is that for it to work, it relies on a very specific combination of plants. Like, we are not totally sure how exactly the tribespeople of the Amazon managed to discover this combination. There are some mythical stories on how they managed to do that. In any case, the result is a drink you will experience tomorrow. Then, the magic happens," she said clapping her hands excitedly, as she quickly finished her sentence.

Her excitable approach to communication made Richard chuckle inwards, as she continued to explain:

"A few minutes after drinking, you will be carried into a fabulous state of consciousness for, like, up to eight hours. Ayahuasca does this thing where it allows this visionary state of mind, which helps you to umm, communicate with, like, a higher nature to, like, find solutions to life questions you have."

She paused for a moment, looking to the ceiling, before happily adding:

"And it can also enhance the richness of your mind at, like, a spiritual level."

To say Richard had a look of confusion on his face would be an understatement.

"Sounds a bit crazy, I know. But most people I know who have travelled with Mother Ayahuasca have stepped outside the realms of time and space and they've all said that they, like, experience this profound sense of bliss, wonder and, like, awe when in her presence."

She paused for a moment, looking at her palms.

Richard welcomed the pause as he desperately tried to keep up with what she was saying. She then continued:

"But, like, it may not be all smooth sailing. In South America, ayahuasca is also affectionately known as "la Purga," as it, like, totally purges the body physically. And purifies the mind psychologically. Some people physically cleanse the body by vomiting and spitting during their journey."

Richard's eyes widened.

"But it isn't as bad as it sounds," Said Zeni, noticing his reaction. *"People usually feel, like, totally refreshed and reborn after going through it. Richard, trust me, it is such a strong and beautiful experience."*

Richard just stared at her.

Not sensing his thought process was about thirty seconds behind her, Zeni then stood up and before walking away, she added:

"Don't worry, you have already met Mother Ayahuasca. You used to talk with her when you were a child. You'll feel comfortable with her, when you meet again."

She turned and walked away.

Richard watched her as she crossed the floor, with the lightest of steps. Almost floating, she barely made a sound on the old wooden floors, before disappearing through the small doorway.

He was still staring at the doorway for a few seconds after she had disappeared through it.

After those few hours of talking and attempting to gain more understanding, Richard went to bed with the words and insights from Zeni running through his mind.

He really needed to get a good rest after what had been a long and remarkable day.

Putting his head on the pillow, he mumbled, *"Tomorrow is gonna be eventful."*

Spraying Sound

As is custom for surfers and those who meditate, Richard woke 6 a.m. the morning of the ceremony. He treasured dawn and liked to be up when the early morning breeze whispers her secrets.

He felt fully refreshed and energised. Following the insights he received from Zeni and the other guests, he was cautiously excited to be reintroduced to Mother Ayahuasca.

As they were not allowed food or drink before the ceremony, he went down and joined the other guests for a group meditation, to prepare spiritually, physically, mentally and energetically for the ceremony.

As they sat through the specially designed guided meditation, the guardians energetically prepared the large tent where the ayahuasca ceremony would be held.

After the meditation, the clock rushed towards noon, and the participants were called to enter the large circular tent. Twenty-four people who had only briefly met entered the ceremonial space.

Individually, they found a place within the space that felt safe to them.

Candles filled the core of the tent, as Amazonian tapestries and art lined the walls.

Dressed in white comfortable clothing, men and women, aged eighteen to sixty-six, got comfortable as they settled onto their mattresses. Securing their journals, puffing up their pillows, they ensured their tissues and plastic buckets were close by.

It was reminiscent of a big white pyjama party as chit chat between the participants gradually faded out and silence naturally descended over the ceremonial space.

At the altar, to one side of the tent, the ceremonial leader poured a milky-brown liquid into a series of glasses organised four deep, six wide.

The ceremonial leader sitting at the front, then declared:

"One per cent of the people on this planet at this time are aware ayahuasca exists. One per cent of those who are aware have access to ayahuasca. And one per cent of those who have access are called to partake in this journey with Mother Ayahuasca, at any one time. If you're here with us now, it's because you were called. You are meant to be here."

She then stood up and overlooked the participants. She asked everyone to contribute one word to signify what he or she wished to gain from his or her meeting with Mother Ayahuasca.

The participants stated, *"Joy," "Safety," "Relief"* and many other declarations. Each was as unique as the individual. When it came to Richard, he loudly and confidently stated the word:

"Knowledge."

That was why he was there. He wanted more knowledge. He wanted to know who he truly was. He wanted to know his place on the Earth and what he could do to make the world better. Ultimately, he wanted to know what his path was. That was his intention as he sat down on his mat.

Once settled in the silence, his guide Zeni presented him with a glass containing a milky brown substance—the ayahuasca.

Giving gratitude for the opportunity to join this secret retreat and for all that had happened to lead him to that moment, Richard humbly drank the naturally brown liquid.

He then lay back on his mat, with his eyes closed. It tasted unlike anything he had ever drunk. Slightly bitter, but nothing as extreme as the nauseating taste others had described.

In his mind, he was saying: *"I am open to receiving. I allow Mother Ayahuasca to take me on a journey for my greater good."*

For 45 minutes, the tent was in complete silence. The ceremonial leader then gave the nod for sound to enter the space.

At opposite sides of the ceremonial space sat a man and a girl, each with a hang drum on their lap. Working together, they filled the space with a melody. It floated in the same manner a flower delivery boy could fill a busy elevator with the scent from a bouquet of fresh cut wildflowers—it softly glided through the air from one participant to the next.

The body of each soul shuddered ever so gently as the frequency of the sound passed through it.

The melody was nurtured and developed as they sprayed sound around the space, coaxing one melody after another from the flying-saucer-shaped drums. The participants were lost in a concoction of sensation.

After an unknown period, Richard opened his eyes.

It was as if all his senses had been turned up.

He could hear clearer. Everything from his skin and hair to his inner core was more sensitive to feeling. His sense of smell was heightened.

However, what was most noticeable was his laser-sharp sight. It was as if before this experience, he had been living his life, seeing through a layer of mesh.

It seemed as if the mesh had been lifted and he could see everything in high-definition. Colours were deeper and brighter. It was as if he was seeing colours he had not experienced before. New colours. Colours that had not existed in his *normal* world.

He could see the faces of the guardians as clear as ever—they mingled through the group, caring for people with water and blankets.

As he observed them, they appeared to be gentle Elven people with pointy ears who seemed to float around the room with the softest of steps.

Observing this in normal circumstances, Richard would have freaked out. However, it all just seemed natural and real at that moment. Richard was completely receptive to everything happening.

He felt protected under the watchful gaze of Zeni, his guardian. As she moved around the room, their eyes would regularly meet. She would flash him a warm and caring smile to show him he was under her protection. It helped him to feel at ease.

Richard had no sense of time. As he delved deeper into the process, he felt the need to lie back and close his eyes. It was at that moment when Mother Ayahuasca really began to come forward.

Lying there on his mat in the foetal position, with his white blanket pulled up under his chin, he was taken in his imagination to another room. He had been told he would receive visions during his journey with Mother Ayahuasca.

The first vision he received carried him as an observer to a social setting. He could not hear anything, but he felt connected to everyone in the room. So much so, he could feel what they were thinking, almost as if he was inside each of their minds.

His initial visualisation was so detailed, as if floating in the room as an observer, connected to the thoughts and feelings of a lady in a moment in time.

Walking across the room, wearing a red dress, black heels and red lipstick with her brown hair casually tossed back. She is focused on whether her male friend will arrive on time, as arranged. Her focus then moves to her new shoes and how one is rubbing on the heel of her left foot and how the little toe in her right shoe is being squeezed a bit too tight.

The entire room is enthralled with her. From the moment she walked in, she brought a new energy. She radiates femininity. A higher vibration. She has the power that can stop all in their tracks. She is a woman in touch with herself, her inner being, her soul, the Earth, the universe. All this power converges into this single soul at this moment, and everyone senses it.

She gracefully moves through the building, hair slightly bouncing at the same frequency as her breasts. Each step pulls her bottom and hips from side to side like a thoroughbred approaching the paddock.

The women are the first to notice her, recognising her energy—they also possess it. Law of attraction. They sense it. The women who have protected their femininity see her as one of their soul sisters and it warms them inside.

Those who have repressed their femininity are the most intimidated by this power from the heavens. The energy surge from the women alerts the men.

Now, the men crane their necks. Their eyes go from her hair, to her eyes, to her lips, to her neck, to her breasts. Then, their eyes trace along her back to her hips, to her bottom, to her thighs. Their eyes then go to her knees, to her calves, to her ankles and to her shoes.

Then, their eyes journey back up the same path. They repeat this journey many times in a few seconds. They are captivated. The conversations fall into a lull. They hold their breath. Their hearts quicken. The feminine women go on the same eye journey as the men, admiring her oozing sensual beauty.

The women who suppress their feminine energy shuffle in their position, attempting to regain the attention of the group. They purposefully lean in the sight of the men. They begin making random statements at the other women and tut and sigh. They are threatened. This sixty-three-year-old woman has maintained the power they once radiated themselves. They suppressed it. They know it. That is what hurts the most.

With her long hair, she has the enhanced intuition that comes with it. She feels the energy of the room focus on her. Now, her thoughts turn from whether she remembered to remove the price tag from the bottom of her new shoes, to a rush of blood—that moment of realisation: "They are all looking at me. I must get to my table."

Richard opened his eyes at that moment and was transported back into the ceremonial space. Zeni was kneeling beside him, looking down at him with her big brown eyes. She was gently stroking his hand.

"You are okay.

"Allow.

"Go with Mother Ayahuasca," she purred with a warming smile, as she looked caringly down on him.

La Purga

Throughout the ceremonial space, there was a hive of activity. Some wept silently, others cried out. One screamed to the heavens at the top of his voice. A few had their faces deep in buckets as they vomited up the very wretchedness that had clung to their body and soul for too long.

Richard closed his eyes. As he began to settle back into the state he was in, he felt an abrupt surge coming from the core of his being. His eyes snapped open.

"Bucket. My bucket."

Zeni had moved away. She was no more than a few metres away, but she may as well have been on the other side of the planet. Split-second reactions were required. Richard needed to vomit.

Rolling onto his side, he grabbed for the bucket with one hand. As soon as he had it over his face, he pulled a stream of gooey liquid from the core of his being.

The level of violence from this projectile vomiting was disturbingly loud and thunderous. Twin streams of the gooey liquid sprayed through Richard's nose and mouth simultaneously.

Commanding convulsions shook his body, starting in the depths of his bowels and traveling outwards to the tip of his nose. It was vicious.

Whilst maintaining a protective gaze over him, Zeni and the other guardians left Richard to his own devices as they sat with other participants.

It was unrelenting, lasting for close to thirty minutes.

He had been on a deep cleansing detox for the weeks leading up to this moment. He had barely eaten anything solid for weeks.

His nasal passage felt stretched from the gooey liquid being squeezed out. His jaw was sore from being jerked open with each regurgitation. The corners where his upper and lower lips met, felt strained and stretched. Tears streamed from his eyes.

This was the infamous ayahuasca purge he had heard about. *La Purga* as it was known in the Amazon.

As violent as it was, and as physically taxing as it was, Richard never felt like it was uncomfortable at an emotional level. It felt welcome and he recognised the purge for what it was: a purification of his body, mind and spirit.

It felt as if Mother Ayahuasca was medicinal first, educational second. She needed to extract the toxins from his body right down to the cellular level. Demons had to be dragged out at the spiritual level. It hurt. Physically, Richard was in agony.

Nothing unwanted that is as deeply rooted leaves without a fight.

Then it stopped. As quickly as it began, it passed.

Richard, head still in the bucket, opened his gushing eyes and took a deep breath. Calmness swept over him.

He scanned his body. That brought his attention to a rumbling in his bowels.

The cleansing was incomplete.

The next stage of *La Purga* was about to begin.

He placed the bucket beside him and grabbed for a handful of tissue. He put the other hand in the air to gain the attention of the guardians as he frantically wiped the goo from his face with the tissue.

Zeni softly and speedily made her way over to Richard, taking care not to disturb any of the other participants in their journey. She took him under the shoulder and helped him to his feet.

There was a series of portable toilets set up along the trees about thirty metres from the entrance to the ceremonial tent. With her help, Richard gingerly made his way to the toilet.

As soon as the cheap plastic door on the toilet banged shut, he frantically pulled down his white shorts. Before he could even get his bum on the toilet seat, a deluge of sludge came gushing out.

It came in waves.

"Where is it all coming from?" he wondered.

Richard was leaning as far forward as he possibly could. In all his years in medicine, he had never experienced such a prolonged excretion.

Then, with his hands strapped tightly around his ankles, his eyes popped open and he realised it was complete. It may have stopped for some time prior.

It was a knocking on the plastic door that brought him back to his senses. It was Zeni, asking if he was feeling okay. He was.

He truly was. With the surety that day follows night, lightness followed *La Purga*.

The cleansing was complete. It felt like his soul had been showered.

He cleaned himself up, scrubbed his hands and face.

With Zeni as a crutch, he made his way back to the ceremonial space. As he returned, the air felt as clean and refreshing as never before. The grass under his bare feet felt as if each blade provided his foot with a tender massage, with each step.

Settling onto his mattress, he realised everyone in the space was deep into his or her own educational journey, with Mother Ayahuasca as teacher.

There were music and singing, crying and chuckling, maddening screaming and frenzied laughter. Amongst it all was a backing track of alternating regurgitation.

It was a scene very few would wish to witness.

Richard closed his eyes again and drifted off into that place between sleeping and being awake. There, he observed all kinds of beautiful patterns entering his mind, coming and going in the most magical of ways.

He was at ease and allowed everything to unfurl in its timeless state.

His internal defences had dissolved as he experienced a deep sense of love and compassion for himself. He felt a contentment and connectedness with his place in the world at that moment.

Lying there, he felt a great trauma he blindly carried had been lifted. It was noticeable by its absence.

His mind felt silent and clear. There was a total sense of knowing. He felt a great understanding of everything.

His life was available for review, with Mother Ayahuasca providing perspective and insight. During times of pain, he saw the beauty and growth. Times of laughter and joy brought gratitude and abundance.

All had a place and was contextualized as part of his human journey on Earth.

He was no longer connected to his soul. He was a soul. He was on the Earth at this time to experience human consciousness.

Everything was one. One was everything.

Mother's Guidance

Then, he remembered: *"Who am I?"*

The intention he had set for this journey was to find out who he *truly* was. He wanted to know why he was the way he was. Why was he always different from everyone else?

In his mind, and maybe aloud, it was hard to tell by then, as he was so deep into the process, he asked:

"Who am I, Mother Ayahuasca? Who am I? Please let me remember my sacred lineage and my reason for being."

By now, his ego had completely dissolved. He felt at one with all. He had returned to this level for the first time in his adult life and he got there by drinking a plant-based mix.

Nothing is as humbling as cutting a deal with a plant, when the plant has complete dominance and control over the proceedings.

Whilst watching the colourful patterns dance and unfurl, a small black hole opened in the centre of his visualisations.

With that, he could hear a buzzing sound.

As the black hole got bigger, the buzzing got louder.

The beautiful patterns were slowly being squeezed to the periphery of his vision and the sound became deafening and painful.

The black empty hole grew along with the buzzing until there was nothing but a small slither of colour at the peripheral of his visualisation.

The buzzing was unbearable. It felt timeless. It was never-ending.

It was as punishing as it was relentless.

Just when he felt he could not endure anymore, the buzzing dramatically stopped.

He was left engulfed in a black empty silence.

Nothingness was everywhere.

This was the first time Richard began to feel uncomfortable. It was the darkest black he had ever experienced and the emptiest silence he had ever felt. How long he remained in this timeless vacuum of nothingness it was hard to tell. Seconds felt like hours.

Emptiness.

The first relief came when he sensed slight rumblings.

Some-thing existed in the no-thing.

Eventually, it became evident there was life in the darkness.

It was a child.

Hidden away in the darkness, a child was whimpering.

Within his visualisations, Richard had free will. He moved towards the child. He felt protective of the child. He also felt connected to it. Slowly, he inched closer to the child.

Going forward in approach, he felt the child pull back in fear.

For the first time, he could visualise the outline of the child.

It was a little boy. He had been ignored, unloved and abandoned.

As Richard carefully went closer, he told the child he was safe, communicating almost telepathically. Words were unnecessary in that sphere.

Getting his first detailed glimpse of the child, the boy was sitting on the ground with his head between his knees, as if wrapped in a protective ball.

As Richard went closer to the boy, he could see he was rocking back and forward. The sense of neglect that resonated from the boy was palpable. At a vital age of his development, he had been abandoned.

Richard went closer still. He was within touching distance of the child. He reached out to gently touch him, by attempting to soothingly rub his head.

Slowly, he moved his hand forward.

Just as he was about to touch the boy, the child popped his head out from between his knees.

Richard gasped, dropped to the ground, falling backwards.

What he saw distressed him.

He scrambled away from the boy. The child stared at Richard with wild darting eyes.

The boy had a face he had seen before. Those eyes, the lips, the high cheekbones, the ears. Maintaining full eye contact, Richard stared back in disbelief.

Neither of them blinked.

Richard knew who he was. He did not want to admit it. He could not deny it.

The child blinked. Those eyes, neither green nor blue, but falling somewhere in-between were the same eyes he had seen every day of his life.

The eyes staring back were Richard's own.

It was Richard. It was he. It was his inner child. They were one and the same.

The moment Richard accepted this, the child instantly felt at ease. It was tangible.

Richard had scared his inner child away when he was nine. Now, he had come into the darkness to reclaim what he had pushed away. Just as the woman on the Hill of Tara had foretold.

He went to the child and, wrapping his arms around the boy, held his head gently against his chest.

At this point, the darkness was less black and the silence held the resonance of sound.

No longer a vacuum. The essence of an environment had returned.

Without deep contemplation, Richard had always known there was a black hole of emptiness at his very core. He had endeavoured to fill the hole with many things over the years.

Education, shopping, sex and football temporarily filled the emptiness. But he was always left wanting more when the initial rush had subsided.

Holding his inner child gently in his arms, he could feel light slowly fill the black hole at his core. He was healing. The energy was flowing and with the light came strength, imagination, power, inspiration and energy.

It also brought another substance. It was a substance he was familiar with as a child. He did not have a word for it. The best way to describe it was as a substance from another realm. It was a substance of *magic*.

He felt whole again. Not since he was nine had he felt that way. He was the one he was meant to be again.

He was whole.

This was the reward for searching his soul. This is what he got for asking Mother Ayahuasca the very simple question: *"Who am I?"*

Once again, he had magic within him.

Magic can only live within the essence of a child. Usually, this power is banished from us by bitter adults before we reach puberty.

Richard had reconnected with his inner child. This reunification was the completion of the first stage of his journey. With the guidance of his inner child, he would now be supported in his development. As long as he maintained the connection with his inner child, his life would be continually enriched.

With his physical body motionless on the mattress within the ceremonial room, Zeni passed by to check on him. The only sign of movement were the tears that gently trickled from his closed eyes.

Deep in his soul, Richard was overcome with emotion as he was reunified and made whole.

Holding his inner child in his arms in that timeless state, the tranquillity was to be violently disrupted as Mother Ayahuasca sent another message.

It came through his sacral chakra like a bolt of lightning.

It was not that he could hear, see or feel the message. It was as if it was all three at the same time, without it being any of the senses in particular.

Richard received the message clearly:

You were a king. You are a king. You are the king. You carry this royal lineage from a past life.

You have lived many lives. In a previous existence, you were a great king who survived a coup as a child. That coup killed both parents, the reigning king and queen of the land. Before your father died, he laid you in the saddlebag of his trusted mare and set her free. The horse was eventually found grazing on the riverbank of a village near Glastonbury in the south of England. You were rescued, reared and cared for by harlots, who were unaware of who you were or where you came from. They named you James.

Growing up in a brothel surrounded by women who loved, protected and cared for you as their own child, you felt very protective of them in return. As a result, you grew to become a skilled swordsman and street fighter within that tough environment. You felt a necessity to protect the women who had become your adopted mothers from the daily violence they faced at the hands of men.

Robbed of your birthright as the king of the land, your life was transformed once you were arrested for enabling tax evasion within the brothel. In a strange twist of events, you came face-to-face with the then-ruling king whilst taken to court. In that moment, looking each other in the eye, you were both forced to acknowledge your true legacy. This brought trouble, yet you fought your way up to reclaim your rightful title as king.

Despite your rise through society, you never forgot the kindness, love and protection afforded by the women in the brothel. They saved you as a child and loved you as their own son. In return, you have always felt protective of women and femininity—you worked during your reign to protect and elevate women. This is a trait you have carried with you across many incarnations. You have carried this trait during this lifetime, as well.

Now, you are being called to rise from slumber, to fulfil your karmic contract. You have been doing the bare minimum with your skills and attributes. You have been using your power only to protect women. Now, you must raise your intentions. From this day forth, it will not be sufficient for you to simply "protect women" when they are in danger. You must utilise your power to go beyond that.

You must work to enable feminine women to take their rightful place as the leaders of society, across the globe. You are a king. Now, your role in this life is to elevate femininity. That is your true self. That is your path. It is your heritage. You are King James.

When Richard came around again, he had his journal in his hands and these were the words he had scribbled down.

Reading it back, he was astounded. He looked up and caught the eye of Zeni, who looked at him from beside the fireplace. With the light of the fire flickering on her face, she nodded and smiled at Richard. It was almost as if she had already known what his journey consisted of.

Nettles Don't Sting

Lying on his mat in the ceremony room, he was now wholly aware of his surroundings. With his journal still in his hands, Richard turned to a new page and began to write.

At the top of the page, he wrote three words, all in capital letters:

I AM SORRY

Then, reaching into the cosmic and connecting with the feelings deep down in his heart and soul, he allowed his pen to move across the page, writing:

Please forgive us. To our sisters, mothers, daughters sharing this world with us, we are sorry. We have treated you improperly and ignored your needs. Please forgive us. We have forced you to conform to our cold, detached machine ways. We are sorry.

We have forced you to change, to forget your true nature, to fit our requirements. We are sorry. All over the world, we have covered you, stripped you, exposed you, hidden you, and all for our selfish needs and desire. We are hurting and we have forced our pain upon you. Hurt people, hurt people.

We have forced you to leave behind your true essence, without consideration to that beautiful little girl living deep in your heart. She is sad. She is ignored. Her voice is beaten down. Her feelings are hidden. Her thoughts are suppressed.

There is no place in the machine mind world for the love, compassion, care, empathy, joy, giggles, lightness or brightness of that little girl. We have forced our feminine friends to ignore, suppress and chastise the little feminine girl who lives in them, who is them. For that, we apologise. We are sorry. Forgive us, sister. I am sorry. Forgive me, sister.

At his very core, he could feel the generations of pain and suffering inflicted on femininity by men and their machine minds. Not just on women, but also on feminine men beaten down throughout history.

Tears started to trickle down his face. Then, he started to wail and cry loudly.

He cried for hours. Weeping and wailing. He was inconsolable.

At 6 a.m., he awoke, back in his dormitory bed without recollection of how he got there. He felt empty. He felt light. He felt cleansed. He also felt very vulnerable and completely exhausted.

His body was physically sore all over. He had not felt as much physical pain since the morning after the beating he had received in the rainforest.

He slowly pulled himself out of bed and went in for a long shower. Hot water felt uncomfortable on his body. He turned it down to lukewarm, but it was still uncomfortable. He had to have the water running as cold as possible. It felt refreshing. He stood under the water, as it seemed to cleanse him at all levels.

Richard spent the rest of the day alone, mostly sitting at the edge of the woodland that backed up onto the old farmhouse. He was lost in his thoughts of all that had happened the day before.

Everything that had been revealed led Richard to ponder on who he was.

He was *acting* his way through life. He fully understood he was not the *personality* he was sharing with the world—that was merely a composite of habits, quirks and behaviours used as a shield to deflect suffering.

Awaking the following morning, he still pondered the big questions around his existence on Earth.

Richard remained in these thoughts whilst in bed, until there was a knock on the door. It was a lady informing him *"the closing ceremony begins in six minutes."*

Richard quickly went in for a sixty-second shower, dried himself down, dressed into his normal clothing and hurried down to the closing ceremony.

The first stage of this was when everyone broke into small groups of six people to share their experiences.

They then all moved into sitting around in a large circle for some closing words from Amanda, the group leader.

Despite all of this, Richard still felt as if he was off the planet somewhere.

He still had not been properly grounded following his meeting with Mother Ayahuasca.

Sensing Richard was not fully grounded, Zeni went to him and called him to the side. She instructed him to remove his t-shirt and footwear.

Taking his hand, she guided him towards the edge of the woodlands, which ran along the back of the ceremony area. Richard was instructed to stay in complete silence until they returned to his shoes and t-shirt. He was not to utter a single word.

They wandered into the ancient forest and soaked up the energy and chi in the silence of the woods. The sun spat its rays through openings in the trees, appearing like laser beams of gold.

As the mud squeezed up through their toes and the smell of sap and pines filled the air, it had a real balancing effect on Richard.

As he wandered through in silence, he let go of Zeni's hand as he was drawn to one big, broad tree of unique appeal. It stood out from the rest because of the twists and turns defining the shape of its trunk. It just oozed character.

Richard walked over and gently put his arms around the tree. The tree was so broad, his long arms just reached slightly more than halfway around.

With his left cheek pressed against the thick, uneven bark of the tree, he felt a massive sense of gratitude for nature. Then, replicating the lady on The Hill of Tara, he put his forehead against the tree and whispered: *"Thank you."*

As he let go of the tree, he turned around to notice Zeni had silently come over and stood beside him. With a smile, she then bent over and began to stroke one of the nettles growing beside the tree. As she did it, she held up her hand to show Richard the nettle had not stung her.

Nettles have hairs on their leaves and stems. These inject chemicals including histamine into the body producing a stinging sensation when touched.

However, the stinging sensation does not affect people who have experienced ayahuasca. They are immune to being stung for some time after as they are more aligned with nature.

Putting his faith in Zeni, without saying a word, Richard bent down, stroked and played with the nettles. For the first time in his life, he did not get stung.

They hugged in silence. Then, with Zeni taking his hand she flashed him a big smile, warmly nodding her head. They then returned slowly to the edge of the woodland, hand in hand, feeling grounded and back in balance.

They arrived in time for the last stage of the closing ceremony, which was heart dancing.

Soulful music gently played on the hang drum and the participants allowed their bodies to take control and move in whatever way it wanted.

Richard started quite sheepishly and gentle on his feet.

Without his really noticing, the pace of the music had gradually increased.

He was soon jumping around and full of life as the hang drum had been gradually replaced with bongo drummers.

As the tempo built in the music, the participants jumped higher and danced harder as beads of sweat gathered on their brow. Extra layers of clothing were removed—men and women going topless.

The drummers banged frantically creating an energy-charged rhythmic sound. It built up to the point where each participant was just jumping up and down and screaming with joy.

And then, silence.

The drummers stopped in unison and all the sound that had carried Richard and the others higher and deeper, now allowed them to crash to the earth.

They fell flat on their backs.

In the silence, the only sound was of heavy breathing as Richard and the others gathered themselves.

Now, he felt fully grounded once again. His feet were again firmly on the Earth and he never felt more cleansed or energised.

Looking around at the people who had shared this experience with him, he knew when they walked back up that tree-lined pathway and out through that strange creaking gate, life would never be the same again.

Each of them had lived through an experience that was pivotal. When they took their last breath on this Earth, and life flashed before their eyes, they would look back at their meeting with Mother Ayahuasca as a defining moment.

Although each of them had significant individual experiences, the sharing of it with a community of people from around the globe enhanced the rewards and reduced the risks. Richard recognised they had been through a process that would bond them for the rest of their time on this planet.

Less than half of the people at the retreat had come from the Netherlands and the adjoining country of Belgium. Most had travelled from around the globe to be there. They shared similar stories. Now, they all had received answers and insight from Mother Ayahuasca that they would take back with them.

It was up to each of them as individuals to take the knowledge and use it in a manner that best served them and their community.

Life is not about overcoming the obstacles. Earth is our karmic classroom. The obstacles are life—they enable us to develop and expand.

Growing up, Richard's grandmother would often remind him: *"Life does not happen to you. It happens for you."*

V

Collateral Connection

On the White Line
Flickers of Lightness
Cosmic Connection
Madness has love
From Music to Lyrics

On the White Line

Arriving back in Amsterdam following the closing ceremony, Richard came out of Centraal Station and sauntered along Haarlemmerdijk in search of a hostel to stay for the night.

As he was unsure of his physical, spiritual and mental state following the ceremony, he had planned an extra night in the city to realign and ground himself again.

He sent Kate a quick message:

> Arrived back safely in Amsterdam.
> The retreat was magical. Will tell you
> about it later when I get some wifi.
> Hope all is good with you? Love R x

Short and simple. Kate always waited for him to check in whilst he was travelling. She wanted to know he was safe.

As he wandered along the street still slightly detached, he lifted his head and across the street was a lady in exact sync with him.

She also lifted her head in that exact moment as they both turned towards each other and locked glaze.

He recognised her. She was familiar to him. He knew her.

"Is it Hannah?"

Physically, she had changed in many ways but even from across the street, those eyes were unmistakable. Her aura undeniable. Yes, it was Hannah.

Both slowing, they had now stopped walking and come to a halt mid-step. They stood still at opposite sides of the street. Staring across at each other. Wordless. Not blinking.

Turning their bodies, both of them had one foot now pointing directly at one another.

Without a change in facial expression, they both gravitated slowly towards each other, one step at a time.

Meeting on the white line in the middle of the road, they stopped when at touching distance. As they stood there, the locals showed their displeasure—muttering in Dutch, they swerved on their bikes to avoid them, ringing their bells frantically.

Richard and Hannah were oblivious to the bikes.

Without saying a word, they embraced in the middle of the road, both leaning in on their left side for a warm hug. It felt familiar.

Her body lined up seamlessly with his, her head slotted perfectly under his chin. Physically, they fit so well together. It was almost as if the final two pieces of a jigsaw, made of magnet, had finally clicked back into place, completing the picture.

More than fifteen seconds later, they remained standing in an embrace in the middle of the road. Neither had said a single word. Time stood still.

Hannah lifted her head from his chest and looked up at Richard with her deep brown eyes.

"Yes, this is Hannah."

He had never seen eyes like hers before. The closest he got to experiencing such depth was when he was working in the Amazon and the Milky Way stretched above him from horizon to horizon. However, that still did not represent the depth and beauty of these eyes, the windows to her soul.

Lost in her eyes, he muttered the words:

"You're ... so beautiful."

The content smile on Hannah's face widened into an involuntary beam as he said it. Her eyes twinkled further, despite the overcast skies.

This embrace may have lasted for about three minutes. What might not seem like a long time by normal standards could seem like an eternity when standing in the middle of a busy road close to Amsterdam Centraal Station. It was certainly too long for the locals, as they rushed by on their bicycles, ringing their bells in discontentment.

Taking him by the hand and pulling him to the side of the road where she had come from, they both spluttered out a magnitude of questions.

"What are you doing in Amsterdam?" Hannah asked.

"Thought you were in Africa?" responded Richard.

Without either answering the questions, Hannah said:

"Okay, we need to sit down. Let's go get some tea."

Still holding hands, their fingers intertwined, they walked to the closest café. They sat down and just looked at each other.

True communication exists in the silence between the words.

Staring deep into each other's eyes, either may have mumbled a few words and a while later, the other may have spluttered a random statement. There was no conversation. They were both lost in the moment. Lost in the memories. Lost in the emotions.

They were startled out of this timeless state by the waitress.

"You cannot sit here if you're not going to order from the menu. Tables are reserved for customers," she snapped.

The waitress had been standing there longer than she had hoped, without recognition from either Richard or Hannah.

They both ordered green tea with a bowl of fruit and *soygurt*. Then, they slowly tread into their catch-up.

They first met six years prior in Uganda on the shore of Lake Bonyuoni, when Richard was backpacking through Africa following his summer exams. Hannah had just graduated from her Ph.D. in medicine and was in Uganda to unwind and celebrate with friends. They clicked instantly.

She had a very prim and proper Jewish upbringing in a wealthy Amsterdam neighbourhood. At the time, she was recovering from a broken heart, following the news her boyfriend of three years was transsexual, and had been using her as his cover story.

She was twenty-four when she met her ex-boyfriend. He was thirty-three. He worked in global finance for a major bank in Luxembourg so was usually absent because of work, travelling around the world. The result being she did not get to see him very often. They had emotionless sex six times in three years after he took her virginity.

In all that time, he never told her he loved her.

In Luxembourgish, there is no phrase for *"I love you."* Instead, they say, what essentially translates to *"I am happy with you."* As a result, her ex-boyfriend used this as justification for refusing to declare his love for Hannah.

As they talked by the lake in Africa at that time, Hannah told Richard about her life in the Netherlands, the circumstances around the breakup with her ex-boyfriend and her hopes for the future. Despite going through a recent breakup, she was full of lightness and joy.

She appeared as if she did not have a care in the world, as they explored the shores of the lake together. In spite of her being a few years older than Richard, he was inspired by her playfulness.

Hannah was a water child. Richard remembered she loved to be around water. She was not one for jumping into the water from a height. Instead, she would always enthusiastically make her way in from the shore, showing complete respect for the water. She adored being in water, swimming and splashing around. Being in the presence of water energised her. Sitting at the side of that lake, she was in her element.

He also vividly remembered her as having the biggest brightest eyes, an immense smile, a joy-filled belly-laugh, an authoritative voice and a powerful aura. She was a leader. A strong feminine leader, who commanded the attention of men and women. She was always open to receiving new information and insight, despite her strong opinions.

At the time, Richard was travelling with Paulo, an Argentinean guy. They had met during the first days of his travels through Africa and shared a tent. Hannah stayed in a bungalow with two other medical students, which was situated further up the hill.

As dusk fell on the side of the lake, the setting sun splattered a blanket of scarlet on the rolling hills. Richard excused himself to return to the tent to put on trousers and a long sleeve shirt to protect himself from mosquitoes and the threat of malaria. As he did that, he realised his friend Paulo's sleeping bag and backpack were gone.

Turning around to put his head outside the tent to check where his friend was, he noticed Hannah close behind him. She pushed him into the tent and climbed in after him.

"I have arranged for Paulo to stay in my bed—you're mine tonight," she purred in a mid-Atlantic accent, derived from her private education.

Pushing him backwards into the tent, she climbed on top of him straddling him with her strong thighs. Sitting over him in silence, she slowly moved her face closer towards his, maintaining eye contact.

Looking deep into his eyes, she whispered, *"eye contact creates 'I' contact."*

They both held the moment for a second, then tempestuously kissed.

Instead of putting on protective clothing as he intended, Richard found himself naked within moments. Her body was like nothing he had ever seen. And he had been around.

Although very white in complexion, her ancestors had come from Suriname, resulting in her having a voluptuous body, with a bigger, stronger bottom than is normal for a European white girl. In addition, she had those long strong legs and large perky breasts that seemed as if they pointed upwards, defying gravity.

Richard did not have a *type* but this lady had set a new standard for him. No one had ever made him feel as turned-on as he was in that tent, by the shoreline.

They both achieved multiple points of sensual climax throughout the night of animalistic lovemaking. They did not catch a single wink of sleep. Neither did the other people camping close by. They moaned, groaned, screamed and talked their way through the night.

Funnily enough, no one in the other tents ever complained or told them to keep quiet.

The hours disappeared and as the sun rose, its rays landing on the tent, the inside further warmed, creating more of a sweat-fest than it already was.

It was a night of magic and connection, playfulness and bonding.

As Richard lay on top of Hannah, naked between her strong thighs, studying the beauty of her sweaty, red, happy face, a voice called out:

"Richard, it's time to go, man. We need to pack up the tent if we're gonna catch this bus." It was Paulo.

As is the backpackers' mentality, Richard had to bid farewell and move on to the next destination. Everything is always perfect.

He had to catch a bus to Kigali, the capital of Rwanda. The bus only passed by there once a week and he could not miss it.

Paulo was energised and refreshed following the tranquillity of sleeping in a bed for the first time in weeks. He had tried it on with both of the other medical students but had no luck.

Hannah had cheekily told him one of them had fancied him, to get him to agree to swap beds for the night. Neither of them had an interest in him. But he was just happy to spend a night sleeping on a bed with a clean pillow and fresh sheets in an air-conditioned room. He talked about how good his sleep was for the first hour on the bus.

As Paulo talked in detail about how nice it was to sleep on a bed, Richard sat at the back of the bus with his head hanging out the window. He was singing along to his iPod, laughing and waving at the young kids who ran behind the bus, as they shouted, *"Mzungu, Mzungu,"* an affectionate slang term meaning "white European wanderer."

The other backpackers on the bus light-heartedly joked and laughed at his expense because they could hear their lovemaking all night.

But for him, it was not *just* about the sex. This was more. It felt like more.

Now, here he was, six years later, sitting in the centre of Amsterdam. Feeling fragile and emotional from a few weeks of detoxing and cleansing, followed by a secret retreat of meditation and ayahuasca.

It was not the optimal state to be sitting across from that girl once again.

He was filled with emotion and extremely fragile.

Their connection paid no attention to distance, time, laws, societal norms, boundaries or borders. A soul will overcome all and it will be pulled to the place where it belongs.

Together again, in a café, looking at each other with a soft and warm studious gaze, they sat in silence, each taking in the subtleties of the other. It felt comfortable and natural.

From time to time, Hannah's eyes would well up with tears that would then stream down her face. It looked beautiful. So pure. So feminine. So strong.

"What are you thinking? What are you feeling?" Richard thought as he watched Hannah's tears come and go, without saying a word, as they slowly picked through their food.

Flickers of Lightness

When they finished eating, Hannah was the first to talk. She explained how she had recently come back to the Netherlands after working in African hospitals.

Bart, her new boyfriend of three years had moved back with her, but he had just gone out to catch up with his friends. Ajax, the local football team, was playing in the Johan Cruijff Arena so he was meeting his friends in the pub for a few beers before the game.

"Everything together is €22.55," said the waitress, in that direct Dutch manner, with one hand on her hip.

As Richard paid for their lunch, Hannah asked, *"Where are you staying tonight?"*

Despite sitting together for over an hour, they had not even asked each other the basic chit chat questions. Much of the communication was non-verbal. As they sat holding hands across the table, it was almost as if they were communicating exclusively at a higher level. Maybe at a soul or cosmic level.

"I'm staying at some hostel in town. My flight doesn't leave until tomorrow evening," Richard responded.

"Oh, which hostel?" Hannah quizzed.

"I have no idea. I was just on my way to find one when I noticed you across the road—there are loads around so it won't be a prob—"

"You should stay with us." Hannah interrupted Richard mid-sentence. *"We have a pull-out sofa bed in the living room. It's not perfect, but it's good enough for one night."*

Delighted she had offered, but trying to seem coy, Richard said, *"Aaww, no. I don't want to be intruding on you and your boyfr—"*

"Don't be so silly. We would love to have you come stay. I'm sure Bart would love to meet you. I have already told him and all my friends about the guy I met in Uganda. So, don't worry, he already knows about you," Hannah insisted.

"She has been telling all her friends about me?" Richard asked himself. *"Now I know her boyfriend* won't *be very happy to see me."*

"Are you sure?" he asked sheepishly, coming out of the café and already walking in the direction of her apartment.

"Yeah, come. I just live around the corner, next door to a nice café. Bart has gone to the football, so I'm totally free all day. Let me show you my version of Amsterdam," she added, invitingly.

The sky was now blue, the sun shone and this woman who had always seemed to reside in the back of his mind had offered the ideal day. How could he refuse?

"Everything is always perfect," he quietly said to himself.

They went up to her apartment to drop off his bag. Inside, everything was in white, with quirky little pieces of furniture and touches of colour. Together, it all combined to create a warm, welcoming and peaceful environment.

As she showed him around, he instantly felt at home. He felt safe there.

They headed out into the beautiful city of Amsterdam for a day of learning and exploring. Unusually, as they walked through the city, Richard was quiet. Hannah did most of the talking.

Richard was listening and observing. Watching how her eyes smiled when she was happy and how they darted when she got excited. Observing how she kindly interacted with people as they passed by. Noticing how she used her soft, slightly wrinkled hands to describe feelings. Listening to the choice of words she used to describe the subject she was conceptualising.

Noticing that despite being physically imposing, she was light on her feet and her steps were silent. He regularly caught wafts of the aroma exuding from her. She did not wear perfume, but her pheromones radiated strongly.

He remembered her as the tall voluptuous Dutch girl of mixed background. She had an exotic look that was a match for her mind and outlook. She was a strong, yet kind and gentle soul—the definition of an Amazonian.

Her grandmother had arrived in Europe from the small country of Suriname, deep in the Amazon, a former Dutch colony. Richard was familiar with the country because of his frequent stopovers there on his way to the Amazon with the logging company.

Observing her, he had gathered that in the past six years, she had physically changed. She seemed smaller and heavier than in the past. No longer tall and voluptuous, she was now more pear-shaped. She carried the weight of her career and past relationships around the energy centres of her lower chakras.

The weight of being a woman in the male-dominated world of medicine had also taken its toll on her face. She carried bags under her deep brown eyes. She had laughter lines, but not the ones that come from deep belly laughs. These lines derived from years of pleasantly smiling and fake laughing to fit in. Trying to carve out her place in a machismo world.

Her beautiful jet-black hair now had strands of white despite being only thirty years old.

From time to time, across the course of the day, they stopped and hugged in silence. It felt so natural. It was as if two souls who had spent many past lives together had finally been reunited, following a time spent wandering alone. There was an instant feeling of trust as they sat together. It felt freeing.

It was exactly what he needed following the secret retreat.

It was exactly what she needed following years of isolation and hard work in politically corrupt African hospitals.

He felt protective of her. It was almost as if despite her strength and power, she was alone in this world.

She was the bright light everyone went to when they had problems. She was the one who always smiled. However, when life got tough for her, she suffered alone.

The world had depleted her once great energy. Moreover, it was taking its toll. The lightness of heart she possessed in Africa appeared only in flickers. It no longer beamed.

But, he noticed, importantly, it was still there—it just needed to be nurtured and brought forward by someone she trusted. Someone she loved. Someone she allowed in.

Hannah was also having problems in her relationship with Bart. A year before, she had returned from work early, only to walk in and find him having unprotected sex, on the stairs, of all places, with the next-door neighbour's black maid. It was one of the reasons that ultimately led to them returning to Europe.

Despite being openly racist, her boyfriend had always had a thing for, what he called, *"black bitches."*

"Whenever I have looked at his browsing history on his laptop, the porn he looked at was usually white men having sex with black women," confided Hannah, confirming the stereotypical Dutch openness.

Prior to going out with Hannah, Bart had a "Coloured" girlfriend, from a military family. His family did not approve of her. By all accounts, she was a fantastic girl with a great career and a sassy personality; the only problem for them was her pigmentation.

"Don't you leave that black girl pregnant. I don't want any of the grandchildren in this family to be Coloured," his mother would say. *"I wouldn't be able to face my friends,"* she continued.

Hannah felt as if they sometimes had a relationship of convenience. She was a white doctor from Europe, brought up in a nice part of Amsterdam and her family were upstanding members of society. She ticked all the boxes. It made Bart's mother and his friends happy.

The irony of it all was despite her light complexion, Hannah's grandmother was completely black. Derived from African slaves brought across from Africa to work the sugar plantations in Suriname.

If her boyfriend had ever bothered to look into her deep dark eyes, he would have noticed the multicultural essence of her heart and heritage. It was where she derived her depth and beauty—her residual splendour.

Instead, he focused more on her being *"a white girl with a black bitch's ass,"* as he crudely said regularly.

Hannah and Richard had some delicious vegan takeaway whilst lying on the freshly cut grass in Westerpark, surrounded by the smell of barbeques and weed.

They then made their way back to her apartment as the sun set over the magical city of Amsterdam.

Cosmic Connection

Back in her apartment, Hannah chopped some fresh fruit and made a big pot of green tea, whilst they sat in her kitchen chatting.

They were halfway through the plate of fruit when the front door flung open and Hannah's boyfriend Bart stumbled in.

He was drunk.

He was also pissed off. His team had been defeated by their bitter rivals, Feyenoord, and he was not happy.

"Who are you?" he snapped at Richard, without acknowledging his girlfriend.

"This is Richard, my friend I told you abo—" Hannah began.

"I didn't ask you," Bart said, interrupting Hannah.

"Hey Bart, I'm Richard. Pleased to meet you, mate. Heard a lot about you," Richard said with a smile, standing up and offering his hand.

"So, you're that guy from the hillside in Kenya or whatever? I expected more," Bart scoffed, gripping Richard's hand a little too tight.

"I have some dinner ready for you, love," Hannah said, trying to move the conversation on.

"I don't want any of that vegan shit tonight," Bart said, still staring directly at Richard. *"I had some real food with the boys. Double burger. With bacon."*

At that, he pushed away Richard's hand and walked into the bedroom. Hannah walked in after him and closed the door behind her.

Richard could hear every word.

"Why are you being so rude? You're drunk. We have a guest."

"You should've told me we were having guests. I would've stayed in the pub."

"I texted you earlier. I told you Richard would be staying for one night. You said it would be okay. You knew he was sta——"

"Okay, just shut up. I am not in the mood for your nagging right now. Get me a beer, I'm thirsty."

"I will get you a glass of water," Hannah responded, through gritted teeth. Embarrassed, yet trying to keep the peace.

Coming back into the kitchen, Hannah said:

"I'm sorry about that. He is such a passionate Ajax fan. He always takes it so bad when they're beaten." She tried to sound upbeat, as if it was acceptable behaviour.

She poured a large glass of lemon water for Bart and went into the room with it. A few minutes later, she came out and said:

"Can you believe that? He was already sound asleep, facedown. I had to undress him and put him into bed. He won't wake until around 11 a.m. tomorrow," she said jokingly.

Richard sort of half laughed along, to kill off the awkwardness for Hannah.

As they spent the night talking in the compact kitchen, they began to appreciate how they had lived their lives in parallel. It was almost as if, despite being on the opposite sides of the world, they had a cosmic connection that allowed them to move in sync through life, together in one direction.

People who vibrate at the same frequency vibrate towards each other. Richard and Hannah had a sympathetic vibration. Scientists may have explained it as a quantum entanglement——it happens when pairs of particles interact and remain connected, influencing each other. Even when separated by oceans and time. It defies all logic.

However, as Richard's grandmother used to say, *"the opposite of logic is magic."*

They had followed a very similar path through life. They had both grown and developed together in a way eerily comparable. They were both now vegan having been vegetarian for many years. Both had recently stopped drinking alcohol. They had been consuming the same books, watching the same documentaries and performing similar daily meditations and yoga.

Yet, it was more than that. The little things they had in common astonished Richard. One thing Richard was very protective of was the unnecessary use of water. Therefore, as he went to use the bathroom, after his *sixth* cup of tea, it came as a shock to him when Hannah said:

"If you are only peeing, please don't flush when you're finished. I also have to pee—I want to conserve water."

This was a small thing, but it was a moment of significance for Richard.

It was something he had said to people many times to conserve water and they always thought it was weird. Now, here was this old friend from a journey through Africa saying the exact same thing he had been saying for years.

As he stood in the little bathroom peeing, all he could think was how this exotic girl was completely blowing his mind.

Without flushing the toilet, he came out of the bathroom and allowed Hannah to go in. As she was peeing, he felt himself having strong feelings towards her. Deeper than ever before.

He paced around her living room. He had a flurry of emotions. His mind was racing. His heart was dancing.

He was growing closer to her but wanted to respect that she was in a relationship. With her boyfriend snoring loudly in the next room, it was hard to forget.

With her in the bathroom, he thought it would be best to end their conversation and call it a night.

He grabbed his toothbrush and went to the kitchen sink to brush his teeth to give her a clue this night had to end—it was bedtime.

Seeing him brushing his teeth by the sink when she came out of the bathroom, she said:

"Can you believe it is almost 3 a.m.? This day has flown by."

With his toothbrush stuffed into his mouth, he widened his eyes and nodded his head in agreement, making a grunting sound.

Hannah went to the room and came out a few minutes later wearing only an oversized orange Dutch football jersey. It had *Cruyff 14* stitched onto the back. Richard had undressed and was under the blankets on the pull-out sofa bed.

As he lay in bed, his mind went back to their first meeting in Africa. One thing she said that resonated with him then was that whenever she found her man, she wanted them to create synergies.

She wanted both of them to be complete and whole in themselves, so they could contribute to the world in a way where together they would become more than the sum of the parts. Richard with his analytical mind described it at the time as, *"One plus one equals three."*

This resonated strongly with Richard because that was exactly how he felt both in Africa and now in Amsterdam. It was another of those weird synchronicities that existed between them, few others would fathom.

However, during the day, he had noticed how she talked about her relationship with her boyfriend as being two halves that created a whole. At best.

Once Hannah finished removing the small bit of makeup around her eyes, she came over and sat on the side of the bed.

"Thank you for a fantastic day. I really needed that. It can be sort've difficult to find someone to have a good conversation with," she said softly. *"Thank you for being such a good listener and thank you for all the advice you gave me today."*

"I didn't really say much today, so I must thank you. You're the one with the mystical understanding of life and great insights into what appears mundane to others," he demurely responded.

With that, Hannah leaned across the bed to hug Richard tightly. In silence, they both embraced.

She then shuffled her hips over beside him and put one leg across him ever so slightly.

Her hand was on his chest.

Richard's hand automatically went to her lower back. It was skin on skin.

As she had shuffled in beside him, her oversized football jersey had risen above her midriff. His once soft hands had become rougher because of working in various kitchens. However, her Amazonian skin was as if it came straight from the rainforest. It was silky smooth, just as he remembered it.

Without thinking, he found his hand move from her lower back towards her buttocks. She was not wearing any underwear.

At this moment, she looked into his eyes, then glanced down towards his lips.

Hesitatingly, she looked back into his eyes—he remembered, *"eye contact creates 'I' contact."*

Bringing her hand up from his chest, she rubbed her fingers through his hair. As she did this, she planted her right leg fully across his body.

Almost like a heat-seeking missile, Richard's hand was guided to the source of most heat. Warmth radiated out from between her legs, where he gently placed his hand—he stroked her with agreeable force from front to back.

She let out a slight gasp.

Having no regard for her boyfriend sleeping next door, she pulled down the blanket to reveal Richard in his underwear.

Throwing the blanket out of the way, she reached down and touched Richard. Without looking up, Hannah pushed down his briefs. Then kneeling up, she pulled his briefs off over his feet and carelessly tossed them across the room.

They held eye contact for a moment, then leaning over him, she took Richard in her mouth. She sucked and licked for a few minutes. As a Jewish girl, his foreskin fascinated her.

As she did in Africa, she sucked and bit on the extra skin with glee before coming up to straddle Richard.

Sitting on his penis without putting it inside her, she rubbed her dripping vagina along him. She arched her back and forced herself down on it, whilst she grabbed her breasts.

Richard was hesitant.

Within a minute, just by sliding along his throbbing penis, she had reached climax. True connection is a powerful force.

In some part of his mind, he wanted to mention that Bart was in the next room. But the guy had been such an idiot, his sympathy for him did not stretch very far.

Anyway, he was snoring so loudly no one needed reminding of his presence.

With her straddling him, he put his hand on her outer thighs. He followed the length of her long legs, then went back up her body towards her breasts.

With her firm, voluptuous breasts squeezed together between his hands he reached tipping point.

The last drops in his tank of willpower had combusted.

He could not hold back any longer.

Lifting Hannah, he spun her around onto her back.

Richard then climbed on top of her and started to slowly make his way down her body, kissing every part of her until he got to her feet.

He spent a minute licking, kissing and sucking on her perfectly pedicured feet. Then, he slowly made his way back up again, repeating the kissing until he arrived back at face level.

When they were eye-to-eye, he paused for a moment. He looked into her eyes.

Richard then gently bit on her bottom lip, whilst slowly sliding himself inside her.

At this moment, her back arched and she let out an almighty groan, digging her nails into his back.

That set the scene.

They noisily made love, disregarding the neighbours, never mind her drunken boyfriend in the next room.

Initially they hungrily clawed at one another. It was frantic.

As the initial enthusiastic burst of energy gradually subsided, their love-making slowed and become more considered and meaningful. Playful yet passionate.

She had completely surrendered to him. She trusted him.

Together as one, they were willing contributors to a truly sacred act: a holy communion and an immersive meditation were they playfully waltzed with the energies of creation.

With their fingers laced together, looking into each other's eyes they climaxed in sync.

As in Africa, both had sweaty, red faces and towel wet hair as they lay on the bed, looking at the ceiling. Richard's back was covered in scratches and nail marks.

Hannah's breasts had love bites on them.

Richard, apologising, seemed more concerned about the marks and the wet sofa than Hannah did.

"He won't even notice," she whispered as she kissed Richard on the ear. *"He will be hung over, eat some junk food and when I'm at yoga, he'll wank off to some black-girl porn."*

As said that, she stood up to look for her t-shirt. It was on top of a bunch of flowers she had purchased for herself, standing in a vase, on the other side of the room. She washed her face with cold water, put on her t-shirt and said:

"I had better go to bed for a while, so he knows I was there beside him. For some of the night at least." She flashed him a cheeky wink.

Looking at his phone, it was 6:03 a.m.

"Yeah, let's try getting some sleep," he responded.

Madness has Love

A_t 11:11 a.m., Richard felt someone shaking him. He suddenly woke up to find Bart looking down at him.

"Man, what are you doing? You're sweating all over my sofa." Bart let out a loud sigh and walked into the kitchen.

"Oh, sorry man. My body is, erm, out of sorts this week as I've ... I have been at an aya ... a wellness retreat," Richard said in a husky broken voice, wishing to avoid a discussion about ayahuasca. And other subjects.

"Hannah's still sleeping as well. Were you two up talking into the small hours? Normally, she's awake at the crack of dawn doing that meditating shit—I remember hearing her say something during the night. Laughing or something?" Bart said.

Ignoring the question, Richard responded:

"Yeah, she was telling me about that. She's really big into meditation and yoga. Great to see her being so passionate. It offers loads of positive benefits ... and, like ... stuff." Waffling on the point, without making one.

"So, are you into that meditating shit as well?" Bart shouted from the kitchen.

At this stage, Richard realised he was still naked. His boxer shorts lay on a chair on the other side of the room, where Hannah had thrown them.

Just at that moment, Hannah shouted from her bedroom:

"Bart, can you bring some water, please?"

With that, Bart filled a glass with water and went to the room. He swung the door closed behind him. Richard could hear him complaining about the pull-out sofa bed being soaked in sweat.

Richard seized the moment as an opportunity to get dressed. First, he had to retrieve his boxer shorts. He grabbed a t-shirt, held it over his man-parts and darted across the room. He hurriedly put on his underwear. Relief.

Getting dressed, he caught his reflection in the mirror. His chest was covered in red blotches and lines. He turned around to quickly inspect his back. A fierce feline, indeed.

When Hannah and Bart appeared from the bedroom together a few minutes later, Richard, now dressed, said:

"Hey, morning guys. Would you mind if I had a shower?"

Helping to take away the awkwardness of the moment, Hannah responded:

"Of course. Yeah, no problem." She went off to find him a towel. Bart let out a beer fart and had a good laugh at it.

In the shower, Richard felt elated following everything that had happened in the past twenty-four hours. His heart was pounding with surging energy; his head was spinning with an array of thoughts and feelings.

Could Hannah be his soulmate, could she be *the one* he would be willing to change everything for?

For Richard, his soulmate would not be someone who crept gently into his life and slotted effortlessly into his day-to-day routine. It would be a person who would force him to question everything about himself and his world.

Entering his world, this person would draw a line, marking a before and after in his timeline of life. This person would be responsible for turbulence, change and friction. Everything he believed up to that point would be questioned. Life would be flipped upside down.

Richard and Hannah had an immediate connection from the moment they met in Africa. The moment they were reacquainted in the middle of a busy Amsterdam street, that feeling was instantly sparked again. It was a connection so strong; they had been drawn to each other, despite the time and distance that had kept them apart.

Hannah seemed to understand Richard on many different levels. She brought a tranquillity and contentment to his world, giving him the space from which to see more of the beauty in life. No longer did he feel like the teacher, but also the student.

Standing in the shower with the water washing over him, he felt a shift. He realised the man he was at that moment was a version of himself that never existed before. He had made an evolutionary jump.

Maybe it was a download from Mother Ayahuasca or maybe it was because he had reconnected with Hannah. Maybe it was the reunification with his inner child. To Richard, it felt like a magical combination of ingredients that led to the baking of the perfect life cake—each of the elements contributed to the process.

He knew he wanted to be more. More of a man. More of a lover. More of a friend. More of a servant to society. He wanted to be a better version of what he had been before.

He realised despite living a wondrous life, he had taken most of it for granted. What others would consider a dream life had become his norm. Yes, he practised giving gratitude for what he had, but he got everything so easy, he did not *truly* appreciate it.

He had been in many casual relationships before, but he would say, at a push, he had three ex-girlfriends. Comparatively multiple times more girls would call him their ex-boyfriend.

Strangely, he had never been on a date before. He had been out with many women, but it was *"just a catch-up"* for him. It was not something he was nervous about. He had never been on a butterflies-in-the-belly-whilst-getting-ready type of date. He was never *that* invested.

Now, he desired a relationship where he was completely devoted. He wanted a girl who was the centre of his world, whom everything revolved around. He wanted a girl to whom he would send a message of support five minutes before she entered an important meeting.

He wanted to do little things for her, like make her tea in her favourite cup every morning and night. When she slammed the door and went to her room mad at him, he wanted to have prepared her favourite dish for her when she came out again.

He wanted to be the only person who could make her cry yet be the only person who could stop the tears. He wanted a girl whom he trusted so much, all his salary was paid into a joint account. An account she controlled because she had a better overview of what they needed as a family.

The girl he desired would be in her element sitting on the kitchen floor drinking hot ginger and lemon water at 6 a.m. talking about the multiverse following a joint session of early morning underwear yoga.

He had a great connection with Anne, but not to this extent.

Maybe Hannah was *the one*. Maybe this was the girl to enter into an *official* relationship with—someone he could call his girlfriend. Maybe someone to call his wife.

Perhaps he could be the father, and the daddy, to her babies? Perhaps he could even be the smiling and patient grandfather of her playful and inquisitive grandchildren?

Richard had never felt like this before. This is what was going through his mind. He had never asked himself these questions before.

When he tuned into his deep-heart, he felt this was the beginning of a love so profound, powerful and intricate, that his life would be redirected onto a new path. Looking deeper into the swirling emotion, his deep-heart brought him back to the rainforest.

There, he had pondered on love as life. As life as a flicker in the darkness. As love as death.

Love has madness. Madness has love.

He again considered the greatest privilege for a lover is to take another's hand and walk through life, hand-in-hand towards death. Back towards the darkness we had come from. Together as one, embracing the challenges of life that each step may bring.

From Music to Lyrics

Coming out of the shower, he took a few minutes to gather his thoughts. At the other side of the door was the girl who had thrown petrol on the candle that resided in his heart, turning it into a raging inferno.

Standing in front of the mirror, he looked directly into his eyes, gathering his thoughts and gaining composure in the reflection.

He could hear his heartbeat. His pupils were dilated. He had those butterflies in his belly.

He closed his eyes, inhaled and held the breath for a few seconds.

Exhaling the breath, he opened his eyes and released the petite latchkey on the bathroom door.

Walking back into the room trying awkwardly to contain his smile, straight away his eyes scanned the living room for Hannah. Sitting on the still dampish sofa, with the bed now folded away, her head faced away from him.

Hannah gazed towards the window. She did not turn around to show recognition of Richard re-entering the room.

To get her attention, Richard let out a weird yawning, moaning sound.

Her head never moved.

Instead, she lifted her feet from the ground and pulled her legs up in front of her, wrapping her arms around them.

Richard could sense Hannah's mood had dramatically changed. He asked her two direct, generic questions, but she was very short in her answers. She responded with an *"I'm not sure."* and a *"No."*

Her body language had changed. Her entire body faced towards the window and away from Richard. She ignored his chit chat. She avoided all eye contact.

The butterflies in his belly had become a lump in his chest.

His head was spinning as he tried to work out what had changed. It did not appear as if they had been arguing when he was in the shower. There did not seem to be any change in Bart, who sat smiling at a video he was watching on his phone.

It just felt like something had clicked in Hannah and she did not want to continue along the unfolding journey as Richard had hoped.

With Bart sitting there, he felt helpless. He could not ask for answers to any of the questions running through his mind. He could not enquire in any way.

Despite being in a room with two other people, Richard had never felt as lonely.

His heart was wide open and exposed. His mind was confused and chaotic. He felt afraid and isolated.

Now, as he wanted Hannah to be all *in* on his life, it appeared as if she wanted Richard to be all *out* of her life.

It seemed to Richard as if at the moment he had fallen in love with Hannah, she had fallen out of love with him.

They were like two ships in the middle of the calm ocean under a star-filled dark sky, sailing off in opposite directions. It almost felt to him as if she was caught up in the passion of reconnecting with an old holiday romance.

Now, it was time for her to get back to reality.

Everything is always perfect.

When Bart seemed like the more hospitable and friendlier of the two, it was obvious to Richard he had overstayed his welcome.

As a busker, music was a vital part of Richard's life. As well as using music for self-expression, he also used it for motivation, entertainment and detachment. He even used music as medicine.

Richard understood that when we are happy, we feel the music. When we are sad, we hear the lyrics. It is the same song, but it transmits two very different emotions depending on circumstances.

During the time Richard was in the shower, Hannah had shifted from being the music in his life to being the lyrics.

6

The Three Phrases

Chipkaart: Expired

Richard packed his things, zipped his bag, went to the door and slipped on his shoes.

Hannah went to her purse in the bedroom. She walked towards the door, gaze down, biting the side of her lower lip—without lifting her gaze, she handed Richard her OV-chipkaart, an e-ticket for travel in the Netherlands.

She then briefly touched him gently on the side of his arm, indicating it was time to go.

Not one word.

She hurried him out, shutting the old apartment door behind him with a bang.

It sent a shiver down his spine.

At times, one moment can be enough to forget a lifetime. At other times, a lifetime is not enough to forget one moment.

He trudged over to Amsterdam Centraal Station. His bag felt twice as heavy. He dragged his feet and hung his head. Drizzle fell from the grey city sky and blew into his eyes.

He was baffled by her sudden change as he stood in queue to top up the travel card. As he attempted to put credit on it, the lady at the information desk informed him it had expired twenty-one minutes before, at 12 noon. She had never experienced that happening before.

"A chipkaart lasts for six years. It is unusual for them to stay connected for so long or not break apart. They're usually replaced long before the six years is up," the lady explained, in a Surinamese accent.

It had expired just as Richard was leaving Hannah's apartment. It was just under six years ago Hannah had met Richard in Africa. She had probably purchased the OV-chipkaart on her way to Africa, where she would have met Richard days later.

He tucked it into his wallet and purchased a standard one-way ticket to Schiphol airport. Sitting on the train as it sped past the new glass-fronted office blocks lining the route to the airport, he thought about his crazy journey of the past week. That Danish guy. The girls for sale. The euthanasia. The messages from the ceremonies. The random meeting with Hannah and their abrupt ending. The insights he received and the many other moments.

His flight back to Dublin was via Stockholm with a Swedish airline. Again, it was the best value option and he had more time than money at his disposal, so he was content to deal with the stopover.

When he got to Gate C33 at Schiphol airport to board his flight, he watched as the passengers departed the aircraft. The aircrew then boarded. Looking immaculate in their uniforms, they held that same weird smile aircrews always seem to have on their faces.

As the passengers waited to board, an announcement came. A lady in her forties, an employee of the airline, stood up and said the flight had been cancelled. The aircraft would return to Stockholm without any passengers. She did not provide a reason.

As she made the announcement from behind the desk, the Swedes and the Dutch who had stood in a perfectly formed queue, rushed en-masse to the desk and started shouting at the woman in unison. Some of the language they used was a tad extreme. *"Talk about shooting the messenger,"* Richard thought.

As this unfolded, Richard realised if he was going to escape Amsterdam that day, he would have to arrive first at the customer services helpdesk. He did not feel like having to go back into central Amsterdam to get a hostel and risk bumping into Hannah again. It would be too awkward.

Without saying a word, he grabbed his bag and walked with urgency towards the helpdesk, situated on the other side of the airport.

As he walked, almost jogging, he wondered if the people would have treated the female announcer in such a way if it were a man making the announcement. People seemed to be quick to criticise in those circumstances when it was a woman. However, he noticed a little more restraint was shown to men.

Due to his quick thinking, Richard was the first from the cancelled flight to arrive at the helpdesk. Before introducing himself, he complimented the lady on her stylish glasses.

"I got them two weeks ago and you're the first person to notice. Thank you very much. I really like them," she said with a Dutch accent, taking off her glasses to admire them for a moment, before putting them back on.

Checking her computer for alternative flights, and still beaming with pride from his compliment, she said:

"Are you in much of a rush back to Dublin? We have a flight leaving for Stockholm tonight, but instead of a quick stop, it will be a two-day layover before you get to Dublin. Of course, we will put you up in a hotel for the two days, if that works for you? The alternative is we can credit you €555 and you can find your own place to stay when you arrive in Stockholm?"

Richard's eyes lit up. He had never been to Sweden and it was a country he yearned to visit. Moreover, being a backpacker and having more time than money, €555 would be a lot more beneficial to him than the two nights at a soulless hotel. He knew he could get a good hostel or a B&B for the equivalent of €30 per night.

"I would be delighted to take the flight tonight with the two-day layover. And instead of the hotel, I would prefer the cash if that is okay?" Richard said.

"Great decision," the lady said, as Richard looked to the sky in gratitude for his great stroke of luck.

"It's perfect, thank you," Richard responded.

As he thanked the lady and turned to walk away with his new boarding pass in hand, she said:

"Enjoy your stay in Stockholm. The girls there are the most beautiful girls you'll ever see." She winked at Richard with a smile. He winked back and they both giggled.

The strange end to his meeting with Hannah was now temporarily banished from his mind and his mood had lifted.

It was a win-win situation. He had heard many positive reports about Sweden. From the outside, it appeared to lead the way in women's rights and worked hard to ensure equality for all. It was the perfect place for him to go based on the information and downloads he had received from Mother Ayahuasca.

He searched online and found a B&B near Pampas Marina on the edge of Stockholm city centre. He could get public transport from Arlanda airport to Västra Skogen station. The apartment he was staying at was only a few minutes' walk from there.

It was approaching 9 p.m. when he arrived in the city, yet it was still bright as the early summer sun began to set in the blue sky. On his left was the lake, with friends and lovers relaxing and barbecuing alongside the water. On his right was a forest with an abundance of magnificent trees.

Västra Skogen translates to *The Western Forest*—it was well named. The apartments were built amongst the trees in the forest, in a manner that still felt natural and at one with the landscape.

It felt like the ideal place for him to spend a few days, trying to figure out all he had discovered in the past few weeks, as well as working out what to do with his new quest.

Don't be a Gentleman

"*Swedish beds are the best beds in the world,*" Richard sighed, as he woke up.

He had not slept deeper since he was a child. At least not since his mother's death. He really needed the sleep, following all the events at the secret retreat and the previous night with Hannah. He woke 9:06 a.m. Very late for him.

For the first time in days, he checked the online messenger on his phone, whilst lying in bed. Nine messages came through. From nine different people. All women.

It reminded Richard of the caring and compassionate nature of women. In contrast to men, they always seem to show consideration for other people and provide support.

The time in the Netherlands was to be a big event for Richard. He told his close friends about it before leaving Galway. They were aware of his discipline in preparing his body, mind and soul for the secret retreat.

He was not surprised none of his male friends reached out to check on him. Not even his father. For the most part, men were usually more wrapped up in themselves, living in the now.

Quickly scrolling through them, he noticed one of the messages came from Emma. He had considered how best to approach the topic of the sex tape. He was unsure how to tell her that this most private of content had been posted online. He decided to wait. They could talk face-to-face.

Richard wrote one large message in response, giving an overview of the events and how it had unfolded for him. Then, he personalised the message for each of the nine ladies who had reached out and he responded to them individually.

He could not go into all the details of the past week, as despite a positive episode, he was still processing it all. However, he assured them he was fine before putting his phone on flight mode. Detaching from his world of online contacts, he then went out to explore the historic city of Stockholm.

As he put away his phone, he realised that Anne was not one of the senders. He pondered on it as he wandered through the city taking in the sights. His mother had told the twins how relationships can be fleeting and expressed the importance of allowing them to run their course.

"People come into your life for a reason, for a season or for a lifetime," she once explained to Kate and Richard.

This insight greatly helped Richard when observing the actions of people who entered his world. It enabled him to gently detach as relationships slowly drifted apart.

At some level, with Anne it felt that a *season* was naturally coming to an end. It was a deep and wonderful time that Richard and Anne had together, but for one reason or another a time-line had been crossed and the wheels of that relationship were now rolling to a halt.

There was no particular reason for this. As time restlessly crawls forth, seasons turn, and things change.

Wandering the cobbled narrow streets, he reflected on their relationship and time together. He realised they had both been using one another as a crutch during a period of toil and stagnation.

During this period, each had looked to others to bring a sense of meaning to their lives. That was the glue that held them together. Now he understood that to obtain balance in life the meaning must come from within himself.

Just after 3 p.m., Richard sat down and had a Swedish *"fika"*—a warm drink and a snack, combined with a chat or a moment of silence—a Swedish custom the locals regularly partake in. His host highly recommended it and said it was a Stockholm must-do.

He chose to sit against an orphan tree by the water. An orphan tree is one that has been factory farmed away from its natural habitat. The tree is then planted in urban settings based on its aesthetic appeal. As these orphan trees grow, they are detached from any natural community of trees and they never know their purpose. Eventually, they are violently ripped out of the ground or chopped down as urban planners come up with new ideas for how they want the city to look.

Sitting beside the water with his back against the orphan tree in the old town of Gamla Stan, he pondered on the beauty around him and how impressive Stockholm was. With its many islands, beautifully coloured buildings and meandering waterways, Richard concluded Stockholm was one of the world's most beautiful summer cities.

However, what really stood out for him was the lack of tourists. Such a beautiful city should be swarming with tourists. The people hired to promote Stockholm to the world could be doing more, Richard resolved.

Upon hearing about his retreat in the Netherlands, his B&B host informed him over tea the previous evening, about the Old Norse burial grounds on the edge of the city of Västerås. It was less than an hour outside of Stockholm and easily accessible by bus. The host insisted he should check it out, as it was a mystical location. It sparked Richard's interest.

He wanted to visit the Old Norse burial grounds at sunset, so he planned to leave Stockholm in the late afternoon.

As he made his way into the Tunnelbana Station, the Stockholm subway system, to return to town, he noticed a lady walking close behind him. In the manner his mother had reared him, he held the door for her. As she walked past, she looked at him with disgust and griped something to him in Swedish.

Whatever she said, it was not very welcoming.

"That was weird," he thought, pausing for a moment. *"Whatever! Everything is always perfect."*

He brushed it off and made his way down to the platform.

At Cityterminalen, in the centre of town, he was the last person to get on the bus just before it pulled away from the station. He was fortunate enough to get the last seat.

Before the bus left Stockholm, it did one more stop in the suburbs. The driver picked up a blonde in her thirties. After using an RFID microchip embedded in her heavily tattooed wrist to pay, she made her way through the bus looking for a seat, walking right to the back. Returning to the centre, she stopped just in front of where Richard was seated, in the middle of the bus.

Even though she was stood holding onto seats occupied by two men, neither offered the lady their seat, despite it being close to a one-hour journey.

Richard observed for a few moments, expecting either guy to offer their seat to the lady. As neither did, he stood up, got the lady's attention and said:

"There you go. You can have my seat. I don't mind standing." He motioned towards the seat and grabbed his backpack.

The lady looked him up and down and in perfect English, with a Swedish accent, responded:

"How dare you."

Then, she moved farther up the bus away from Richard and stood closer to the front. Again, she stood between two men, neither of whom offered their seat.

As Richard sheepishly sat back down on his seat feeling rather embarrassed, the guy beside him could hardly contain his delight. Trying to conceal his laughter with coughs, he said:

"You're not from here, are you?"

"No. I just got into town last night. I'm on a stopover," Richard responded.

"*Okay, let me help you. My mother brought me up to always respect women and the elderly. However, as a rule of thumb, I never offer my seat to white girls in Sweden—if she looks Swedish, I just ignore her and let her stand. But if she looks like an immigrant or someone who is not from Sweden originally, then I will always offer up my seat,*" the man explained.

Further confused, Richard asked:

"*Is that not, like, racist?*"

"*It is not a race thing, my friend. It is a feminist thing,*" he explained. "*You see, in Sweden, women are taught when a man offers up his chair, holds a door or shows any table manners, he is being sexist. They simply believe he is treating a female differently from a male and so these acts are frowned upon here.*"

"*That's crazy,*" Richard exclaimed, in a high-pitched tone.

"*Welcome to Sweden,*" the man laughed. He had spent most of his life in Sweden, immigrating as a refugee at age six from Sarajevo during the Balkans war.

Feeling frustrated, Richard went on to explain:

"*When I hold the door for someone, it is not because of their gender. It is because they're human beings and I want to show we are part of the same community—that I respect them as a human. I was always told by my mother to offer my seat to women and to my elders—both men and women. I've done that my entire life. When I'm in a waiting room or I get a seat on the bus or any other public transport, I almost expect I'll have to stand up at some stage of the journey. It's how my parents brought me up. I do that to show respect, not to insult. If it had been an older man, I would have done the exact same thing.*"

"*Well, just be careful here. Things are very different in Sweden. The story they sell to the world is very different from the reality,*" the man explained.

After relaying the story of the lady who snapped at him earlier for holding the door open, as one example that day, Richard and the guy delved into a conversation on the true essence of Swedish society. They talked in detail until the bus pulled up at the stop, near the village of Irsta close to the old Norse burial ground at Anundshög, outside Västerås.

Richard had been in Sweden for less than a day, but he had already grasped it was quite different from his expectations.

He had seen Sweden topping many international indexes in happiness, health care and others.

However, from being around town, he found the people to be anything but happy. Beneath the Botox and the gym-toned bodies, they certainly did not seem carefree or friendly.

In fact, as he made his way through the central station, a few times that day, he found that people routinely banged into him. They pushed past him without as much as a sideward glance, never mind an apology.

As he was getting off the bus, one statement from the man really affected him:

"Forget about all the things you read about Sweden in the international media. What Sweden is good at is PR. No other country does public relations like this one. Sweden is great at telling the world what it wants them to think it's good at. Sweden is good at ice hockey, but it is the world champion in PR."

The Labyrinth

Arriving at the old Norse burial site helped Richard forget about his ordeal on the bus.

A magnificent site, Anundshög was nearly 2,100 years old and carried powerful energy.

The site consisted of six boat-shaped "stone circles" and several burial mounds, with one large mound in the middle.

Richard went straight to the largest mound and climbed to the top, where it was said the legendary King Bröt-Anund of Sweden was buried.

Lying back down on the grass, on top of the mound, he was staring straight up at the perfectly clear blue sky.

His face held a faint smile. There was a genuine feeling of contentment.

With an infestation of energy and noise, three adolescents from Belgium and their mother joined him on top of the sixty-metre-diameter mound. They were on holiday and had researched the site in a school project prior to visiting.

With enthusiasm, they informed Richard how the area was an important centre of power and how a fantastic ancient labyrinth was hidden in the forest beside the site.

What struck Richard, more than their eagerness, was that none of them were holding a mobile phone, never mind staring at it. Very unusual to see teenagers with both hands unfurnished with their *black mirror.*

Having sufficiently inspected the largest mound, the family were going in search of the labyrinth and invited him to join them. He considered their polite invitation and appreciated their liveliness and enthusiasm, but felt it was something he would prefer to experience alone—to completely absorb the energy from the visit.

He politely declined the offer and went down the other side of the mound to examine the stone circles.

As the Belgian family went off in search of the labyrinth with a rumbling of noise and vivacity, Richard explored the ancient formations.

He snaked inwards to the middle of the largest formation. A round rock was dug deep into the ground. Laying his hand on the rock, Richard felt a tangible energy radiate from it, as it gave off a deep warmth.

It felt inviting. Following his intuition, he turned around and lay back down on the rock, allowing gravity to stretch him. His head fell backwards, and his arms and legs fell outwards, hanging in the air.

It was uncomfortable, but the gravitational stretch felt so right as it opened his body.

He lay in that unnatural position for maybe fifteen minutes giving gratitude and counting his blessings for all he had and for the experiences of the past week.

His eyes followed some small clouds as they slowly meandered overhead, dynamic in shape.

He received a few strange glances from others at the site.

When he was done, he rolled over onto the grass and lay on his stomach for a while. Realigning on a bed of daisies and soft natural grass.

Getting up, Richard dusted himself down and walked into the forest in search of the labyrinth. Having walked for about twelve minutes through the trees, he deduced he might have gone past it.

The sun was low in the sky and, as it cast magnificent shadows through the trees, he assumed he had missed the entrance to the labyrinth in the poor light.

Just as he decided to turn around and go back, he noticed a pheasant come out of an opening just a little further up. Going to inspect, he noticed it led up to an elevated platform.

He rambled up the slight slope and getting to the top he lifted his gaze. There it lay: a great big labyrinth, carved into the soil of Mother Earth.

It was surrounded by a circle of tall trees that had protected the labyrinth from the harsh weather of the region throughout the ages.

It was the largest labyrinth Richard had ever seen. More than likely, it was also the oldest.

He stood in admiration for a moment, before going to the *opening* of the labyrinth. Starting at the edge, Richard threw off his backpack, and followed the path of the labyrinth, circling his way into the centre.

He carefully placed each step as he spiralled ever closer to the middle. When he arrived there, he looked around and admired the large trees that afforded a wall of protection. He felt a sense of *sanctuary*. It felt natural for him to lie down. It felt very peaceful. He sat down on the centre spot for a minute.

Richard then lay on the soft grass and curled into the foetal position. After a few moments he closed his eyes.

He did not fall asleep, but he felt himself drifting off, almost into a trance, as he lay on the centre of the labyrinth. He felt safe surrounded by the whispers and protection of the great trees.

Feeling is Knowing

When he came to and opened his eyes, dusk had taken hold of the forest. Although it was not pitch dark, visibility had dropped significantly.

He sat up, looked around and was given a slight shock. He noticed a figure standing just metres from him at the entrance to the labyrinth.

It appeared to be a woman, upon closer inspection.

Wearing light-coloured, airy clothing and brown sandals, she looked towards the ground as if meditating or praying.

Looking up, in a welcoming manner, she held Richards gaze.

"Är du okej?" she asked.

"Yeah, good. I just … um, yeah, of course," stammered Richard awkwardly.

She smiled. Then without saying anything else she again lowered her gaze and started to circle her way into the centre.

Noticing what she was doing, Richard jumped to his feet. He had leaves, bark and little sticks clinging to his clothing and an acorn stuck to his forehead. He dusted himself down as the woman weaved her way towards him.

He followed her movements closely, spinning his body as she circled ever closer to him.

As she arrived in the centre, she came right up to Richard. Without much effort, their bodies could easily have bumped together. Personal space did not seem to be an issue for this lady.

She stood there in silence, right beside him, looking down at the ground. Even for Richard, this was a little weird.

Slowly, she lifted her gaze from the ground. Standing centimetres from Richard's face, she looked up. Straight into his eyes.

Her strawberry-blonde hair was falling loosely over her face and she was quite a bit smaller than he was, but instantly he could see one thing. She had those eyes.

Her left eye was a leafy green and her right eye was a piercing blue. Each eye sparkled more than the other.

"Det är trevligt att träffa dig," she said, looking up at Richard with a wondering gaze.

Eyes can tell you everything about a person. He could see who she was. Now, he was at ease. Smiling back at her, feeling she had offered a nice welcome, Richard simply responded:

"Thank you. Tack så mycket."

Whenever Richard entered a new country, there were three phrases he learned to say: *"Please," "Thank you"* and *"I love you."*

Of course, he was unsure of the *exact* translation of what the woman had said. But he was aware only seven per cent of communication was verbal. When tuned into his surroundings, he could generally understand what people were communicating from body language, hand gestures, tone of voice and other non-verbal cues.

He had maintained an inquisitive interest in languages as he travelled the world. He cherished the appreciation of the local people when he would say these few words in their native tongue. It vastly enhanced his interactions and general travel experience. The cultures and languages that defined the countries he travelled through fascinated him.

"I said, 'it is a pleasure to meet you,'" the lady explained, with a giggle.

"I know. I could feel *that."* Richard chuckled.

Earlier in the day, he learned the word *"känner"* was the word for both to *"feel"* and to *"know"* in Swedish. The word resonated with him.

What she said from her mouth was less important to Richard. Her eyes held their own vocabulary. There, he understood all that she was.

The lady smiled back.

Without saying another word, she again looked down and reached for both his hands.

Holding them in her warm soft palms, she closed her eyes and put her head down, chin tucked in against her chest, as if praying.

Considering all Richard had been through recently, he just went along with it.

Without looking up, she said:

"Today, you've seen a glimpse into your challenge. A closed bud can never go to seed. It must open itself and surrender to vulnerability in order to flower. This also applies to you. You will need to embrace your vulnerabilities to succeed. You have many obstacles to overcome as you go on your journey. If you attempt to empower femininity, then those who will resist you with the fiercest of determination will be women. Those kept as prisoners behind the invisible bars, those enslaved in the mind, are the ones who most fear freedom."

The woman paused for a second before explaining further.

"Mental oppression is a state of mind that enhances the confusion between freedom and serfdom. It is a state where the people enslaved become trapped by misinformation about their self and their environment. People can be trained to believe and say anything, even if it goes against their greater good. They can go out and march for women's rights. But deep down they will happily settle for a slightly more comfortable invisible cage."

Richard contributed:

"Yes, I understand. They don't believe the person who comes to rescue them is their liberator. They see the liberator as someone damaging the bars of the cage they have grown to cherish. In return, they will attack the liberator and dig deeper into their state of oppression."

"Correct. It is the ultimate version of Stockholm Syndrome," added the lady.

"Yes. Stockholm Syndrome. Of course," muttered Richard.

Richard mulled over the irony, considering he was just one hour outside Stockholm. He now more clearly understood why this phenomenon was associated with the city.

The woman, with her head bowed, continued to talk whilst holding Richard's hands:

"Mental oppression is more dangerous than physical oppression because the invisible bars and chains are binding for generations. If the oppression was physical, then the oppressed would break free within one generation. They would rise up and free themselves. They would use their numbers to overcome their captors."

As she talked, Richard briefly thought back to the tribeswomen in the rainforest, kept behind bars. For a moment, he pondered on the levels of emotional scarring derived from physical bars and psychological bars.

His attention was brought back to the woman as she continued to explain her insights.

"People do not like change. All over the world, we see people fighting to keep themselves in slavery. Slavery of the mind. Their approach is simply: 'Better the devil we know.'"

Richard added:

"You are right. To them, being freed from slavery of the mind is like being awoken from their sleep during a house fire. They get mad at those who have woken them. They don't yet sense the threat."

"That's a great analogy. Is that the right word in English? Analogy?" queried the woman.

Richard simply nodded in confirmation. The woman made a mental note, then continued:

"When people are led to believe they are already free, based on manipulation spoon fed to them via education, religion and mainstream media, they block themselves from attaining their full potential. They never obtain true freedom or reclaim their power. The objective is not for femininity to have power over men, but for women to realise their own power, as individuals. As women."

The lady paused.

With her chin still against her chest, she sat down in the centre of the labyrinth with her legs crossed. Whilst sitting in silence, she let go of Richard's hands and motioned for him to join her.

That Dirty Word

He clambered down, crossed his legs and looked directly at her.

She sat in silence for a moment and then she began to explain:

"Femininity is the strongest power on this planet. It is connected to the purest form of love. It is love with the earthly touch and a sprinkle of joy. No love is stronger than between a mother and her child. That power, strength, knowledge, wisdom, happiness and ecstasy is the definition of femininity."

Without lifting her eyes, she then asked him:

"Think about this: How many times this year have you said the word 'femininity' or even heard it mentioned?"

Thinking for a moment, Richard responded:

"Honestly, I have said the word 'fem-in-in-it-ee' so few times in my entire life that I actually find it difficult to pronounce the word. I have to take care when pronouncing it, so I don't trip over the syllables."

The woman then looked up at Richard and asked:

"It is the same for most people. So, why has this essential word been stolen from our society? It has almost become a dirty word. Why is this powerful word associated with frills, bows, cuteness and the colour pink?"

Richard was stumped. He had never considered the essence of femininity had been *"stolen"* and intentionally devalued.

He looked directly at the woman.

"Why are they so afraid of the feminine energy?" asked Richard naively.

The woman answered his query with another question:

"What we should really examine is, who is responsible for this theft?"

Richard had assumed she was asking him a direct question. He pondered for a moment, but before he could respond, the women answered for him:

"We know at our core who the culprits are. We know it is the machine-minded men who have stained femininity. These masculine machines have replaced femininity with feminism. Yes. They have taken the most beautiful power on the planet and turned it into an 'ism.' Feminism. They know best how to control and manipulate the 'ism' to meet their needs and wants. Feminism is little more than the machine mind of men transplanted into the mind of women. It is the stimulus to give precedence to the thoughts of the mind over the feelings of the heart. It is the encouragement to follow the path of man and to play by his rules. Those who do will be rewarded by sitting at the table with men. However, those women that sit at their table will rarely get their own plate."

He paid close attention to her words. As his grandmother had said, he was *"a good listener."* The lady continued:

"It is difficult for someone to go against her true nature and all she stands for. Despite all the education, media, sororities and promotions to convince her otherwise, she knows this is the anchor truly holding her back. Deep down, she knows pandering to the machine mind brings only pain."

The woman looked up at Richard.

"Combine this with the fact man and his machine mind are a natural fit. When a woman enters his environment, no matter how indoctrinated she is in his machine world, she will find it very difficult to compete near the peak. It is hard for her because the machine-minded man would drag her down to his most base level and there, he will often beat her through experience."

Richard maintained his silence, as the woman continued to explain:

"The machine-minded man at the very top of the game is a master craftsman in the art of debauchery. Just consider the competition he had to overcome to get to his level. What destruction, disorder, death and dis-ease has he left behind on his relentless pursuit of the next short-term goal? No consideration is given to the long-term impact of his actions. No empathy. No compassion. No love."

The woman looked up at Richard. She paused for a moment.

During the moment of silence, Richard, almost in a hurry, spat out:

"Greed and the desire for profit come from the mind. Love and compassion are from the heart."

As a spluttered one-liner, it sounded almost childish in delivery, but energetically, he was right.

"Correct. And it is this greed that has left our planet, Mother Earth, calling out for help. Calling out for relief from the scars that go deeper by the day—through mining, fracking, exploration and, worst of all, deforestation."

Richard, with a slight frown on his brow, slowly nodded along as the woman spoke.

"It is this approach that has seen animals and plant life become extinct and wiped from the planet. Gone for good. It is this approach to our human brothers and sisters that sees widespread cancer, heart dis-ease and depression around the globe."

"They continually tell us this system is broken. But it didn't break. It was designed this way," Richard added.

Again, his delivery was almost nervous, but the woman was in harmony with him. Nodding in agreement, she continued to explain:

"It is all by design. So, what this world needs is a new approach. A new way. A new order. An order with women leading from their hearts. Making decisions that will lead to greater advances as well as holistic

profits. In the long-term as well as the short-term. And for the greater good of all. That includes animals, plant life, the seas and land, as well as Mother Earth holistically. Men, women and children across the planet, no matter their race, religion, colour, creed, gender or femininity must benefit. In the new order, this is the endgame."

"Yes!" Richard nodded enthusiastically. He was being very childlike in his approach to the woman. It was very unlike him.

"Our planet, birds, land animals and fish are crying out for help. Human beings around the world are desperate. Our Mother, the Earth, is broken. Despite this, the machine mind of man continues with the relentless pursuit of short-term goals despite the mass destruction," she explained.

"So, how shall we proceed?" Richard asked.

He did not feel anyway inferior, but Richard was aware he was in the presence of a soul of vast power. It made him feel a bit giddy and uneasy, but not in a manner she was extracting energy from him. Quite the opposite.

With his question, the lady paused and for a moment, she looked directly at him. Then, in a very low and calm tone, she slowly responded:

"We must call on our sisters, mothers and daughters to correct this. Bring your femininity to the world—the strongest power of all. That is how we shall proceed."

With those words, the woman let go of Richard's hands, allowing them to drop onto his lap.

She then dropped forward onto her knees. In the centre of the labyrinth, she put her hands on the Earth. The woman stayed in that position in complete silence for around thirty seconds and then in Swedish mumbled towards the Earth.

Richard sat still with his legs crossed, overlooking her, feeling protective of her.

She then bowed down and kissed the ground. As her face was at ground level, in English with a Swedish accent, she said:

"Mother Earth, we will protect you. We will heal you. We will work for your betterment. The Age of Aquarius has arrived and brought with it the revival of the feminine energy. Womankind is awakening. We will correct the wrongs of our sons. We will protect you Mother, as you have protected us."

Then, without looking at Richard, the woman stood up.

With her gaze to the ground, she turned away from him and began to retrace her steps back out of the labyrinth.

Reaching the edge, she raised her head, spent a few moments looking up and around at all the large trees that provided the cover.

Without looking back, she then went on her way, back through the nature into the night.

VII

Grounding the Downloads

I Love You, Brother
Not a Feminist
Not Fighting Back
Drop that 'ism'
Just Staying Dry

I Love You, Brother

The following day, Richard's return flight to Dublin was departing in the early evening. He wanted to maximise the time, so he packed early, thanked his congenial host and left.

The sun was shining, and the birds were chirping in the trees. He felt the freedom that comes with a warm spring day. He wanted to walk along the beautiful coastline that leads from Västra Skogen past Pampas Marina along Kungsholmen and into the city centre.

According to the maps on his phone, the entire walk would take about sixty-three minutes, but Richard was in no rush. He wanted to obtain a deeper understanding of the beautiful city of Stockholm and the psyche that resonated in the people of Sweden.

As people passed by, he wondered how they appeared so free and easy. But based on his interactions, internally they appeared detached from their hearts and clouded in their minds. Sweden seemed to Richard as a very paradoxical society. A country with so much potential for happiness and lightness, yet the people carried a heavy hidden darkness.

The walk into town was enjoyable. He sauntered for nearly three hours, such was the beauty, easiness and carefree nature of his walk towards town, with detours.

As time quickly passed, Richard needed to eat something before going to the airport. He considered it would be cheaper to eat in town first, before going to the airport. He popped into a fast-food chain close to the central station in the hope of getting a salad.

He was pleasantly surprised to learn half of the menu was dedicated entirely to vegan fast-food. He ordered a Mexican-themed Oumph burger, with fries and water. This reminded him Sweden was leading the world on many fronts, such as the wide availability of vegan food.

Sitting in the outdoors dining area as the sun shone, enjoying his fast-food, he noticed a couple with large backpacks sitting close to him. Anxious about the high cost of public travel in Sweden, he enquired:

"Do you guys know the cheapest and quickest way to get to Arlanda airport from here?"

"Aye. It's the Flygbussarna—the bus that goes direct to the airport. It's not the quickest, but it's the cheapest. We're going to the airport once we finish this food. So, if you're leaving soon you can follow us, if you want?" responded the man in a strong accent.

"Yeah, that'll be fantastic. My flight is in three hours, so I was planning to go there soon. Great, I can follow you, thanks," Richard said.

"No problem at all, mate. Just give us a few minutes and we'll be on our way," the man said.

He sounded Irish, but not like the people from Galway or Dublin, whom Richard had become familiar with during his time there. *Maybe he is Scottish?* thought Richard.

"Cool. So, where you guys from? Scotland?" he asked.

"Oh, no. I'm from the north of Ireland, County Tyrone to be exact. And she is Swedish," the man said, nodding towards his partner. *"We have been living in Stockholm for the past three years. We met in Australia nine years ago, when we were backpacking."* Then extending his hand, he said:

"Hi, I'm Keith. And this is my girlfriend, Sonya."

The Irishman had dirty-blond hair and arresting green eyes, to match the bright blonde hair and pale blue eyes of his Swedish partner.

Keith was open and inquisitive. Before the bus even pulled out of Stockholm's Cityterminalen, he already had Richard talking freely. They had both extensively backpacked around the world. Keith had been to more than 120 countries and Sonya had travelled to nearly 90 countries, despite still being in her twenties.

The result was they both had an open mind, calmness, solidity and balance, unusual in people who valued *stuff* over experiences.

It was not long before Richard was discussing his ayahuasca experience. That sparked the attention of Keith and Sonya.

The couple mentioned that whilst travelling in South America, Keith had participated in an ayahuasca ceremony in Peru. Sonya had guided him through it but did not partake herself. When Richard asked why, Sonya responded in her Swedish accent, with the hint of Irish wording:

"I didn't feel the calling at that time. Mother Ayahuasca calls us when we're ready and when the time is right. I wasn't ready then, but the calling is getting louder now. I can feel it much more vividly now, so I can."

Richard felt at ease with the couple, so he opened up and told them about his time with Mother Ayahuasca. He explained the downloads he received during the ceremony. Including the insights into his past life as King James and how his new role in this life was to empower femininity.

To say that on a bus to people he had just met felt strange. He almost expected a negative response. However, when he looked up, they were both nodding along in wide-eyed agreement, as Richard spoke.

As he continued to tell his story, the bus pulled up to the airport. They grabbed their bags and got off at Terminal 5. As Richard went down the steps of the bus, Keith was waiting on him. With outstretched arms, he took one step towards Richard and embraced him. As the men held each other tightly, Keith said:

"I love you, brother."

It felt strange for Richard to be embraced by a man in this way, as he did not have such a relationship with his father or any of his friends. It felt natural.

True masculine love is a powerful force. When Keith said he loved him, as a brother, he felt protected and secure.

At one level, masculinity is about bonding with men, wanting to relate with other men, wanting to celebrate one's essence. It is a feeling of appreciation of masculinity in others.

Men have left behind their true masculine energy. They have been sold false substitutes counterproductive in filling the hole left behind.

In young frustrated men, the result has been anger, which usually does not serve them. Anger can be a good servant, but it is a dangerous master. If not controlled, it can become an act of self-punishment for being connected to another's mistake.

Still holding Richard having listened carefully to his words, Keith leaned back and looked into his eyes, saying:

"I am proud of you—you've been on a difficult journey. But I know you will achieve your goal by listening to your inner child. That's where your strength will come from."

To hear these words from another man, one so connected to his masculine energy, made Richard feel empowered.

As with femininity, masculinity is broken. Being disconnected from one's essence can bring pain. This makes life harder, but broken crayons can still provide colour and create beautiful pictures.

In the manner the sexes need interaction with the opposite energy to repair ourselves, we also need interaction with those who hold our predominant energy. That is the case for femininity as it is masculinity.

For millennia, those with the machine mind have steered society away from true masculinity, glorifying the male and the mind. At the same time, they have demonised the female and the heart. This has left an imprint on the DNA computer that, via genetics, has passed through the generations.

The result has not only seen the systematic ruination of the feminine in humans, but in every aspect of the feminine across all living things, including our Mother, the Earth. This has been the root cause of the orderly destruction of this planet.

However, change is afoot. The Age of Aquarius has awakened the song of the feminine. Women have come alive with these vibrations and tones, as the songs of praise have echoed positivity for the feminine and all that it radiates.

These songs of praise for the feminine are not an attempt to demonise the masculine—the demonisation of one energy was what gave rise to the machine mind.

Rather, these feminine songs are the rebalancing of the energies in a global alignment. This rebalancing will guide us to abolishing dis-ease and destruction and enable a better understanding of cause and effect.

With this dawn, we hear the singing of the *Yin*. This sound fits melodically with the chorus of the *Yang*.

The labels associated to each of these energetic forces are now slowly being peeled back and released. Balance is now slowly being restored.

All on the same flight back to Dublin, they made their way through security.

As they walked towards Gate 22, Richard was in the middle with Sonya to the left of him and Keith to his right. All walking in a line and facing forward.

Having considered Richard's insights, Keith said:

"To be successful on your journey, Richard, you need to proceed as a man. You need to tap into your masculine energy and balance it with the strong feminine energy everyone has at his or her core. The reason you've been chosen for this journey is that as a man, you are highly attuned to your feminine energy—it just resonates out of you, mate. Yet, you have maintained a balance with your masculine energy. You have a good understanding of both sides. That's a real blessing."

"Yeah. Energetically, you're well-balanced." Sonya added, looking Richard up and down. *"To empower femininity, you must work with*

men. Men are the rulers of the planet at this time and you must reveal to them the destructive impact of their habits. And if you're going to succeed, you must proceed in a way that is non-confrontational."

Stopping, putting his hand on Richard's shoulder, looking at him dead in the eye, Keith said:

"You must work within the system already in place. To operate in any other way is to create war."

Then, he looked forward and continued walking towards Gate 22.

Richard paused for a second before quickly catching up with the couple.

Not a feminist

Having grown up with many female friends, Richard considered himself a feminist, so he was slightly taken aback with what sounded like a mixed message coming from his new friends.

Pondering on the conflict for a moment, he turned to the couple and asked bluntly:

"Do you consider yourselves feminists?"

"Not anymore," Sonya answered promptly. *"I did during my teenage years, but now I know better."*

Richard pondered on her response for a moment, then said:

"I'm a feminist, and I—"

"Of course you are. You should be. You're a man after all," Sonya interrupted him.

"What's that supposed to mean?" Richard said, taken aback by her sudden sharpness.

Leaning towards Richard, Sonya responded:

"Have you ever considered maybe it was men who set up the feminist movement? Have you ever considered maybe it was men who had the most to gain from the feminist movement?"

"Well, obviously not. The feminist movement has been about obtaining more rights for women," Richard declared, leaning back.

"On the surface yeah. But the reality is, the only right it has given women is the right to add more complexity, more struggle, more tasks, more decision-making and more pain," Sonya said.

Sonya held the space for a moment. Richard did not say anything as he considered her words.

"Do you know what a commodity is?" Sonya asked Richard.

"A commodity?"

"Yeah. A basic commodity. Do you know what that is?" Sonya asked, slightly raising her voice. She was an economist.

"A commodity is a thing or substance of value," Richard confidently answered.

"Correct," Sonya said. *"You're exactly right. Okay, let's consider this. Let's go back a generation, to when the most valuable commodity on the planet was sex. For a man to have sex with a woman, he had to find a girl he was attracted to. Then, he had to build up the courage to ask her out on a date. If she accepted, he would have to go to her home and collect her. After meeting her parents, he then had to take her for dinner and maybe then take her to the cinema. He had to romance her, wine and dine her. Maybe even buy her flowers. He had to be willing to do this for months on end and sometimes for years. Then, he was tasked with asking her parents for permission to marry her. If her parents agreed, the next step was for him to buy her an engagement ring. Maybe with a diamond?"*

As she said that, she held up her left hand.

The only jewellery she wore was a friendship ring on her right middle finger. It was carved out of wood with Keith's initials inscribed on the inside of the ring. Keith had a matching ring.

"Once a suitable ring was purchased, he would have to take the girl out for an extra special night. When the moment arrived and he overcame the nerves associated with this life-changing event, he would humbly get down on one knee, present the ring and make a marriage proposal. If she deemed his proposal acceptable, they would then agree to get married. Together, they would begin planning the wedding, for which the man would have to work extra hard to save money, or he would have to take out a loan."

Sonya pointed at Richard and said:

"Please understand that even after all of this, the man still had not achieved his objective of having sex with the woman. This is the natural instinct of adult humans. To achieve this objective, he would have to go

through a marriage ceremony, where the couple would stand in front of all their friends and family and pledge to stay together for the rest of their lives. Until death do they part, and all that malarkey."

Keith had heard Sonya present this argument before, so followed along silently.

"It was only after all this, on the wedding night following the ceremony, that a man would finally obtain the honour of having sex with his new bride. Just imagine that. Again, this was only a generation ago. This is what men were willing to do just to have sex.

When a substance is rare, in high demand and highly desirable, it becomes very valuable. So, if sex was a commodity, then you can see it was the most valuable commodity there was.

Can you tell me anything else on this planet that a man would want to obtain so much he would be willing to put in even one per cent of that effort?" Sonya asked.

"Okay. I get your point," Richard responded, looking away.

They arrived at Gate 22, and sat by the window, looking out over the airplanes on the runway.

Taking her seat, Sonya continued:

"Compare that to today's 'market.' Feminism has sexually liberated women. The result is that the hardest thing a man must do today to have sex is to swipe through an app on his phone. Girls are increasingly pressured to send sexualised images of themselves to prove their physical worth before they are invited over. They are resigned to sending these images because the practice is now the norm in 'dating.' If the guy is sufficiently impressed by what she has sent, he may then invite the girl to come to his place. She then jumps into a taxi, which she pays for, has sex with him and leaves, without them even having a conversation. He doesn't pay for the sex. He doesn't even have to make her a cup of tea."

This was all too familiar to Richard. Not only was he aware of this being the new norm in dating for many, but his own father acted in this manner.

"If the guy considers the girl to have performed well enough, and deems her to have sufficiently satisfied his needs, she may even be asked back again. Allowing her body to be used as a mere sex aid. The next generation of girls are growing to accept they are little more than sexual service stations for male gratification. Moreover, it is other women who are normalising these attitudes. They actually believe they are the ones in control. "Empowered" if you like.

In this world where bondage and S&M have gone mainstream, girls feel pressured to perform sex acts to receive tokens of affection. Keep returning to the same man and performing well and eventually, he may even give the girl a kiss."

Sonya glanced over at Keith as she continued to talk.

"Oh, and I suppose I had better add the small point that we have now arrived at a stage in this society where marriage is now reserved for the rich. The rest of us end up in what is known as 'single-parent households'—if you want to be P.C. about it."

She dramatically waved her left hand, devoid of any jewellery, in the air to get her point across. Keith glanced at her then looked over at Richard, who was smirking. Seeing Richard trying to contain his cheeky smirk filled Keith instinctively with giddiness.

For a split second, the two boys held the gaze. Both felt that deep urge to laugh. Not at what Sonya was saying, but just at the moment and at the extra slice of matrimonial pressure being applied to Keith.

To release the pressure, Keith began to cough. Richard inhaled deeply, then bit his bottom lip. It was almost like trying to contain a laugh in church. A smile restrained can develop as a fit of unwarranted giggles, right at an inappropriate moment.

As the boys fought to retain their composure, she continued to talk.

"And on the point of 'single-parent households' a single man, when given the choice between two women: one who will make him a home-cooked dinner and the other who wants to have sex with him, will now generally choose the warm plate of dinner, over the sex.

"Just think about that. Women, in our most vulnerable, when offering our bodies to a man we like, can be turned down for what is basically a plate of vegetables. In one generation, we have gone from being more valuable than gold to becoming worth less

than a few cooked potatoes. And we think that we've been empowered?"

The two boys had now fully regained their composure. Hearing the realities of the game of modern-day dating laid out in this way really struck a chord with them.

They were both aware that sex was widely available. However, an invite to the home of a woman they liked, with the promise of a warm nutritious meal, prepared with love and care would be hard to turn down.

The bond Richard had with Anne, derived from sitting across a table, laughing and chatting as they savoured an array of her experimental dishes. The time they spent in her kitchen was more valuable to him than the time spent in her bedroom.

"Are women really the winners in all of this?" Sonya asked. *"Today, we live in a hypersexual society, where sex is still in high demand and it is highly desirable. But it is widely available. For free. The result is that sex has gone from being the most highly valuable commodity on the market to the lowest. Feminism has taught women this is a good thing and they are the ones gaining. The feminists are right on some level; women should be sexually liberated, of course. But it doesn't take a genius to understand the big winners in all of this are men."*

Sonya took a moment.

Richard was astonished by her passion and consideration for the trials of women. He appreciated her insights into the unseen struggle of females. She had reframed many socially accepted arguments and provided fresh insight. It left him with a lot to consider.

Not Fighting Back

Keith sat quietly. He had heard Sonya debate these points before.

Internally, Richard was pondering on the fresh perspective she had delivered. Just as he went to enquire further into her point on marriage, Sonya again began to talk, with the same passion and vigour.

"It is the same in the workplace. Women have gained more stresses and strains, but men have not lost anything. Women still have to complete all the jobs and tasks they always did. Now, they must also study for degrees, master's and doctorates that keep them occupied past their mid-twenties. Then, they join the workplace that offers them additional stresses and strains, on top of everything else women must go through. These short-term solutions create long-term problems."

"Bear in mind, women must climb as high up the corporate ladder as possible before their mid-thirties," she continued. *"At this age, they are then under pressure to find a man to be the father of their children, if they listen to their feminine instinct to be a mother. If a woman decides not to give birth, then I must wonder how they will occupy themselves from age forty onwards. Because when all their friends are preoccupied with children*

and grandchildren, they could well face a barren future, if their lover leaves them for a woman who can fulfil their desire to bear children and continue his lineage."

Keith contributed to the conversation for the first time, adding:

"Well, they will focus on their careers," he said it with a shrug of the shoulders. *"Women today are increasingly encouraged to compete for the top jobs. And that's a good thing. Equality and all."*

Sonya stared at him for a moment. Then, with a sigh, she sarcastically responded:

"Yeah, that is one option—to fill our time 'representing womankind' in the hypercompetitive world of manic men obsessed with hitting the pinnacle of global business structures. How much fun it would be to enter an environment where those with almost psychopathic tendencies work nonstop in their dog-eat-dog world, flat out all the time to get ahead of the other guy."

She paused for a moment, still staring at Keith, before adding:

"Yeah, that's a real healthy position to be in."

She turned back to Richard and continued:

"Of course, if these women do not make it to the top, then they are almost accused of letting down other women. Other women who, need I say, dropped out of the race to have family and work a job more suited to their individual tastes."

"That is a bit harsh, Sonya," complained Keith, without conviction.

Nevertheless, she persisted:

"How about this? Maybe we should stop pressuring women to enter this world. Instead of asking why there are so few women in these positions, we should ask another question."

She stared directly at Keith.

He knew he had to say something. So, he said:

"Okay. What is the question?"

"Measuring a woman based how well they can play a man's game is a waste of a good woman."

"Agreed. You know I agree with that. But that is not a question," Keith added.

Sonya tilted her head to the side and gave Keith a look.

He got the message.

"My question is not based on why there are so few women in these positions. It is why are there any men at all who want the pressure and

overwhelming responsibility of these roles, where there is a handful of hungry wolves always on their tail actively plotting for them to fail.

To encourage women to compete with these adderall and cocaine-fuelled psychopaths is to feed an already broken system. After a few years in that world, most men realise there is more to life than that. So, why are we pressuring women to set themselves against this unattainable standard?"

Without stopping for a moment, Sonya put her hand on Richard's arm and said:

"Can I ask you another question, Richard?"

"Yeah, of course. What do you wanna know?"

"Why are men not fighting back?"

"Not fighting back? Fighting back against what?"

"Why are men not fighting back against the feminist movement? Why are they not fighting back against women taking their jobs?

There can only be one CEO, there can only be one managing director and there can only be one president. Those roles are being increasingly given to females to fit the feminist agenda. So, why are men not fighting back?" She almost insisted on an answer.

"Well, you know why," Richard said. *"You've just said it there. Very few men are stimulated by those positions. Most men have no interest in fighting their way to the top of a debauched hierarchy. Only a finite number are even willing to accept the pressures that come with those roles. In the same way most women are not willing to work eighty to ninety hours per week and be constantly travelling, men don't want that, either. As long as a man can provide for his family and have a little bit leftover for some leisure, he is content.*

The political narrative of the day is all men compete to get to the top. Most men, including me, drop out of that race within the first three years of their career. They just want to live. Fighting back? We've no desire to fight for something we've no interest in obtaining. If someone, man or woman, is crazy enough to aim for those roles then good luck to them."

Happy with Richard's answer, Sonya's pitch lowered and her stance changed.

"Yeah, that's what I think as well." Sonya said. *"So, why all the pressure on women to enter these male-dominated industries and compete for these roles? Each gender has its own troubles and unfairness to deal with. What frustrates me so much is women being encouraged to take on male problems as well as their own. It's sold to us under the pretence of more*

freedom. But freedom and happiness aren't the same thing—women are less happy now than in any of the prior decades."

She was genuinely frustrated and her eyes began to well up.

With her hands in front of her, palms up, she said:

"I want to have a family and get married, but if I say that, I get attacked by other women. It's almost as if we're deemed slaves if we serve a meal to our husband and children, but we are strong and empowered when we serve our employer for forty-plus hours per week. I really ... I really ... don't get it."

Seeing an opportunity to contribute to the conversation and show Sonya support, Richard responded:

"I hear ya. It makes sense when you put it like that. For example, we men no longer have the stress of being the sole provider to the family. Now, we can also have our wife or girlfriend working full-time. This massively lessens the dependency on us to be the breadwinner. It removes so much pressure from our shoulders."

"Exactly, Richard. Thank you." Sonya said. *"And that's just one example. With feminism, the big losers are women. The big winners are men. Look at every area of feminism and you'll see it has ultimately brought more heartache and stress for women, as men sit back and reap the benefits."*

This got Richard thinking. His mind went back to the rainforest when the loggers were excited to download the newest images each weekend from the latest "Slut Walk" organised by feminists somewhere around the world.

The guys used to laugh at *"how stupid women were"* for thinking that walking down the street dressed *like sluts* in a naked or semi-naked state was some sort of stance against men. At least that is how the loggers saw it.

With a tear in her eye, Sonya concluded:

"So, you consider yourself a feminist? I'm not surprised. All men should."

She buried her head into Keith's chest.

Putting his arm around his girlfriend, Keith said:

"This world owes so much to feminists. They have worked so hard, day after day, to change the world for the better and to create opportunities for women. However, the progress has been slow because they've worked against the system. They have fought and been confrontational towards men and women who thought otherwise. That is what has hampered their progress and slowed their development. Despite this, they've made amazing

strides in achieving equality for women. We must never forget what they've done for womankind specifically, and for Mother Earth in general."

Richard nodded along in silent agreement as Keith continued to talk.

"Now, as we move into the third decade of this third millennium, the objective is no longer about gaining equality for women. The goal is to empower femininity, and all that consists of, and place feminine women in the positions of leadership around the globe. To make this possible, femininity will require the help of true masculinity. The world needs open-minded, well-balanced, thoughtful, deep-feeling and connected men. Not because women can't do it on their own, but because men respond better to other men. And we are now in a hurry."

Sonya silently leaned her face against Keith's chest as he further explained his point:

"Although most men aren't even aware of it, they have been programmed from birth, and maybe long before, from conception, to believe they're superior to women. Therefore, they don't take the word or actions of women as seriously as they take those of men. Richard, that is why you have been called.

You must believe in the power of one. The power of one committed person with a heart filled with good intentions can be the catalyst for bringing change to the world. That person can be the pebble that drops into the lake and through their actions can help the ripples of progress to find their way to shore. Everything starts with one. The power of one can change the world. Actually, it's the only thing that ever has."

Keith was interrupted by Richard's name being called over the speaker system.

Slightly worried, he walked up to the man at Gate 22 check-in desk.

He was surprised to learn his seat had been upgraded to business class. When Richard enquired why this was, the guy was not completely sure, but assumed it was because he was a frequent flyer.

Richard had never flown with the airline before, so was astonished at the events. Nonetheless, he happily and gratefully accepted the free upgrade.

"Everything is always perfect," Richard said to the man, as he politely responded with a smile.

He was then invited to board the plane and settle in before the other passengers arrived, as was the norm for business class passengers.

Before boarding, Richard turned and waved to the couple. They enthusiastically waved back, then he joyfully turned to board the airplane.

However, just before he scanned his ticket, he caught himself. Stopping still, he paused for a moment.

A wave would not suffice on this occasion. He turned around and looked at the couple. They were both looking directly at him. He bounded over, eyes locked on Keith. Arms open, they met each other with a big hug. Tight, but just right.

Keith was the first to ease his grip.

Without saying anything, Richard then turned to Sonya, reaching down to hug her, being a bit gentler with his grip.

Richard looked at each of them, slowly nodding his head.

Sonya smiled.

Keith nodded back.

Neither said a single word. The communication did not require sound at that time. Richard turned and accepted the opportunity to board the plane without the usual hustle and bustle associated with economy class.

Settling into the big comfortable chair with extra legroom, he declined the offer of free champagne from the stewardess. There, it struck him how increasingly lucky he had become since meeting with Mother Ayahuasca. From reconnecting with Hannah in Amsterdam, to getting a cash windfall from the airline to stay in Stockholm and now the upgrade on the flight—and all within a few days. It felt like he was on a path of new possibility.

Drop that 'ism'

Touching down in Dublin airport, Richard thought long and hard during the flight about Sonya's insights. Maybe she was correct and men did create feminism. It is conceivable men did support and manipulate it for their own needs. Perhaps men were the true winners from the advances of the feminist movement.

However, maybe they once again underestimated the power of women. One real benefit of feminism was it had enabled women to organise. It brought women together in a sisterhood. It had taken them out of their homes and reconnected them. As a collective, women had grown into a powerful force, gathering momentum by the day.

The human race has forever lived with the perpetual choice between discussion and violence.

Finger pointing, victimhood, greed and the blame-game have carried us on a path towards implosion and explosion. Dialogue, awareness and cooperation will take us to a world of understanding and collaboration.

One thing Richard's mother had told him to always consider during times of change was that the arc of the moral universe is long, but despite the challenges of life, it does bend towards justice.

> Every time women come together to discuss big issues, the world becomes a slightly better place to live for everyone, and the pace of the destruction of our Mother, the Earth, eases slightly.

Sooner or later, women will be ready to drop that "*ism*" men enforced upon them with femin*ism* and reconnect with their true feminine power. Moving away from femin*ism* and returning to femin*inity*. Journeying from the mind to the heart.

Richard slowly became conscious that everything was perfectly becoming. The energy had already been ignited and the forward motion of this power had begun.

He felt more excited and content about the future of this planet than he had in a long time as he went through immigration at the airport. He felt relieved about the future whilst his passport was scanned by a trainee immigration officer, as his female superior stood behind, directing him with a smile.

Richard collected his bag and, instead of exiting the airport, went around to departures to see if he could get on a standby flight to take him home. He had been on a massive journey, physically, mentally, spiritually and energetically. He wanted to get back to familiar surroundings and be reacquainted with people who knew him.

He enquired at the information desks of the various airlines, but all flights were overbooked because of the forthcoming bank holiday weekend. His option was to sit in the airport and hope a bunch of people would not turn up for a flight so he could get a last-minute seat.

However, following everything he had experienced, one thing he really valued now, more than anything else, was his time.

He wanted to live his life. He wanted to make the most out of every moment. He could not justify sitting around an airport waiting to get on a flight. Life was now too short. There was a flight departing in three days slightly above his budget, but compared to the alternatives offered, it seemed like a good deal. He booked it.

Outside the airport, he jumped on the DublinBus going into the city centre. On the way into town, he reached out to Therese to see if he could stay with her again for the few nights.

Therese was on her way to the airport at the same time. She went to work that morning only to be told she was needed in Jerusalem and the task would take between three and six days. She really liked her job in the tech company, but it did not allow her to have much of a life outside of work.

In the company headquarters, they provided her with breakfast, lunch, dinner and all the snacks and drinks she could handle. Nevertheless, she was expected to be on call at all times. For example, she was now going to the Middle East to work over the bank holiday weekend, without really knowing when she would return or how long she would have to pack for.

Each promotion added an additional one-hour to her working day. Twelve-hour days were common. Eighteen-hour days were not unusual.

At times, Therese was requested to travel to a foreign country to complete a two-to-three-day task. In reality, she could end up being there for two-to-three weeks.

Not surprisingly, she was single, was not seeing anyone and had no friends outside of work. The company was her life. By design.

Despite the great PR garnered for its dedication to sexual equality, Therese was adamant the world-famous tech company she worked for was still *"an old boys club, where females came second."* In fact, a high percentage of the company's web traffic came from users viewing pornographic images, videos and gifs.

This was something the company embraced behind closed doors, but never mentioned in public. Pornography was responsible for *"keeping the numbers up."* Revenge porn videos were particularly well received.

As they would not be catching up, Richard sent Therese his regards saying:

"Good luck in Jerusalem, beautiful lady. It is one of the world's most storied cities so make sure you take some time to see the sites there. See you on the other side. XX"

When he stayed with her, Richard noticed a large hostel right in the heart of Smithfield Square, tastefully integrated into the site of the old whiskey brewery.

As he made his way from O'Connell Street, walking through the hustle and bustle of the street market, avoiding the forklifts and pallet trucks, one of the forklift drivers pulled up beside him, saying:

"Ah, it's yer, man. Are ye back again? I thought ye were going off somewhere?"

Richard was slightly confused.

After looking behind him to check there was no one else, he pointed at his chest and mumbled:

"Me?"

"Aye. Yer the man from the pub, aren't ye? I never forget the face of a man who buys me a pint. Especially when he doesn't drink himself."

A lot had happened since Richard was in the Irish pub, even though it was only a few weeks before. He had talked to so many people in the pub. He did not remember all of them. However, this guy in his overalls and slightly grubby appearance did have a familiar face, despite the dust on his brow and cheeks.

Richard had still not amply responded.

"Here, wait there a minute, mate." The man jumped off his forklift, now abandoned in the middle of the street.

Disappearing into one of the buildings, he returned thirty seconds later with a large bag of fresh fruit, all the colours of the rainbow.

"There ye go, mate. Thanks for that pint. I was totally broke. Sure, I only got me wages during d'week." He handed Richard the bag of fruit.

With that, he swung back onto his forklift and accelerated away with his pallet of fruit for loading on a delivery truck.

Richard never said a word. He stood there for a few moments looking at the fruit and wondering what just happened.

Again, he recognised, that since his meeting with Mother Ayahuasca, he had been exceptionally lucky. Good things seemed to happen in the most unexpected ways.

Normally when Richard stayed in a hostel, he booked into the largest dormitory room available. If it was a ten-bed dormitory room, he knew he would automatically have nine new friends. However, as he was feeling a bit fragile and vulnerable since the ayahuasca experience, he opted to book into a four-bed dormitory room.

Entering the dormitory, he noticed three of the beds had bags on them, but no one was in the room. He placed his bag on the lower bunk closest to the window, which was the bed he would have chosen if the room were empty. He climbed into the bed and started picking out some pieces of fruit to snack on.

He was snacking on an apple when he closed his eyes.

The next thing he knew, it was the following morning and the three people from his room were getting ready to leave. He was fully clothed, lying on top of his sheets, with bits of apple floating around in his mouth. His roommates were going to catch the bus to the historic Boyne Valley.

The group consisted of one Brazilian guy, one Australian girl and one German girl. None of them was travelling together, but they had all met in the hostel bar the night before and agreed to go on the trip as a group with some others.

As Richard awoke, they each introduced themselves, and invited him to join them.

"The bus leaves in fifteen minutes. It's supposed to be magical—you should come," one of the girls said in her Australian accent.

His mind was willing, but his body needed rest. He graciously declined the offer.

They arranged to meet him later that evening at the hostel bar. Richard was happy, as now he had the room to himself for the entire day, allowing him to catch up with his thoughts and his journal.

Just Staying Dry

Richard did not leave his bed the entire day. Between naps, journaling, daydreaming and eating his fruit, he was taking it easy and was fast asleep before his roommates came home.

He awoke 6 a.m. the following morning totally energised. Based on the smell of alcohol in the room, it seemed as if the other three had had a good time sampling Dublin's famous nightlife.

The German girl was completely naked and sleeping on top of the Brazilian boy. He was in the top bunk, fully clothed lying upside down under the German, with her foot on his face. The Australian girl was snoring loudly and appeared to be curled up and hiding under her blanket.

"Hostel life, eh? It's good to be back," Richard chuckled to himself.

He filled a bag with everything he needed for the day and departed the hostel, walking up the river, along the quayside, away from the city centre. He came to a set of large Victorian gates at the main entrance to a park.

It was Phoenix Park, one of the world's largest enclosed recreational spaces within a city, and a truly remarkable site.

Walking through the main entrance, he stopped to read a plaque just inside the gate. It contained overview information about the park, which he was reading with interest until interrupted by a young boy letting out a big enthusiastic: "WOW"

"WOW. Look. Mummy, look. There is a deer crossing the road."

At this point, Richard spun around. There was, in fact, a deer casually sauntering across the road near the gateway to the park. He was amazed at the sight unfolding. Very unexpected considering the proximity of the park to the busy city centre.

The young boy went to run towards the deer, but his mother instinctively pulled him back. She then hunkered down beside him, and with them both still looking at the deer, she said:

"The deer isn't crossing the road. The road is crossing the park.

Remember this is her home and we are her guests. We must respect her and her environment."

This insight was as powerful to Richard as it was to the little boy.

With that, he wandered off from the roadway. With no objective in mind, he strolled through the grass, past one of the lakes and through an opening in the trees.

As he came out through the opening, the sight that greeted him was astonishing. Popping his head through the trees, a few hundred fallow deer stood looking directly at him, nervously anticipating his next move.

Richard slowly sidled away from the deer, until he had his back against a tree.

He calmly sat down.

Once he was on the ground, the entire herd went back to grazing, largely ignoring him. He sat there watching the beauty of nature reveal itself.

Richard had become very comfortable with being in a timeless state. He no longer wore a watch and his phone was on airplane mode most of the time. For hours, his mind wondered and wandered as the deer peacefully grazed.

Just as he considered going back towards town, a torrential downpour swept across the park.

Sitting under the big leafy tree provided the perfect shelter as the smell of rain on the wild grass filled the air. As he sat there admiring the beauty of the rain, an old lady rushed in under the tree for shelter.

Richard packed his journal and water bottle into his bag.

He prepared for his conversation with the old lady. She stood three metres from Richard, on the other side of the tree.

Picking up his bag and clearing his throat, Richard tentatively walked over to the old woman.

"Hey, I'm Richard." He held out his hand.

The woman looked up at him. Then down at his hand and back into his eyes.

"I'm the one you're looking for," Richard began. *"I'm ... I'm Ja—"*

Interrupting him, the old woman, in her thick Dublin accent, looked scornfully at Richard and said:

"I dunno what yer on, but the only thing I'm looking for is shelter. So, ye can feck away off, so ye can. Ye weirdo."

She then darted out into the pouring rain, across the opening and in under the next closest tree. Under her breath, she continued to curse Richard's intrusion.

Richard stood in shock for a moment, and then exploded in laughter.

It was a humbling moment for him. It was what made Ireland so special.

It was the land of magic and mysticism as he had expected. It was also a land of people with big hearts who kept their feet on the ground and showed their feelings.

The next morning, he departed from Ireland filled with gratitude for all he had learned during his time on the Emerald Isle. Including a big reality check: Not everyone believed he was King James and wanted to deliver a message from the unseen.

Some people just want to keep dry.

VIII

Finally Understanding

Revenge Porn
Full-Frontal Naked Selfie
I am a Man
Lacy Underwear

Revenge Porn

As the anniversary of their mother's death approached, Richard decided it would be best to stay with his sister Kate for a while. Despite their regular online correspondence, he had not seen her for a few months.

Throughout the events of the past few weeks, one thing weighed on Richard's mind. Even more than his mother's forthcoming anniversary, he worried about Emma.

He wondered how best to tell her about her sex tape being shared on pornography sites across the Internet.

Emma was a high achiever. She did well in everything she attempted. As well as being captain of the sports team, she came top of her class academically. In addition to all of this, she was one of the kindest and sweetest people imaginable. As opposed to having a "personal PR routine" of self-promotion, she regularly downplayed her achievements, preferring to shine the spotlight on others.

A high-flying finance professional in the city, she was quite petite. But with her well-proportioned athletic figure and a sassy personality, she always seemed larger than she was.

Some people create happiness wherever they go, but other people create happiness whenever they go. Emma was certainly the former. She filled a room with joy when she walked in. She had a powerful aura.

Richard arranged to meet Emma for food and a casual catch-up after she finished work. Strangely, his flight landed early because of strong tailwinds, so he went straight from the airport to their usual café.

Despite his being early, Emma was already there working on her laptop—she always arrived early to avoid leaving anyone waiting.

Greeting him with the usual big hug and a smile that could light up any room, Emma was excited to hear about his trip and ayahuasca experience. Unlike many of his friends, she had no desire to sell everything and go travelling. She loved her job. It was her passion.

Richard was being awkward. He gave her some insights into his journey since leaving for Ireland. But she sensed he was not his normal energetic and enthusiastic self.

He was distracted and she knew it.

Richard wanted to tell her about the sex tape. He wanted to tell her how it was widely available online. He did not really know what to say, or how to approach the subject. But he cared for Emma enough to know he had to tell her.

He had to be the carrier of bad news. He had to be the one to inform her this most intimate of content was being freely shared online, despite what it may do to their friendship.

During a lull in the conversation, when Emma asked him why some of his teeth were missing, he had to tell her the full story.

He began by telling her exactly what happened in the rainforest. He explained how he was drawn to the video by the recognisable sound of her voice, coming from the TV, as he tidied up. How he unplugged the TV to stop the loggers from watching and how he woke up in the first aid room, broken and bruised and missing a few teeth.

He explained how he had wanted to tell her sooner, but as he recovered in Anne's apartment, he did not know how best to approach it.

Before departing for Ireland, Richard arranged for his friend Pádraig to locate all the websites that hosted the video—he worked for an Internet security company. Richard had printed out the list and brought it with him. It was three pages, front and back. Handing the pages to Emma, he said:

"We can work together through the legal system to remove the video from all these sites—it worked for the celebrities. We'll do what they did. We'll get rid of every single copy." He tried to sound upbeat.

Emma did not look at the pages.

Not even a glance.

It appeared as if she was looking at Richard, but her gaze ended somewhere before it reached him. It was almost as if she was looking at a flicker of dust in the air, halfway between them.

She was in a state of shock. She did not cry. She did not get angry. She calmly said:
"Now, I understand."

Richard held the silence. After a few moments, Emma continued:

"I just couldn't work out what was going on. I couldn't put my finger on it. But now ... now I understand. Now, I get it."

In a low tone, Richard said:

"Do you ... want to ... explain?"

Emma, looking at her perfectly manicured nails for a few moments, then delved into the details.

"About six months ago, the guys in the office really changed in their attitude towards me. It was almost as if they lost respect for me overnight. They started using very specific words and phrases when talking to me. It really stood out, because it was inappropriate language. Especially for a work environment. But more than that, it just seemed out of place for the conversations."

"Such as?" Richard asked.

"They would say: 'Oh, that must have been a pain in the butt' *and* 'what an asshole' *or* 'such a dick.' *This was in scenarios where*

it was neither required nor appropriate. It was really bizarre. Because it almost started coming from all the guys at the same time. And they did it with a smirk on their face."

She took a deep breath.

"Around that time, a guy I really liked—he was a friend of a colleague—asked me out on a date. I haven't been out with anyone since my ex-boyfriend ghosted me and disappeared into thin air, all those years ago. I was so excited about it, Richard. On the day of the date, thirty minutes before I was due to meet him, he sent me a bland text cancelling. He didn't give a reason.

I was already in a taxi on my way to meet him. I wanted to be early, so he wasn't waiting for me. I was wearing a new outfit I bought specifically for the occasion. I had taken a half-day off work to go get my hair and nails done. I had even purchased new lingerie. I was really excited, Richard. Really, really excited."

Richard was staring directly at Emma as she talked. Listening with his eyes.

"Leading up to the date when we talked on the phone or sent messages, he was a complete gentleman. Really fun, kind and attentive. He was such a nice guy that when he cancelled on me, I assumed something happened he didn't want to share. So, I brushed it off, ordered some nice takeaway from that new vegan place and went home to read on the sofa. I text him a few times since, but he never responded. He just went dark on me. His friend whom I work with also went very cold on me around that time."

Speaking in a slow, almost monotone manner, absent of her usual bubbly energy, seemingly detached from her words, Emma continued:

"I also had a lot of creepy guys from the office coming up to me and asking me out. Almost acting like they were doing me a favour. Allowing me to go out with them. And this was not just from guys in the lower levels of the team. Some of these sleazebags are partners in the firm.

A lot of married men in work have really been coming on strong over the past few months. I could deal with all that. That's what women have to deal with every single day."

Richard's mouth was dry. He reached for his cup. He had already finished his tea.

"But two things really annoyed me. I have thought about them for a while and I could never work them out. Two very specific things. The first one is that I was almost guaranteed a promotion this year. It was almost

assured. I was so confident, based on the feedback I had received within the firm, I had started arranging the celebration dinner with my parents."

Emma turned to look at Richard for a moment. He was looking directly at her, listening attentively. Following a second of eye contact between them, she turned back to talking into mid-air.

"I had done everything and more to ensure I was promoted. Then, at the last moment, I didn't get it. I got a nonsense explanation from the senior partner. I learned the next day a guy a year behind me, and a lot less qualified, was promoted instead. I couldn't work it out. I was baffled. But I accepted the decision. I had to. There was nothing I could do."

Richard again reached for his teacup, desperate for something to quench his thirst. He again realised it was empty and put it back on the table.

"The second thing that really annoyed me was that the women in the office also went cold towards me. They would huddle together and ignore me as blatantly as only women could.

Now, when I think about it, the women have been the worst. It has almost died down with the men, but the women are still on it. Every single day. At every opportunity. I could never put my finger on it. Now, it is so obvious. Now, I get it."

Listening to every word, Richard was worried. She was still talking in monotone. Totally detached.

She showed no emotion at all.

Richard leaned over to hug her. She did not lift her arms to hug him back. She just sat there like a lifeless mannequin in a shop window, with her eyes open, gazing into space.

Richard was stumped. He had nothing to say.

She calmly thanked him for dinner. Then, slowly grabbing her designer handbag and umbrella, she made her excuses to leave.

Just as she was walking out the door, she turned around, looked at Richard across the café and said:

"I am sorry you got beat up and lost your job in the rainforest because of me."

Then, she was gone, walking across the street in the pouring rain, with her *Kate Spade* umbrella down by her side.

Full-Frontal Naked Selfie

Arriving at his sister's apartment, Richard worried about Emma. He wanted to talk with his sister and get her take on what to do next.

Letting himself into the apartment with the key she had given him, he was surprised to find she was still in bed. Going over to the open door of her bedroom, he noticed Kate was crying. She was sitting up on her bed, holding her pillow.

She looked tired and pale.

Going over to comfort her, he held Kate in his arms. With one hand across the centre of her back and one hand cradling the back of her head, Richard pulled her close, in a brotherly manner.

Although he had not seen her for months, he observed the silence and just held her. Kate sobbed into his chest as they sat on the bed.

Then, with an abrupt jerk, she lifted her head and said:

"I'm sorry. I'm just being stupid. Sorry about this. How was Ireland?"

Looking back at her, Richard responded:

"Don't worry, just relax. Allow the emotions to flow. Better out than in, as Mum used to say, eh?" He pretended to chuckle. He then added:

"Don't worry. I miss her too, Kate. Time is supposed to be a healer. But with every passing year, I miss her more."

Still sobbing, Kate responded:

"Yeah, that's right. Mum's anniversary is coming up in a few weeks. I need to arrange the flowers for Dad again."

This confused Richard. He assumed she was crying about their mother.

To get his thoughts correct on how he should approach this issue, and everything that had happened with Emma, he offered to make a cup of tea. It would give him time to think.

Kate was a stunning girl. Her eyes really set her apart: they possessed a soft glow, whilst simultaneously sparkling. In addition, her features were perfectly symmetrical. Like her twin brother, she was tall. However, her body mass index was very high and doctors had warned her about the impact it would have on her long-term health if she did not lose weight.

With her mum passing away at a vital time in her development into womanhood and her dad emotionally unavailable, she had no one to remind her how beautiful she was, during those awkward times, as her body morphed.

She was so used to her features, she was unaware of how beautiful she looked to strangers. She did not recognise her worth. As a result, she would comfort eat at night, despite being so careful with what she ate throughout the day. Like a fuel-tank, her willpower was slowly depleted with daily use, leaving her open to suggestion at night.

As twins, Richard and Kate were close in some ways. But not close enough to discuss the everyday details. Especially not the details of their love lives.

As Richard was making tea, she came out wearing yoga pants and an oversized hoodie, having brushed her hair and washed her face.

Turning to Kate and handing her a cup of green tea, Richard asked:

"So, what is going on?"

"Uumm, nothing to worry about. Just stupid boy problems." She downplayed it.

"I sort've picked up on that. You and Terry having problems again?" Richard asked.

Kate put her tea down on the coffee table and fell back into the sofa. She took a moment to compose herself and said:

"I don't know what to do. I'm just so disappointed in them."

"In who?" Richard asked.

"A few weeks ago, I received a dick pic' from Terry, just out of nowhere, with the caption: "You asked, so you shall receive,'" she said. *"He was out with the boys in the pub. When I woke the next morning, I received it with a timestamp of 3:33 a.m. He didn't even remember sending it. When I confronted him about it, he said it must've been him joking with the guys. He palmed it off as nothing more than a joke. He had never sent me a dick pic before that. We're not that type of couple."* She almost overexplained the point to her brother.

"And then, when he was here yesterday, he went to shower after we had sex. The sex was really unusual. It was almost as if he wasn't there. As if his mind was somewhere else. As he was in the shower, he got a notification on his phone. Now ... I know ... I know I shouldn't have opened his phone, but he's been so possessive of it recently, I just felt the urge. So, I did. And when I loo—"

Filled up by emotion, Kate could not finish the sentence.

Richard went over and sat beside her, cuddling her in his arms. He asked:

"What was it? What did you see?"

"When I looked at his phon—" she stammered, before getting caught up and wailing loudly again.

"You should know never to look at anyone's phone. Things can be taken out of context. When you read something without having the full story, it may seem worse than it is," Richard said.

Pushing him back and sitting up straight, Kate looked at Richard straight in the eye. She gritted her teeth, then said:

"Trust me, Richard. I got the full story."

She wiped her eyes with the sleeves of her hoodie, then tucking her feet under her bottom, she continued:

"It was a message from a number saved as 'John Work.' It said, "I hope you had a good time with Kate this morning, but I hope you saved some for me?" *As I was reading it, a photo message came through. It was a full-frontal naked selfie of Jennifer, kneeling on her bedroom floor and touching herself."*

Trying to put everything together and understand what he had just heard, Richard said:

"What? Who was this? Which Jennifer?"

"JENNIFER!" Kate screamed back. *"MY Jennifer. OUR Jennifer."*

"Jennifer? Your best friend Jennifer? No way. Are you sure?" asked Richard in a high-pitched tone of disbelief.

Kate and Jennifer had been best friends since they were nine. They had come through school together. They had gone on holidays together. Their lives were intertwined.

Richard fell back into the sofa. In his early twenties, he had had a one-night stand with Jennifer and she pleaded with him never to tell Kate. He never did, and nothing ever happened between them again. They simply picked up their friendship and continued as normal. When they were teenagers, Kate and Jennifer had made a pact never to sleep with each other's family members.

He could not believe what he was hearing. How could Jennifer do this to Kate, her best friend?

How could Terry do this to Kate? How could he be so blatant? How could he be so stupid?

Richard did not know what to say, as his twin sister lay on the sofa with her head in her hands crying loudly.

Looking at Kate, he gathered she probably had nothing to eat or drink for at least twenty-four hours. After much persuasion, Richard got her tidied up and they left to have a fruit smoothie.

She did not want to go to their usual hangout, as she did not want the people there to see her in that state. She was normally the bubbly and enthusiastic girl who knew everyone there on a first-name basis.

They sat in the newly opened organic health food bar. Yet, before Richard even had a second sip out of his large forest berry smoothie, Kate had finished her small kale and pineapple smoothie.

Without asking, Richard went up and ordered her another. He got her a large one this time. Once again, she finished before Richard got halfway down his cup. She was hungry and tired to the extreme.

I am a Man

Back at the apartment, Richard made Kate a hot water bottle, like their mother used to, and tucked her into bed. She instantly fell asleep. She was exhausted.

Richard put on the kettle for a cup of green tea. Whilst waiting for it to boil, he sat down at Kate's dining table. On the table was a notepad and pen. He lifted the pen, opened the notepad and at the top of the first page, he wrote:

I AM A MAN

He pondered for a moment, allowing his mind to drift off.

His mind drifted back to the sights that unfolded as he sat in that large tent, in the Netherlands, dressed in white.

As his mind scanned the revelations of that time, he felt a sudden bolt of energy enter his root chakra from behind. It powered through his body, lighting up every cell and strand as it went, before exploding out the top of his crown chakra.

A brilliant white light filled his world, along with a comforting silence.

As the white light faded and his senses returned, he felt dazed.

He realised he was hunched over the table. He had his head on his arms.

With his eyes still closed, a very clear and exact insight had crystallised in his mind.

Pen still in hand, he sat up straight and blinked open his eyes.

Looking down on the notepad in front of him, he composed himself for a moment. Following a deep inhalation, he began to scribble this new insight on the paper. He wrote:

I am a man. To be a man is to be a servant to the world, to our mother, to our sisters— our leaders. We go out into the world to bring home the food and sustenance they require. We bring home what our leaders need to help make tomorrow better. We are hunters and gatherers. We are workers. We use our physicality to fulfil the requirements of our feminine leaders. We encourage and support women to make the decisions, and to debate the matters of importance. We are there to protect our goddess. We are there to give in to her needs. We are there for our feminine leaders.

There is no tool more effective in rebalancing this world and protecting our planet than the empowerment of femininity. When men support women, incredible possibilities unfold. The empowered feminine woman possesses a beauty beyond description and resonates a power beyond measure. As men, this is our role. Empowered masculinity empowers femininity

Arriving at the bottom of the first page, he eagerly flipped over the notepad and continued writing, in green ink, on the second page. The words flowed through him with ease.

I am a strong man in that I know the needs of my woman and respect her as the leader of my tribe. I know my role is to provide for her and her babies. I know she is a sexual animal that requires a release. She is a strong mother and leader in the day that commands respect. But at night, away from the searching eyes of the public, she is a playful kitten that wants to be bitten and spanked, touched and scratched, brought to orgasm. Her animal instincts scream out for her man to dominate her with his masculine energy in a safe and playful manner.

Allow her to let go of the seriousness of life and allow her inner child to be released, to be set free. She loves to laugh, play and be silly and to roll on the floor and sit against the wall, and write and draw and sing and hum and tidy away. In her element, she enjoys adding little touches that turn a concrete block into a warm, loving, inviting home that is a safe and welcoming place for her babies.

The feminine woman is gentle and soft, yet strong and tough. She possesses a drive and focus that sit easily with her moments of laughter and timelessness. Her kindness and affection co-exist with the ferociousness and wildness. In mankind, we desire power when we wish to cause harm. Otherwise, love is sufficient to achieve our goals. Now, is the time to love, embrace and empower femininity.

Scribbling the final words, he then gently placed the pen on the table beside the notepad and sat back into the chair. With another deep inhalation, he gathered his thoughts.

Baffled by the abstruse nature of what had unfolded, but in no way feeling uncomfortable, he lifted the notepad and began to read the words aloud.

Richard was astonished. He could not believe he had just written these words in a state of subconsciousness. The words had been delivered to him. From where, he was unsure. He pondered. Maybe the words were channelled directly from Mother Ayahuasca?

He went to the kettle and poured the water for tea. The water was lukewarm, verging on cold. How long had he been crystallising those thoughts, he wondered?

He switched on the kettle again.

The words he wrote felt strong. They were real. At his very core, he believed them. They felt natural.

Since meeting the Irish lady at the Hill of Tara, he had been away from social media—on a complete digital detox.

Despite this, he felt the urge to take what he had written and, word for word, post the message to his social media.

Opening his sister's laptop, he logged into his Facebook account, typed up what he had written and posted it.

As he submitted the post, his sister came out of her bedroom. She stood behind him and read down through his words on the screen.

"You sure about this?" she asked. Richard did not respond, as he pondered on her question.

"You really have been on a big journey."

His sister's comments planted a seed of doubt in his mind. He questioned whether he should share the thoughts with his friends and followers. He reconsidered. Maybe the world was not ready for these words yet.

Men, in general, were not ready for those words—they would say he sounded like *"a bitch."*

Women, in general, would reject the words—they would say he sounded like *"a cuck."*

Feminists would pour scorn on those words—they would say he sounded like *"a sexist."*

Having second thoughts, he deleted the post.

Just as he confirmed the deletion of the post, a notification popped up on the corner of his screen:

> One person has shared your post.

He clicked on the notification and it went to a page that said:

> This post has been removed.

Turning to his sister, Richard said:

"So, that's deleted for good now? Or is it out there somewhere on the Internet?"

"I think it is been deleted. It should be gone now." Kate replied.

"Let's hope so," Richard said, as he got up and walked towards the kettle, to finally get that cup of tea.

Lacy Underwear

The following morning, Richard struggled to complete his meditation and stretching routine—his meeting with Emma and how it had ended weighed on him like an oversized wet sweater.

He needed to check in with her.

He turned on his phone and sent a message of support.

> Hi Ems,
>
> Sending you a massive virtual hug this morning. I won't even pretend to imagine how difficult this must be for you. But please know my heart has been breaking since the moment I saw my most beautiful, kind, funny and loyal friend up on that screen. I'm going to do everything I can to help you along this process and ensure we get that stupid video removed from every single site. I am 100% committed to that. Sending you a big green heart of luv for today. Call me at any time if you wanna talk. Otherwise, I will call you when you get out of work 2night, to see how you're feeling.
>
> Much luv. Richard

At around noon, Richard turned his phone on again. Emma had still not responded to his message.

That was very unusual. Despite being a high-flying professional, she would respond to messages as soon as it was possible for her to do so. Otherwise, she would simply acknowledge the message responding, *"I'll text you later."*

Richard left his phone on, keeping it on him. He eagerly checked it every few minutes, anxiously refreshing it.

Just after 1 p.m., when she would be at lunch, he still had not received a response, so he decided to call her. It went straight to voicemail. He left a message, gently checking in and asking her to call him when she got a moment.

At 2:30 p.m., Emma had still not responded. He called her again and left another message.

Feeling a bit anxious, he called her office number, which was directed through to reception. The receptionist told Richard she had not turned up for work that morning and was unreachable.

Richard asked the receptionist:

"Can you please clarify that? Did she not turn up? Or did she call in sick?"

"She did not turn up. Some of her clients have arrived here today for meetings and were unable to get in touch with her. No one has heard from her today. Would you like to leave a message?" the receptionist responded.

Without saying another word, Richard ran straight out the door.

Down on the street, he hailed a taxi, jumped in and ordered the driver to take him to her place, across town. Now, he was deeply worried.

Emma was the most professional and dedicated employee he knew. He did not remember her ever calling in sick or missing a day at work. This was totally out of character.

Arriving at her apartment, he went straight up to her door and rang the doorbell. There was no answer. He rang the doorbell once more whilst simultaneously knocking on the door, shouting Emma's name, yet trying to sound calm.

Maybe she was on the toilet or in the shower, he thought. If she was, he did not want to create any more stress for her by banging on her door, after everything that had happened the night before.

Despite his best efforts, he was starting to panic.

She did not respond.

Whilst searching for the number of the apartment administrator, he casually checked the door handle. He was surprised to find the door to her apartment was unlocked.

He barged through the door, hurried into the living room, to the kitchen and then to the bedroom. She was nowhere to be seen. Everything was perfectly in place throughout the apartment, as it always was.

Until he noticed the clothes she wore the evening before, in a heap outside the en-suite bathroom.

He then detected something very bizarre above the heap of clothing. A black and a red bra were attached to the door handle and were stretched up and over at the top of the closed door.

In a panic, he rushed to the door.

It was locked from the inside. He did not try the handle for a second time. He ran at the door with his shoulder and burst right through.

On the other side, naked and slumped in a heap was his big-hearted friend Emma.

She had the other straps of the black and red bras double-folded around her neck.

He quickly lifted her weight to help take the pressure of her airways. He then removed the straps from cutting into her flesh.

He checked her pulse.

It was faint, but it was there.

He doubted himself. It crossed his mind the slight throbbing may have been a result of his own pounding heart.

He took a deep breath, closed his eyes and focused hard. Yes. It was Emma's pulse.

She was unconscious, but still alive.

This was not a cry for help from Emma. This was a genuine suicide attempt. She had truly wanted to end her pain.

Richard performed mouth-to-mouth resuscitation—his medical education and training kicked in, as he delved into emergency response and resuscitation autopilot.

It appeared as if the bras had held for long enough for her to lose the supply of oxygen to her brain and she had blacked out.

However, the lacy designer bras were never designed to hold such a weight for a sustained time, even someone as small as her. Fortunately, the bras had ripped, sending her petite frame crashing to the floor and to relative safety.

Richard immediately dialled for the emergency services. Twelve minutes later, they arrived at the front door of her apartment. By a stroke of luck, they had received a prank call from some young boys to pick up another person in the neighbourhood.

For Richard, it felt like hours had passed. He had never been more stressed than he was during those long drawn-out twelve minutes.

Although he had been confronted with these situations numerous times during his medical education, all the training in the world could not prepare him for being in this situation with a loved one.

As the ambulance rushed through the city towards the hospital, Emma was strapped to the gurney in the back, surrounded by medical professionals. Everything was going in slow motion for Richard. It was as if time had stopped. All Richard could do was sit back and wonder how this could have happened to his wonderful friend.

Why did her ex-boyfriend upload that intimate and most personal video for the world to see?

Why were the loggers in the rainforest entertained by watching a girl wriggle in pain as a man twice her size attempted anal sex with her?

Why did her work colleagues share the video around the office?

Why did the women who worked with Emma every day since graduation think this was an acceptable stick with which to beat her?

Why did I not think this through properly before telling Emma?

Why did I not have all the videos removed from the Internet before I met her?

Why did I let her walk out into the rain on her own last night?

Why did I not go to her apartment sooner?

These questions and thousands more beginning with "*Why?*" babbled through Richard's mind. Sitting in the back of the ambulance, strangers worked frantically to save the life of his soul sister.

And all of this, because this kind soul wanted to make her boyfriend happy.

9

One By One

Our Mantra

With Emma on the hospital bed in a coma, Richard maintained a bedside vigil. Holding her hand, he repeatedly whispered a mantra to Emma as she lay motionless.

He hoped something close to her heart would trigger a memory and would help her come around. He gently whispered:

> "I am whole.
> I am perfect.
> I am strong.
> I am powerful.
> I am loving.
> I am harmonious.
> I am happy.
> I am perfectly healthy.
> I am abundantly wealthy.
> I am filled with love."

As the nurses came and went during their shift, they stopped for a few moments. They would listen as Richard calmly and warmly whispered the mantra into Emma's ear. Towards the end of his shift, one of the nurses said:

"What you're saying is so beautiful."

His words startled Richard. He glanced around at the nurse. *"Thanks,"* he politely responded.

"What's the origin of that?"

Richard took a moment to compose himself, and then gently told him:

"It's just our thing. Emma and I came up with this little mantra when we were teenagers; it started out being a lot simpler. We started it one day after I got into a fight with a few guys who had been rude to Emma. They were calling her a 'skateboard' saying she was 'flat and hard to ride' because she didn't have any boobs yet."

"That's rough," said the nurse.

"Yeah, it was a tough time for both of us. I was coping with my mother's death and Emma was having a difficult time as she was late going through puberty. So, following that fight, Emma and I designed a mantra to help us feel empowered. People think it's a bit childish, but when we started, it was only three lines. It was simply:

> *I am perfect.*
> *I am powerful.*
> *I am happy.*

Over the years, we have added to it, to the point it's now a list of ten."

"Ohh, that's so cute."

"It has been like this for about three years now, so we won't be adding more to it," Richard said. *"Having a mantra of ten powerful statements just works for me on a practical level."*

"So, have you built it into your routine in any specific way?" the nurse asked.

"It's completely part of my daily life. For example, when I'm in the gym and doing reps, instead of counting to ten, I can just talk through the mantra to get to ten."

"Of course. That's so smart."

"If I'm ever going up or down steps or stairs, I always say the mantra, one line for each step I take," Richard said. *"It helps me bring my mind back into the moment. And the steps are always a good reminder to do it, y'know? We all have a few steps we must climb, every day of life."*

"And is that how Emma uses it as well?" the nurse asked.

"Emma has got a few other ways of using it. When she is brushing her teeth in the morning, she always stands on one foot and talks through the mantra in her mind. She does this so she has a strong, positive start to her day. And it strengthens her core—it's why she has such a flat and strong stomach." Richard smiled from his eyes. He then turned back towards Emma.

As Richard talked, the nurse wiped a tear from his eye. Then, he said:

"I really like that. I'm also going to build your mantra into my life, if you don't mind?"

"Please do." Richard held the faint smile.

As the nurse walked out the door, he stopped, turned to Richard and said:

"You're right about that. We all have a few steps we must climb. Every day of life."

Nodding, Richard turned back to Emma and continued whispering the mantra.

Richard again got lost in time as the hours past.

He was startled when he felt a firm hand on his shoulder.

He jolted in surprise.

Richard had fallen asleep with his head on Emma's legs during the night. His face was covered in drool. Only one thing surprised him more than being awakened in such a manner. It was the realisation that the hand on his shoulder was his father's.

Standing behind him holding a large bunch of flowers and a teddy bear was Mickey.

Not only that, but he was wearing a crisp white shirt under a navy suit. Richard had not seen his father in a suit since he was a child.

Since Mickey's wife died, he had let his hair grow wild and had been wearing t-shirts and vests along with jeans and trainers.

Mickey had a sombre look on his face and his head was hanging slightly, like a dog that had just ripped apart a new cushion. He had only returned to the rainforest a few weeks earlier, meaning he was only halfway through his shift. He should still be there, by Richard's calculations.

Mickey did a lot of soul-searching after flying back from the rainforest with his son. He began to take stock of the man he had become.

In his small apartment, he had only one sentimental item. It was a framed photo of Angel. He usually kept it behind his record player, as he did not want her searching eyes on the photo to see the man he had become.

Following the events that ended with his only son being beaten up, by people he considered friends, he took a long hard look in the mirror.

With the framed photo of Angel in his hands, he apologised to the mother of his children for the mistakes he had made. As a father. As a man.

He promised Angel changes were coming.

"Son, I'm sorry for what happened to Emma. I came straight up when I heard."

He handed the flowers and teddy bear to Richard, who gently placed the teddy bear on the bottom of the bed at Emma's feet—carefully propping it up so that it was looking towards Emma with its big teddy bear smile. He then delicately put the flowers in a vase beside the bed.

As Richard turned to face his father, Mickey motioned with his arms out to give him a hug. They both stepped forward and embraced one another, squeezing tight.

It was the first hug Richard had received from his father since he was a child. His father did not hug him at his mother's funeral, and he had not received one since.

As Mickey squeezed tight, Richard could no longer contain his emotions.

He started to cry.

Tears of pain escaped down his face.

Then, he started to wail out. It was a combination of everything that happened over the last few days. From his sister's heartbreak to Emma going through her ordeal. Then, his father turning up at the hospital after years of neglect—it all caught up on him.

As Richard held his father, it felt as if Mickey was also crying, by the way his body was shaking. But when they eventually let go, Mickey did not have any tears in his eyes.

He had been suppressing his emotions since the death of his wife and he did not know *how* to cry anymore. Tears could not physically leave his body. It was as if the pipes in the waterworks had been emotionally blocked.

As they looked at each other, Mickey said:

"Son, your mother would be so proud of you—the man you've become. I know that. I really know that. Because I know I feel so proud of you.

The room descended into silence for a few moments.

Richard tried to comprehend what his father was saying. After Mickey gathered his thoughts, he continued:

"I'm going to work hard to become the father you and Kate deserve. I am sorry. I'm truly sorry, but I will make it up to you as best as I can. If I can. If you both will allow me to?"

"Thank you, Dad," Richard said. *"It means a lot for you to say that."*

In reality, Richard could not believe what he was hearing: Had his father just apologised?

"Yeah, and another thing," Mickey said, *"that backpacking thing you were saving for? It's looking up for you, kid. The company will be paying up the full amount of your contract. Signing off on that beating as an 'accident' under duress is not going to cut it. I put a bit of pressure on the guys when I got back. You will have a few non-disclosure legal docs to sign, but then you will get full payment for the rest of the year. You deserve it, kid. You worked hard down there."*

"Seriously? Seriously? That will be fantastic." Richard had his hands on his face.

He was delighted. He needed the money after everything that had happened during his trip in northern Europe. Again, he noted for a moment how his luck had changed since his meeting with Mother Ayahuasca at the retreat.

However, he was not overly excited. His good friend Emma was in a coma, lying in a hospital bed one metre from him, with tubes coming out of her nose.

"Okay, I'm going to go now. You know how much I enjoy being in these places," Mickey said, waving his arms.

"Okay, Dad, I understand. I'll let you know if anything changes," Richard responded as his father turned and left the room.

As Richard sat down beside Emma again, his father put his head back inside the door and said:

"By the way ... loved your post."

Mickey flashed him the *thumbs up*, and then he was gone.

This was slightly confusing. Richard had no idea what his father was talking about. He considered for a moment the peculiar meeting with his father.

"Was my father really wearing a suit?"

The thoughts regarding his father lasted for only a few seconds—he had more pressing matters to consider.

He went to the sink in the room and washed the drool and tears from his face, then turned his attention towards Emma. Again, he started repeating their mantra.

This time, he decided to repeat each line three times before moving on to the next.

> *"I am whole. I am whole. I am whole.*
> *I am perfect. I am perfect. I am perfect.*
> *I am strong. I am strong. I am strong.*
> *I am powerful. I am powerful. I am powerful.*
> *I am loving. I am loving. I am loving.*
> *I am harmonious. I am harmonious. I am harmonious.*
> *I am happy. I am happy. I am happy.*
> *I am perfectly healthy. I am perfectly healthy. I am perfectly healthy.*
> *I am abundantly wealthy. I am abundantly wealthy. I am abundantly wealthy.*
> *I am filled with love. I am filled with love. I am filled with love."*

He continued across the ten statements, saying each of them three times, until he got to the end. Then, he started again.

This continued for hours.

Richard lost track of time, as he stroked Emma's hand and continued whispering the mantra to her repeatedly.

Richard was almost in a trance, blank expression, eyes open, looking down at Emma's hand as he stroked it.

> *"I am whole. I am whole. I am whole.*
> *I am perfect."*

As he said the first *"I am perfect,"* it was almost as if someone mumbled it with him. He repeated it for a second time:

"I am per—" he said, stopping halfway through.

Looking up at Emma, who with closed eyes, emotionless face and lips barely moving, finished the statement with:

"...fect."

Looking at her, her eyes still closed, Richard stayed silent as Emma then mouthed the third:

"I am perfect."

He jumped up in amazement with his hands on his head. Then started screaming:
"Nurse. Nurse. Quick. Help. She is awake. She is awake."
As he shouted for the nurse, Emma continued with the mantra:

"I am strong. I am strong. I am strong.
I am powerful. I am powerful. I am powerful.
I am loving. I am loving. I am—"

Then, just as she murmured, *"loving"* for the third time, her eyes sprang open.

At that moment, two nurses rushed into the room and went through the various protocols required in those circumstances. They demanded Richard leave the room.

Richard, fully aware of the protocol for friends and family in those circumstances, went outside the room, stood against the wall. Looking in at Emma as the nurses calmly worked, he slid down into a seated position on the floor.

Here, he held his head in his hands and just cried with joy.

"I am perfect. I am perfect. That was what woke her up. That is what saved her. I am perfect. Those are the words that brought her back," Richard whispered, looking upwards as he cried with relief.

Viral Post

Richard turned on his phone to call his sister and father to let them know Emma had come out of the coma. Unusually, he dialled his father's number first. Mickey was at a restaurant with an old friend, but he answered the call straight away and listened eagerly as Richard relayed the good news.

As Richard talked, he could feel his phone vibrating constantly—messages and notifications continually came through.

His father was relieved to receive the news and it was soothing for Richard to hear his father talk and respond in a compassionate manner.

After saying goodbye to his father, he called Kate, but her phone was busy—she was already on a call. He decided to call around the circle of mutual friends he and Emma had in common. But his phone continued to vibrate, as messages came through in a constant stream.

He had mostly been off the grid in the months leading up to that moment. With that and everything that happened to Emma, he was expecting to receive some messages, but this just seemed a tad excessive.

He went to his messages and found he had 111 unread texts, with more coming through by the second.

Flicking down through the list of messages, many of them came from people he had not been in contact with for years. Many other messages came from numbers with no name saved to them.

He opened the message from Anne first.

He had not been in contact with her since she told him they would not be going backpacking together. Their last contact was when he left her the note saying he needed to get some space to heal. She did not know about the ayahuasca ceremony.

As Anne was finishing her master's degree, he just thought it would be best not to worry her. But at a deeper level, he came to believe she was becoming too *"left-side-of-the-brain"* to fully understand that stage of his life journey. He noticed as she cared for him, she was increasingly communicating from her head than her heart.

He could sense slight changes in Anne during their few days together, at her apartment. He got a feeling despite everything they had in common, she was probably spending too much of her best years in formal education. It was having a negative impact on her spiritual health.

Now, with her planning to do a Ph.D., she would go deeper into her mind, leaving her connection to her heart further behind. Possibly to her detriment. For someone who had always been so connected to her heart, Anne was now becoming increasingly mind orientated.

She was getting to the stage where her schooling was beginning to interfere with her education.

The message he received from Anne read:

> U r everywhere. U r such an amazing man. I am so proud to have you as my boyfriend. Your post was beautifully written. It's almost as if it just poured out of your heart. Can't wait to see you again huni. Much love. PS Answer your phone. PPS Call me.

Richard was confused. *"I'm her boyfriend now?"* he mumbled.

After all that had happened, he was not ready to make that commitment, especially as they had both discussed not getting into any kind of official relationship just a few months earlier.

She had a beautiful mind; he really enjoyed their conversations and her insights. However, what he liked about Anne was her big heart. It was the strong connection to her femininity that differentiated her from other girls. It was why he was excited to go backpacking with her.

Now with a distance of time and space since their last communication, Richard had more perspective on their relationship and the direction they were both growing as individuals.

She was beginning to do more thinking than feeling around unfamiliar subjects. Especially something a little leftfield like ayahuasca. It was not her fault. She was becoming a product of her environmental training.

Richard could not handle her mind-based questions before he left for Ireland and went to the secret retreat. It was why he did not share it with her. Despite it only being a number of weeks since she had been caring for him on her sofa, he felt a gap had opened between them. A season was coming to an end.

Love is an uncontrollable master.

"I need to call her," he muttered as he opened the next message.

> Hey bro, I always knew that you being a big softy would make you famous. Well-done man. I have really been getting into this girly feminism stuff these past few weeks. We need to start supporting our women man. I'm 100% with you on this. Let's catch up for a beer this week. Give me a call. Tariq.

The message came from a number he did not recognise and had not saved any contact details for.

Next message said:

> Hi Richard
>
> This is Rachel from Cosmo. Everyone here in the office totally loved your post. Would love to have a quick chat today, as we are going to have you featured in the mag. You're exactly what the world needs right now. You embody a strong masculine man, who's in touch with his feminine side. Let's talk. Rachel. X

Richard opened another message from a phone number with no saved contact details.

> Richard, Marcus from The Times here. Really love to talk to you about your post. Give me a call on this number.

Richard was now completely confused. He flicked down through the messages on his phone and they all mentioned a *"post."* Then, he remembered his father also mentioning something about a post earlier in the day.

Richard closed the messages. Whatever was going on, he did not want to have to deal with it. He opened the photo gallery on his phone. He scrolled to a selfie he had taken with Hannah as they sat in the park, engulfed by the smell of freshly cut grass and groups of friends smoking weed.

The light in the photo was perfect. The sun was shining directly on them and it brought out the bliss on their faces. Her brown eyes sparkled with inner joy. The smile on Richard's face was as natural as it had ever been. Both had messy hair from lying down, watching the metamorphosis of the clouds as they went by. Richard's mind wandered back to that moment.

Startled, his phone began to ring.

It was his sister. He answered it immediately. Kate instantly began talking:

"Richard. Wow. Can you believe this? I can't believe it. I'm just so proud of you and everyth—"

"Kate. Kate. Kate. Please. Stop. Stop for a moment. Please." Richard attempted to get his sister's attention and find out what she was talking about.

"What is going on, Kate? I have just turned my phone on and it has been blowing up with messages. I am getting messages from so many random numbers. From people I haven't heard from in years. Every second message seems to come from someone within the media industry. What is going on?"

"It's your post. It has gone viral. It is everywhere. It is absolutely everywhere," Kate explained with excitement. *"I have been trying to call you. My phone has been blowing up, too. All our friends and family have been reaching out. I have even had some reporters calling me, because they can't reach you."*

"What are you talking about? What post?"

Despite the obvious, Richard was so tired, he could not think straight. He just did not make the connection. It was too far-fetched for him to even consider.

"Your post. The post we deleted. The post about empowering femininity," Kate said, sounding almost annoyed her brother was still not getting it.

"The post we deleted?" Richard frowned his forehead.

"Yes. The post. The one we deleted. It was shared. Remember?" Kate sighed. *"When it was shared, it was captured on screen shots and then shared again. The post has gone viral. Your post has been discussed on the local news. Vloggers all over the Internet are talking about you. You're appearing on blogs and being discussed all over social media right now. You're trending globally under two hashtags. Depending on the region, it is either* #ForgiveMeSister *or* #EmpoweringFemininity. *You've gone viral. I am so, so proud of you, Twinny."* Kate finally stopped for a breath.

As Kate stopped talking, she waited for Richard to talk.

She expected him to sound excited.

He did not say anything.

"Hello, Richard. Are you there? Hello? Richard. Richard. Damn phones. Can you hear me?"

"Yeah, I can hear you loud and clear. I am in the hospital right now with Emma. She is here because something private to her was shared all over

the Internet. So, to have something of mine I purposely deleted being shared across the Internet is not exactly what I want to hear right now," Richard sighed.

"Sorry, I didn't know. I wasn't thinking."

There was a silence.

"No, I'm sorry. I'm sorry for snapping. I was just calling to tell you Emma has woken from her coma. Things are looking up." Richard gained his composure.

"You won't believe what woke her. I was saying our 'I am' mantra to her over and over again," he said. "When I got to 'I am perfect', Emma finished the sentence for me. She muttered it. That is what connected her and brought her back. It was so powerful."

"I'm so happy to hear that. That's so amazing. Whenever you tell people about your mantra, it is always the 'I am perfect' they struggle with most. That is so awesome, Richard. Please tell her I send my regards, will ya?" Kate said.

"Yeah, it is awesome. Truly, mind-blowing. How are you feeling now? Have you fixed things with Terry yet?"

"Aaww don't worry about that. I'm completely exhaustipated with him right now."

"Exhaustipated?"

"Yeah, I'm too tired to give a shit. We can talk about that another time. Please focus on Emma for now, as you will have enough to deal with when you come out of there."

"Okay. I am going to turn my phone off again, because as we are talking I have various calls waiting and a stream of messages coming through. Take care of yourself and make sure you are eating properly and getting plenty of rest. I will let you know if there is any further progression with Emma. Love you."

"Love you, Richard. Call me la—."

"Wait, Kate. Hold on," interrupted Richard.

"What? Yeah, I'm still here. What is it?"

"Good. One last thing. Who shared the post? What made it go viral?"

"*Yeah, I traced it back. It was one of your Facebook friends. If I remember correctly, her name was Eva. Eva something. You know the one. The famous vlogger?*"

"*Eva? I don't ... have a Facebook friend ... called Eva.*" Richard was perplexed.

"*I think it was some German name. Eva Von something,*" Kate trailed off.

"*Eva van Persie. It was Eva van Persie. It's a Dutch name. I met her and her brother on a train in the Netherlands. Their mother had been recently euthanized. I didn't know she was a vlogger,*" Richard said.

"*Euthanized? Are you serious? They allow that in the Netherlands?*" Kate stated in surprise.

"*Yeah, euthanization is legal there. I will tell you all about it another time. I had better go now. Thanks for everything, Kate.*"

"*Love you. Take care and let me know if you need anything.*"

"*Thanks, Kate. I appreciate that. Love you.*" They both hit the red button on their phone screens.

Orange Seeds

Kate understood she had been a tad insensitive towards Richard. The last thing he wanted was to hear about a post going viral, considering one of his best friends was in intensive care for that reason.

Kate had been so caught up in her brother's fifteen minutes of fame, and the subsequent light shone on her. She was giving radio interviews and talking to the media and bloggers. She forgot the essence of the message Richard had posted was to empower femininity. Not just women, but true femininity.

The power of femininity exists as strongly in some men, particularly gay men, as it does in women. The essence of Richard's post was not about empowering a particular gender— it was about reconnecting with a power that was caring, nurturing, compassionate and loving. Bringing it to the surface. Freeing it from the machine minds of men. Giving it back to women. Normalising it.

Richard's message was about elevating femininity, by first granting individuals the space to look within themselves.

Bringing out their power and clearing the path to their rightful place on the global stage.

It was not about creating a movement. It was about allowing individuals to tap into their inner goddess at their own pace. Listening to the little girl who lives in us all and bringing her to the forefront.

With that, Kate decided to turn down the radio and turn off her phone.

She walked to her kitchen table, powered down her laptop and flipped open a notepad with the intention of writing a mantra for Emma. For herself. For womankind. For femininity.

The *"I am"* mantra Richard and Emma had developed was already a part of her life. Now, she was inspired by how it had helped deliver Emma from her coma.

She understood the power of being able to say, *"I am perfect."* Kate knew this because their mother taught it to them just days before she died.

Kate remembered that day as if it was yesterday. It was a rainy Tuesday afternoon and the three of them sat looking out the window at the pouring rain. They were all eating slices of oranges as they admired the beauty of the sheets of rain lashing down. When a young Richard complained about the bad weather, Angel corrected him and said:

"There is no such thing as 'bad weather.' There is only one type of weather and that is 'perfect weather.' All weather is perfect, because it is exactly as it needs to be. We need the summer, autumn, winter and the spring. All are different. All are perfect. Everything is always perfect. It must be so. This is true of every aspect of the world and every person in it."

When her kids looked at her in a state of bewilderment, she said:

"Because something is perfect does not mean it is complete."

Peeling the next orange for the three of them to snack on, she continued:

"No one anywhere is complete, but so far as each of us has travelled along our path in life, we are perfect in our development at that moment. Although not complete, the world and all that exist on it are perfect at this moment."

Her kids tried to grasp what she was saying. Seeing the look of confusion on the faces of her children, she continued to explain:

"Consider nature as an example and you will agree all things associated with nature are good; there is no bad in nature. Nature is perfect, but it is not complete, as it will continue to grow.

That applies to us as individuals. All of us are growing. All of us are advancing towards completeness. It pertains to the societies we live in and our governments we elect. All are advancing towards completeness. As nature is not bad, people are not bad. Things that appear to be incomplete are often seen as being bad. The machine minds have trained us to think this way."

Noticing the blank look on the faces of her twins, Angel changed her approach in explaining.

"Okay, take this seed from the orange as an example. A seed could be considered ugly now, but it will eventually grow into an orange tree. So, it would be stupid for us to condemn the seed based on how it looks at this moment when we know it will grow into a beautiful tree and will light up our garden and provide us with more yummy fruit."

The twins looked attentively at the seed as Angel held it up to the light. As she did this Mickey came up behind her, lovingly kissed her on the top of the head and gently placed another three oranges on her lap.

"The seed is perfect as it is; it is a perfect seed, but it is an incomplete orange tree. This is how we must learn to see ourselves and those around us. It does not matter how we look or feel at this time; we are perfect in this stage of our progress and we are all on a journey towards completeness. Saying, 'I am perfect' does not mean you are vain or detached. It means you understand yourself in the here and now. It means you know life is a journey and, on this journey, everything and everyone is perfectly becoming."

Sitting at that window, that rainy afternoon provided Kate and Richard with a life lesson they carried with them through the years: Everything is perfect. But not complete.

Orange seeds played a reminder of their mother's words and wisdom from then forth.

Kate decided to write a new mantra for Emma and for womankind. She headed it up at the top of the page:

The Womantra

Then using a free-writing technique, she continued:

I am not my cute friend
I am not my ex-boyfriend
I am not my dress size
He may find that a surprise

I am not my family
I am not my followers
I am not my frenemies
Nor will I pretend to be

I am not my education
I am not my bank account
I am not my job title
My self-esteem is vital

I am not my phone
I am not my car
I am not my address
I am no longer your waitress

I am not m—

"No. No. It's not right!" she screamed out, in frustration. *"It's too negative. I need to be positive. I must focus on the actuality of what it is to be a woman."*

She put a line through it, flipped over the page and started again.

"It has to be positive and empowering, but it has to be real. Too many mantras dedicated to women are unrealistic. They try to make all women out to be superwoman. It has to fully encompass the ups and downs of being

a woman and why our challenges and struggles make us who we are as we work towards completion," Kate thought, aloud.

With a fresh piece of paper, she went to the top of the page and wrote:

From Femininity, For Femininity.

She closed her eyes, took a deep breath and asked herself out loud:

> *"Who am I?*
> *Who are we?*
> *What are we?*
> *What does it feel like to be a woman in this world?"*

She then opened her eyes, took another deep breath, put her pencil to the page and began to write:

I am a woman, I am fierce,
I am a lioness, as the scars will tell,
I walk through this world, head held high,
You may see me now, but not the pain gone by.

I am a woman, I am powerful,
I walk into a room and the energy rises,
My vibe is high, my pulse is low,
I carry your baggage, but you don't even know.

I am a woman, I am weak,
I can open my mouth, but I cannot speak,
Everyone stares, nobody cares,
The world drags me down, but still I flare.

I am a woman, I am abused,
Friends, family and lovers, they all use,
I paint on my mask and pour into my jeans,
Everyone takes their slice without making a scene.

I am a woman, I am true,
I think from my heart and listen from my soul,
Everywhere I go, I feel the people of the night,
They gravitate to pure, like moths to a light.

I am a woman, I am here,
When you need me, I will always be there.
For those in my world, compassion, kindness
and care,
But, to dishonour a lioness, I beg you to dare.

She crushed the final full-stop on to the page, following the word *dare*.

Then, she violently threw her pencil across the room, allowing it to crash against the wall.

As it fell to the ground, she stood up from the table and yelled:

"Yes! We are lionesses. We have the power to bear our scars. Despite our challenges, we've the strength to continue. We will rise from slumber."

With a smile, she put her hands in her hair on the back of her head. She squeezed and pulled for a moment.

She then let her body drop to the ground, spreading herself across the floor like a starfish. With a look of gratification, she stared towards the roof, without her gaze ever quite reaching the ceiling.

Enjoy the Champagne

As Kate lay on the ground, she realised she had some tidying up to do in her own life. She had to be true to the words she had just written.

She knew the world was a good place full of good people. However, good people are capable of doing bad things when stressed or anxious.

She understood the difference between *the* world and *her* world.

The world was perfectly becoming. It was advancing and moving forward as a whole for the greater good.

Her world was turbulent and ever-changing. It was in *her* world where all her pain and suffering derived. The heartache she felt did not come from the wider world, but from those closest to her—her friends, lovers, colleagues and family.

Her father had emotionally abandoned them since the death of her mother. He had developed into a horrible, sexist pig as he struggled to deal with the death of his wife.

Her boyfriend Terry could be emotionally void and cold and was sending her best friend Jennifer *dick pics*.

Her brother, Richard, had floated around the world drifting between jobs and girlfriends. He was detached and unavailable to her when she needed him most.

Her best friend, Jennifer, had become increasingly resentful as Kate progressed in her career and life. Now, she was sending naked pictures of herself to Kate's boyfriend.

To make matters even more frustrating, she was also the ultimate *"askhole."* Jennifer was that friend who would constantly ask for advice yet do the opposite of what Kate advised her. The two people in whom she most confided, Jennifer and Terry, were sleeping together behind her back.

The big bad world, as portrayed by the mainstream media, did not bring heartache and pain to Kate. Her friends and family were the cause of her heartache and sorrow. All the pain in her life came from those closest to her. It was time to tidy up shop.

She decided the best way to remove the pain was to get rid of those hurting her most. People will treat us exactly as we allow them. They take their permission from how we treat ourselves.

Kate would deal with her dad and her brother after her mother's anniversary. But she would not let another day pass before dealing with her best friend and her boyfriend.

She sent both Jennifer and Terry a message telling them to meet her that evening 6:30 p.m. at her favourite restaurant. She had chosen this restaurant because she worked there during college and she still had a great relationship with the owner and the staff. She made the separate messages sound urgent and told them both to come well-dressed.

Terry arrived a few minutes early and as he waited, he scrolled through his phone, as normal.

At 6:45 p.m., Jennifer arrived. She was always late and usually left Kate waiting whenever they were due to meet.

Jennifer was confused when Terry was standing alone just inside the restaurant door and there was no sign of Kate.

"Hey, where is Kate?" she asked, looking around the restaurant, keeping her distance from Terry.

"Dunno. She must be running late. Didn't know you were coming to dinner with us?"

Jennifer did not respond.

This was out of the norm and she sensed something was up. Female intuition.

Before they could get down to discussing what was going on, the head waiter who hired Kate and was now a close friend, invited them to sit. Jennifer's mind was racing, but she settled slightly when offered to sit at a table for four people.

Facing away from the door, Jennifer glanced around the restaurant before whispering to Terry he was looking hot, in his suit and tie.

Terry winked back, with a smothered smile.

After complimenting them on how well they looked, as Kate had instructed, the waiter presented them with a bottle of champagne. They gratefully accepted it. Terry watched with hungry eyes as the waiter slowly poured.

With every bubble that swelled out of the bottle, Jennifer's anxiety level grew.

The moment the waiter finished pouring, Terry greedily reached for his glass and held it up to Jennifer. She had no option but to reciprocate.

Her heart was now filling her chest like a boom box.

As they swallowed their first sip, the waiter pulled a note from the front pocket of his apron.

Jennifer's left hand was frozen.

She held the glass mid-air, halfway between her mouth and the table.

He presented them with the note, a single piece of paper, folded over with both of their names on the front. He laid it in the middle of the table.

Gently.

Dramatically.

Like only a French waiter can.

Jennifer, understanding this was not a good sign, swiftly snatched for the note with her right hand and flipped it open with her thumb. Still holding her glass mid-air with her left hand, she silently read the note.

Allowing the note to fall on the table, she put her hand over her mouth, which was wide open.

Not gathering what was going on, Terry had been too busy looking at Jennifer's breasts in her low-cut dress, to realise something was not right.

Her glass crashing on the table got his attention.

Immediately, he reached for the note. He shook away the champagne that had spilled on the note, and then read the contents one word at a time. Kate had written:

You both had my love, respect, trust and time.

Now, all you have is each other.

I wish you the best in your relationship together.

Enjoy the champagne, on me.

Goodbye

Kate

Cleaning Shop

On the morning of the anniversary of Angel's death, Mickey invited the twins to an address in the suburbs.

Kate and Richard were unsure of what was going on. This was unusual.

Normally, they would go to the church and have a quick service. Both Richard and Mickey would say a few words, lay some flowers and they would then go to the pub for some food and drinks.

Arriving at the address, Richard and Kate feared the worst when after ringing the doorbell, they were greeted by a very pretty girl wearing a sundress. She looked like she was in her late teens.

After being invited inside, they were astonished to find their father in the kitchen. He was wearing an apron with his sleeves rolled up, preparing a fully vegan meal. Beside him, wearing a matching apron, was a woman who appeared to be in her mid-thirties.

Under Mickey's apron, he wore a designer white shirt, freshly pressed with care. He wore red braces attached to a pair of well-pressed black trousers and a pair of well-polished new black shoes. His long shoulder length greasy hair had been cut into a "*short, back and sides*" style. It took years off him.

The lady beside him wore a tightly fitted black dress with red sequins. The dress went well with her red heels. Her hair was in a ponytail. The scent of freshly squeezed lemon filled the air.

As Richard and Kate entered the kitchen confused, Mickey turned around with a big smile and said:

"*Aww, they're here.*"

He quickly cleaned his hands, walked over and gave each of them a warm welcoming hug. Mickey held each of his children for that little bit longer than necessary.

He then turned to the lady and introduced her as his new girlfriend, Tracy.

"*His girlfriend?*" muttered Kate, under her breath. The twins glanced at each other in disbelief.

Mickey had met Tracy many years before, as he was a friend of her husband Joey. Mickey and Joey had worked together in the logging industry for many years, until Joey died prematurely from his alcoholism.

Mickey and Tracy bonded because they both experienced losing a partner to an early death and bringing up children as single parents. They had always been friends, however, they were never romantically involved, until the day Mickey went to the hospital to visit Emma. As he was leaving the hospital, he met Tracy in the elevator. She was there to visit her mother who was undergoing a routine operation.

They went for coffee, which led to dinner that evening. They had been inseparable ever since.

Tracy was thirty-nine. Still much younger than Mickey, but it was better than the nineteen-year-old girls he had been meeting for sex. The girl, who opened the door and invited Kate and Richard in, was Tracy's daughter Mia, and she was nineteen.

Mickey liked Tracy because they would talk for hours, they laughed together and liked the same music, both being fans of dance music from the early 1990s. The one thing Mickey had forgotten was how impassioned and impulsive sex could be with a truly feminine woman. A woman who was connected to her deepest instincts.

Being in bed with her felt fun and nourishing—it was explorative. He was no longer the one in control, which was unusual for Mickey.

Because Tracy was so connected to her femininity, she allowed Mickey to reveal his true masculinity.

From the moment he first slid inside of her, he felt so present. His mind was clear and content for the first time in a long time. Sheathed by her soft and warm embrace, he felt safe. It humbled him. There was lots of kissing and eye contact. He wanted to provide her with a gift she was open to receiving. They both enjoyed every moment.

By the end, they were completely spent, both lying *spread eagle* on a bed of giggles and sweat.

It made him feel like a man.

As a result, he once again began acting as a man should: a proper gentleman. Once again, he felt he had a purpose as a man.

The day after first having sex with Tracy, Mickey deleted the dating apps from his phone. He informed all the girls he was sleeping with he was *off the market*.

This was before he was even sure Tracy wanted to get into a relationship with him.

He realised the vulgar hypermasculinity prominent in his world had become more of a disorder than a strength. Masculinity had been twisted and broken.

Mickey began to understand true masculinity was not something given as a birthright, but rather something to be gained. Masculinity is gained moment to moment by winning small life battles with dignity and honour.

Being male is a consequence of creation. Being a man is a consequence of time. And being a gentleman is a simple choice.

Kate and Richard could hardly believe the man with a big smile and soft shoulders, who was getting ordered around in the kitchen, was their dad. The tough guy, sexist pig, who worked in the rainforest cutting down precious trees and causing untold damage to the planet.

This guy ate microwaved meals, lived in a square box apartment and regularly had sex with teenage girls disconnected from their feminine power. Now, he was well-groomed and beamed with pride as he prepared an avocado salad.

On a few occasions over the years, Mickey's employer offered him a promotion, overseeing the operation of all the logging sites. He had refused the role because he did not like the thought of having to work in an office. He often said he preferred to be involved with the camaraderie that came with being on site with the loggers.

The reality was he had turned down the promotion because he did not want to work for, and take direction from, a woman. As incompetent as Stig was, at least he was not a *"nagging woman,"* was how Mickey justified it.

However, it was reading Richard's post and seeing the impact it had on people around the world that provided him with the incentive to make real changes in a positive manner.

The devastation of seeing his only son beaten, bloodied and unconscious shocked him into genuine reflection. Nothing can prepare a parent for facing their child in that state. The pain was compounded by the fact that it was his friends and colleagues who were responsible.

More than just becoming a better person, he wanted atonement for his sins.

He had failed his son. He had failed his daughter. But what hurt most was that he had failed Angel, the love of his life, the mother of their beautiful children.

Shame is a horrid and rotten emotion—a feeling of pain derived from the realisation of who he had become as a person. Upon reflection Mickey felt shame quiver through every strand of his DNA.

Change is not gradual or sloping. It happens abruptly and in bursts. Deriving from heartache or growth, we are faced with life events that change how we see our place in the world.

If we do not change with the world, then the world will change us. It is inevitable.

Helplessly nursing his wife towards her passing drove Mickey to change for the worse.

Seeing his son beaten unconscious forced him to change for the better.

Heartache is the most confrontational portal to transformation. Pain leads to alteration and renewal. For Mickey, this was absolutely the case. As it was pain that brought the sickness, it would be pain that would administer the cure.

Not one to do things in half measures, he accepted this evolutionary jump with vigour. Changes would be forthcoming with the same doggedness he approached all areas of his life.

He contacted the female CEO of the logging company and informed her he was now interested in the role. Her offer would put Mickey in charge of the loggers on all the sites

After accepting the new position, he went back to the site for a few days to inform the loggers of his promotion and to *clean up shop*.

He sat with his old friend Stig and in no uncertain terms told him a few home truths. The way the site was run was totally unacceptable. Porn would be forbidden from being shown on any public TV. Any man found watching porn in a public area would have his contract terminated immediately.

In addition, he told him that within the team the general approach to work on site had to become more courteous and considerate.

The remaining tribespeople, particularly the tribeswomen, had to be given the utmost respect as matriarchal leaders. They were caretakers of this Earth and they must be treated as such.

Mickey told Stig they had to raise their standards as a team and as the on-site leader he should set the new benchmark. He wanted to give Stig a fair chance to clean up his actions. They had been friends for a long time.

However, he made sure to let him know if he reverted to his old ways and changes did not happen, then not only would he lose his job, but their friendship would end.

Mickey then called all the loggers together for a team meeting. As he stood in front of them, he congratulated them for their hard work and the difficult job they had done in challenging circumstances. As a team of workers, he could not have asked for a more dedicated bunch of guys, he told them.

He reminded them, as individuals and as men, they had let themselves down when it came to their behaviour. Particularly their attitude towards women.

Initially, the men on site thought Mickey was joking. They laughed along. However, he had earned the respect of the loggers over the years and they soon came to realise he was serious.

His body language left them in no doubt—everyone can subconsciously read the signs.

They all knew their behaviour, individually and collectively, left a lot to be desired. None of them disagreed. For many of them it came as a relief, as the toxic environment had become tiring.

"All the girls you talk about or watch on that screen are someone's sister, mother or daughter. You all have a sister, mother or daughter at home. None of us would want the women in our lives to be treated the way we've been treating women. I've been as bad as anyone here, so I have to take the blame as well," Mickey told the loggers.

The room was silent as the men hung their heads.

Breaking the weighty silence Mickey declared,

"Don't look, see."

He looked around the room at each of the guys before adding, *"Guys, don't just look at them, see them."*

The loggers lifted their heads and looked at Mickey quizzically. He held the space for a moment.

Then he explained, *"See them as the wonderful souls they are, with all the pain and suffering that comes with being a woman in this world at this time. See them as the giggling daughters they were just a few years ago, and the loving mothers they will become in just a few years. Don't just look at them. Don't look at them as if their only value is their body and how they can use it to entertain you. Guys, the world is changing. Deep down you are all good guys. Don't get left behind. Trust me on this. Don't look, see."*

He reminded them of how they had beaten up his son, simply because he tried to protect his friend. A friend who possessed an inner beauty Richard could *see* since they were children. He then told them Emma had attempted to commit suicide as a result and had nearly been successful.

The loggers began to realise all actions have consequences—there is a butterfly effect.

As Mickey relayed this to Richard and Kate, they felt a deep sense of pride for their father and the man he was becoming.

Nevertheless, without saying anything directly, they both wondered if he was for real, or if he was doing it to impress his new girlfriend.

They had their doubts as they stood in the kitchen. It just seemed like too big of a change too quickly.

Unlearn and Relearn

Mickey sensed the hesitancy of his children. He understood their position—there was a vast change within a short timeframe.

He removed his apron and motioned to the twins to follow him to the back garden. Under the warm sun, he performed a very unusual act of dropping onto the grass in the middle of the garden and asking them to join him.

He had a newspaper in his hand, which he had picked from the garden table as he passed by.

He handed it to Kate for her to sit on, so she would not get grass stains on her green and violet summer dress.

As Kate opened the paper to sit on, Richard noticed Mickey reacting, craning his neck to read a headline.

Instinctively, Richard glanced down and, just before Kate sat on the paper, he caught a glimpse of the headline that had so distracted his father:

**PROMINENT DOCTORS ARRESTED
IN SEX SLAVE STING**

A few days earlier, Mickey had anonymously tipped off the local vice squad. He alerted them of the people trafficking operation the doctors had openly facilitated, by allowing girls to be kept in cages below their practice.

When Mickey had turned up at the location with a mutual friend of John who he met in the strip club following a late-night drinking session, he witnessed first-hand the conditions the girls endured. It made him heave.

To see girls forced to exist in such an environment made him feel sick. He blamed his gagging on the combination of alcohol and the heat in the basement and made his excuses to leave. John's friend stayed. It had haunted Mickey ever since.

Kate and Richard dropped down onto the grass with their father. Mickey gained his composure, then spent a few moments looking both in the eye before saying:

"I am sorry. I'm sorry. Now, I can see the error of my ways. I've been a terrible father and a horrible man. When I think back to how selfish I've been since your mother's death, it breaks my heart to think of the man I've become. Words are hollow. I know that, so I don't expect you guys to believe anything I say.

I will work to prove my love to you both with my actions over the coming days, weeks, months and years. I think I must explain what has happened over the past few weeks, so you can obtain a better understanding of what has changed in me."

"Yes, you really need to explain this to me." Kate said as she glanced back towards the kitchen. *"I'm so confused right now."*

Mickey took a deep breath.

"Okay, when I arrived back in the rainforest after my suspension, the three-man team that usually works in the kitchen was still down to two men. The replacement they had found for Richard was let go after a few days because they thought he was not performing his tasks. They later brought in two more guys to cover for you, increasing that team to four," he said, nodding at Richard.

"And what about the new on-site medical personnel?" Richard asked.

"No, they still haven't found a new first responder either. The place is a mess," Mickey said. *"Arriving back there and seeing how messy and untidy the kitchen, dining hall and living quarters were, really opened my eyes. It helped me understand how much effort and care you put it into*

your daily tasks. Without you there, diligently cleaning up after everyone, really putting effort into your tasks, we all noticed a vast difference in the homeliness of the living and eating quarters.

You quietly ensured everyone had a clean and healthy environment in which to eat the wholesome meals you prepared. You were noticeable by your absence."

Richard's lower lip quivered. As he was at the home of people he had just met, he took a deep breath to try and regain his composure. He did not want to embarrass his father in front of his new girlfriend.

"There were so many complaints from the loggers, a few of them directly asked me in confidence whether it was possible for you to return, Richard. By my third day back on the site, even Stig was asking if you would be interested in coming back. In return for a substantial raise, of course."

Richard sat cross-legged with his head bowed, rolling a blade of grass between his fingers.

With his gaze lowered, he held back his tears as his father spoke. Mickey continued:

"It really hit home for me," he said. *"I was taking my only son for granted. I had failed to support him. I never bothered to offer a word of encouragement during the entire time we were in the rainforest together. I never even bothered to take a moment for a quick chat to check and see if everything was okay."*

"It's okay dad. You were doing…"

"No, it's absolutely not okay," Mickey said, interrupting his son. *"How could that ever be considered okay when the result was the people who I called friends thought they had the go-ahead to beat up my son for protecting the decency of his friend? What made this harder was they thought they were doing me a favour by beating my son unconscious. What does that say about me as a man?"*

"Wait! What? Richard got beat up in the rainforest? On your watch?" Kate said as she stood up.

"What am I hearing? You let your son get beat up by that group of idiots?" She was standing over her father as she demanded an answer.

Mickey hung his head.

"Kate, please. It's not as bad as it sounds. Please sit down again," Richard said, as he grabbed for his sister's hand and pulled her back into a sitting position.

Richard glanced back towards the kitchen as Kate stared directly at Mickey whilst she fixed the newspaper back into place.

"I can't believe this. What am I hearing? Dad?" Kate said, settling back on to the newspaper on the ground and tucking her summer dress in under her bum.

"It's nothing Kate. Please," Richard responded.

"Is this why you quit your job?" Kate asked Richard.

"Please, Kate. I will tell you all about it later. Let dad talk," Richard pleaded.

Kate was looking directly at her father. Tears ran down her face. Mickey kept a low gaze.

As the twins waited for their dad to speak, Kate pulled a packet of tissues from her handbag. Mickey, looking at the palms of his hands, paused in silence for a few moments.

Richard had never seen his father like this. He could see Mickey's eyes had welled up. A tear ran out of his right eye. He looked so vulnerable.

Without wiping the tears from his eyes Mickey began to talk again.

"I was in the middle of a morning shift, chopping down trees and I was having all these thoughts running through my mind," he said. *"As I thought through everything that had happened, it really held a mirror up and showed me the man I had become. Honestly, I just stopped what I was doing. I turned off the machinery, climbed down, slammed the cabin door and walked back to the living quarters. I had a cold shower. I stood in that cold running water for maybe thirty minutes. It wasn't that I was just washing the sweat and dust off my body. As I stood there, it also felt as if I was washing away the toxins built up in my body, mind and soul. I was cleansing from the inside out. I know it sounds weird coming from me, but that's just how it felt."*

Richard was completely on board with what his father was saying. Kate, not so much.

Mickey composed himself for a moment, before continuing.

"Following the shower, I tried to call you, but your phone just rang out," said Mickey to Richard. *"I really wanted to have a chat with you. So, I called Kate to see if you were with her and she told me you were at a retreat in Germany or somewhere."*

"I told you he was in Holland," snapped Kate. *"I never mentioned Germany."*

"Yeah, sorry, it was Holland. That's right." Apologised Mickey.
Richard glanced at his sister.

"When I hung up the phone, I just felt like doing that thing I used to see you do in the mornings," Mickey continued. *"In my bare feet, I walked out into the trees, touching each tree gently as I walked past. Then, after a few moments, I came across this big tree. I just felt the desire to sit down. So, I sat there with my back against that old tree and I just did nothing. I just sat there. I dunno for how long. It felt good."*

"It's called forest bathing," Richard said, blowing his nose and wiping the tears from his face.

"It has a name? Forest bathing? Yeah, sounds about right. It really felt like my mind was being cleansed as I sat against that tree, looking out at the forest, in silence. But it was more than that. With my mind being cleared, it was almost as if I had opened up some free space in here." Mickey tapped his head with his knuckle.

"It felt like I could once again access the old memories of Angel and I in our younger days. Of us as a young family, as well. But mostly of your mother and I together and all things she used to say."

Turning towards Kate, Mickey said:

"Your mother had very specific insights regarding women and femininity. She was the only person I ever met that talked about femininity as a power. She would talk about how the female body was the perfect vessel to carry this feminine power."

Kate was still furious. She listened closely to her father's words but swirling around in her mind was the question of how one member of her family could allow the other to be bullied and physically abused.

"When we were young, before we had any children, we would regularly go to the countryside and make love under a big leafy tree," he said. *"In fact, you were conceived in the countryside under a tree. After we made love, Angel used to adore sitting under trees and chatting for hours on end. We would sit there watching the sun set and the moon rise. We never seemed to feel the cold then. I would sit between her legs with our backs to a tree, looking out."*

As he talked, he glanced up and could see that Kate's eyes were piercing through him. He lowered his gaze and continued to talk to his children, whilst looking at his hands.

"In the countryside one Sunday afternoon in the late summer, your mother said something that didn't mean much to me at that time. But as I

sat against that tree in the rainforest, it really struck me. She said a woman is more than man. A woman is a womb-man. She told me that was where the word 'wo-man' came from."

Kate instinctively put her hand across her lower stomach as she listened to her father talking. She had a strong will and Mickey knew his daughter well enough to understand he would not get away with what happened to Richard in the rainforest. It would not be the last that he would hear of it. Like her mother, she had grown into a strong woman. A true matriarch.

Richard was completely lost in the moment. He hung on every word his father uttered.

"So, when mum said that a woman is a womb-man and more than man, what did she mean?" Richard asked.

"Of mankind, but with a womb," Mickey responded. *"Capable of creating life, carrying life and bringing life to the world. The only force sufficiently formidable to act as the portal for unborn souls to voyage from the spiritual realm to the physical world. A true superpower if ever there was one. With this superpower, she said all women should be treated in the same way we treat these superstars. They should be held up in society as leaders, protected, encouraged, listened to and followed. Women should lead. They should rule our world because it is the natural instinct of women to preserve life and facilitate growth, she would say."*

Tears ran down from both of Mickey's eyes now.

"That's beautiful. Yeah, okay. I get it," Richard added.

It was obvious to Kate, despite everything that had happened, Richard held no grudge against his father. As she listened intently to her father, she softened. She was beginning to understand that he was quite pathetic.

He was not the *Superman* she had always thought he was. Mickey was lost and he needed their help. He needed their love. He was just a man.

As a consequence of the times he lived in and the environment he worked, he had bottled up all the grief of Angel's death. To reveal his pain was considered a weakness, so he had found outlets that encouraged reckless behaviour as a way of masking it.

Kate realised that being angry at him was not going to benefit any of them. Not now. Not when he was finally facing up to his actions and wanting to rectify the pain he had caused.

"Your mother was my leader," Mickey said. *"I followed her around like a puppy dog. Everything she said, I would take as gospel. Her words were everything to me. Although I have ran from them in recent years, at that time, I never doubted them. She was my best friend and the most fascinating person I have ever met. She carried a strength only a deeply feminine person can carry."*

Kate leaned forward and took his hand in hers. Her soft manicured hands were engulfed by his big, rough, dry spade of a hand.

"Everybody dies, but not everybody truly lives," Mickey continued. *"Your mother lived every moment and that was what made it harder for me. She loved life. Yet, the way her death stalked her and snatched her from us after such a short sickness left me totally exposed to the world. I was unprepared for life without her guidance and the result was that without my best friend, my leader, my Angel by my side, I went off the rails and became the pig I am. That I was."*

Mickey's voice trembled as he corrected himself. He inhaled deeply and composed himself.

Kate squeezed his big hand with both of hers.

"I'd been carrying the weight of rage for so long I had forgot it was a mass of sorrow," he said. *"I blamed the entire world for stealing my best friend away from me and I hurt many people as a result. Ultimately, I now know I was only hurting myself. When I look at you both and see the great adults you have grown into, despite having me as father, it makes me so proud."*

Kate pressed a tissue into his big hand for him to wipe his eyes. He glanced at her and continued to talk.

"More than anything, it reminds me of how amazing your mother was to plant the seeds of such strong morals and ethics that flourish within you both. Without any help from me, you both overcame the trials and

tribulations you have faced. As I read Richard's post, I could hear his mother's voice in the words."

Mickey took another deep breath.

"I can assure you, from now on things will be different," he said, as he straightened up. *"I will prove to you through my actions I am worthy of earning a place in your lives as a friend and as a father. I recently read that in this information age, the illiterate are not those who can't read and write, but those who can't learn, unlearn and relearn. I owe it to you both not to be information-age-illiterate. I will relearn."*

Leader of the Family

Mickey then made a move that shocked both Richard and Kate, leaving them in no doubt of his intentions. He stated things would be different in their family from that day. His first decision was that when it came to family matters, the four of them would vote on anything important.

When Richard suspiciously asked where the four votes would be becoming from, Mickey casually said:

"Well, your mother, my Angel, may not be here in body, but maybe you have both noticed she is here in spirit? And she always had a strong opinion on family matters. So, that's why Kate will cast her mother's vote from now on."

"Sounds good to me," agreed Richard, with relief.

"There is one more thing I've been thinking about," Mickey said. *"When we cast our votes, each feminine vote will weigh one and a half times a masculine vote. So, if both guys cast their votes in opposition to Kate's vote, then they lose three to two. The result is the decision would go towards Kate's preference. The power of femininity must be given precedence over masculinity. Moreover, it starts today."*

As Mickey said this, his girlfriend stood at the kitchen window, silently listening with a smile as she peeled the potatoes.

Richard's mouth dropped open.

He was in complete agreement with his father's decision, but he could not believe these words were coming from Mickey, of all people. He was dumbfounded at how much his father had changed from the man who, merely weeks before, was talking about having sex with girls kept in cages.

Looking at her brother and father, Kate composed herself and said:

"I appreciate you thinking the power of femininity must be given precedence over masculinity," she said. *"But I do not agree each feminine vote should weigh one and a half times a masculine vote.*

The result of every family decision would be based on my desires and that is not balanced or realistic. So, if I'm to be the leader of this family, then I want us to cast our first votes together on an issue important to me."

"Okay, let's do it," Mickey said, wiping the tears from his face.

"So, my first proposal is each feminine vote will weigh exactly the same as a masculine vote," Kate said. *"One for one in perfect balance with nature: Yin and Yang. I will still have Mum's vote, so if we find ourselves in a two versus two situation, then we can flip a coin, like mum used to do, and leave it to the universe to guide us.*

Men have had greater rights for generations. To accept a greater level of rights for women over men would now be hypocritical of me. Especially after years of working for equality and parity."

Interrupting his daughter, Mickey said:

"Darling, please. Let's try it for at least a few months? Let's just see how it plays out for a while and we can vote on it then. We can take a vote on my birthday. That's just a few months away."

Richard contributed:

"Yeah, come on. Let's give femininity precedence over masculinity in our family until Dad's birthday. Let's see how it plays out?"

Kate was uncomfortable with this, saying:

"No, Richard. Listen. I do not want to be hypocritical. It would neither be fair nor just. As a woman, it is equality I desire, not revenge."

Then, thinking back to the tribeswomen in the Amazon, and how they repaired the trees, Richard continued:

"I hear what you are saying but remember there is only one way to correct a tree bent out of balance. A tree will not grow into an upright position by holding it up straight. To achieve balance, we need to overcorrect the bend of the tree far to the opposite side, so when we let go, it can spring back into an upstanding, straight position and be aligned again. It's the same with empowering femininity. We must overcorrect the balance of power beyond the level of equality so when we 'let go,' the balance of power will spring back into an equilibrium."

Nodding her head, Kate understood his analogy:

"Okay, we can give it a go. But Dad's birthday is when we 'let the tree spring back,'" she said, making air quotes with her fingers.

Mickey nodded his head and said:

"Kate, you are now the leader of this family. As leader, it would be a great honour if you, as my daughter, would give the speech at your mother's service today. I will take responsibility for the flower arrangements."

Kate's mouth dropped open.

She was overcome with emotion. This was a massive honour for her.

She crawled over the freshly cut grass to her dad and hugged him. He squeezed her tightly.

Normally, she was only responsible for choosing the flowers as Richard and Mickey did everything else. Now, as the family leader, she would be the one talking on behalf of the family.

Richard looked on as his father and sister hugged. With big smiles, both had their eyes closed as they squeezed one another tight. It was a beautiful father-daughter moment. He had an emotional lump of love and joy stuck in his throat, choking him up as he savoured this point in time.

Change happens, not in gentle rising slopes, but in evolutionary jumps. It now felt that within the microcosm of his family, they had gone through positive transformational change.

Whilst dressed in all white, in a tent in the Netherlands, Richard was tasked with empowering femininity. In addition, he was steered to do it by appealing to the spirit of men.

The main guidance Richard received was he simply must remain true to himself and be sympathetic to the feminine—that would be sufficient to *begin* to influence men.

The last person he thought would help him to elevate and empower the feminine was his own father.

Getting an understanding for the extensive change in his father caused him to reflect on the journey he had been on.

It brought him to the realisation that the positives had come from negatives.

Getting beaten by his colleagues in the rainforest was the catalyst that thrust him upon this leg of his life journey. That led him to Anne's sofa and the darkest moments in life.

His grandmother once told him, *"There is a path that leads over every mountain, but it is rarely seen from the valley. Only when we begin to climb does the path reveal itself."* Now he understood her words. Now he appreciated her timeless wisdom and patience in gently planting the seeds of knowledge in his young mind.

He was lost and searching for his path. But in the darkest black, a flicker of light can be enough to light the path. This flicker was the beginning of his empowerment, as a simple whisper from Anne enabled him to get up, to remember who he was and take responsibility.

From that moment he was open to the synchronicities of life. He was open to the signs and followed the unfolding path with a curious determination.

He had set a firm intention and the people he met showed him the short cuts and the hidden paths of life—they pointed out the direction and he followed through. Getting lost along the way, was part of the path.

With hindsight, he understood that if we are open to receiving, the people we meet all have something to teach us when in flow with synchronicity.

For a while after the secret retreat, he believed that his meeting with Mother Ayahuasca had created more 'luck' for him.

Now Richard understood that the secret retreat was not a new beginning, but rather one step along his path that unfolded daily. More than that, he realised that when we return to our true path, goals are more easily achieved when allowed to unfold.

To those still swimming upstream against the current, off their true path and ignorant to the importance of the flow of energy it may appear as 'luck.' They fail to appreciate that force and pressure are unnecessary, reckless even.

During the ceremony, as he lay on the mat embraced by Mother Ayahuasca, he was not blessed with '*luck*,' but what he had received was simply enhanced clarity. Reconnecting fully with his inner child brought a sense of harmony and wholeness.

Now, by being true to himself, sharing his words and bringing his balance of masculinity and femininity to the world, he was already seeing the direct impact that one person can have by setting an example.

Men know at their core change is needed.

They also sense their actions as a collective have led to the near destruction of this planet, our Mother, the Earth.

The love and respect men have towards their mothers and daughters is the power that can stop them in their tracks towards self-destruction. It is that power of love now in play.

The road is long, the challenges are vast but as Richard was told, men will embrace this change one by one, as the ripple of feminine power resonates out across our Mother, the Earth.

Order from Chaos

As the family packed up to go to the church, Mickey's phone rang. It was a call from his boss.

On this day of all days, he was hesitant to answer. She knew it was his wife's anniversary, so it must be a pressing matter for her to call at that time.

Reluctantly, Mickey answered.

During the call, he hardly said anything. He was listening intensely.

Richard instinctively knew it was important, so he stood staring at his dad throughout the call.

An emergency board meeting had been held at the logging company.

When Mickey returned from chastising Stig's team of loggers in the Amazon, he delivered a package to the company CEO. It detailed the actions of the on-site loggers and how they had been treating the local tribespeople.

In the package he also included video footage of the soldiers from the private military keeping female tribe members in cages whilst initially securing the area.

Upon review, the CEO forwarded the evidence to the board of directors, detailing how the tribespeople had been treated.

Two male members of the board resigned immediately.

Those who remained on the board of directors were fully aware of the negative impact the information would have on the company if leaked to the media. The board knew if it got out, it would end the company.

The CEO immediately tasked a team of her closest allies within the headquarters with finding a remedy to overcorrect the mistakes made in the region controlled by the Myayama tribe.

They came back with a proposal that would pre-empt any negative feedback. The team reported the appropriate overcorrection would consist of a combination of healing both the planet and women who had been sexually abused.

They planned for a reforestation of the Myayama tribal region of the rainforest. In addition, they would invest in helping women in remote areas who were the victims of sexual and physical abuse.

It was estimated it would cost $6.9 million to rectify the problem and bring a level of order to the chaos created.

Stig's team would be dismantled. Following the signing of a non-disclosure agreement by each of the loggers, they would then have their contracts terminated. In return, they would receive full pension along with a substantial golden handcuffs payment, based on years of service.

The company had also signed off on a $3.69 million donation to a South African charity called GreenMoM. For many years, this organisation had been at the forefront of "*A growing Treevolution*" in the world's most rapidly urbanising continent: Africa.

GreenMoM was appealing because it was a non-governmental organisation using the act of planting trees to enable the healing of women who had been sexually and physically abused. GreenMoM actively supported volunteers who had been sexually abused to join in this work as a way of enabling their healing. The women were empowered to get back into nature and rehabilitate themselves, by being a part of a bigger project.

As a highly respectable NGO, GreenMoM maximised the value of every cent donated. It had perfected a method of dense tree planting that allowed for the re-establishment of vital waterways to enhance the existing conditions in regenerating the natural vegetation.

When the logging company talked with the GreenMoM founder, she detailed how their approach to regenerating the Amazon would consist of creating habitats that stabilised the soils and watersheds that provide lifeblood to the grasslands of the area.

The rainforests could then return to being a vital supply of food, medicines and building materials for the Myayama tribe over the coming years. It was not a perfect solution for the tribe, but it was a good start.

The fact it was a South African NGO was specifically appealing to the logging company because of the serious nature of the crimes under the tenure of the private military and board members believed it would enhance the feel-good factor of the PR campaign.

Teams of African women would fly in for three weeks at a time and help reforest the area. This was also done as a mark of respect for the female members of the Myayama tribe.

The board was happy to pay for all travel and boarding costs of the female teams from Africa to fly into the Amazon, as they volunteered on rotation to help regenerate the region.

The board would send in an all-female media team to collect footage of the events unfolding. Within six months, it was planned the organisation would pass the land back to the tribespeople, in a handover ceremony, which would provide impactful PR for the company's website and social media channels.

The company was doing it to limit negative PR. Nonetheless, for the tribespeople, those healing from sexual assault and for the health of Mother Earth, this was a massive step in the right direction.

After finishing the call, Mickey then hopped into the passenger side of the car. He was silent as Tracy drove him, her daughter and the twins to the church for Angel's memorial service.

As the car pulled off, Richard noted the only words Mickey said throughout the call were:

> *"You have my full support."*
> *"This is the appropriate response."*
> *"Thank you for making this happen."*

Richard then knew his father was for real. He had genuinely changed. He wanted to not only rectify the mistakes of the past, but he wanted to prevent them from happening again.

Mickey's actions would lead to his closest friends and work colleagues losing their jobs. He knew that would happen. It was not a decision he had made lightly. However, he knew it was for the greater good. Changes were needed and he understood he had to begin with the man in the mirror.

On this day, Angel would have been smiling down on Mickey, knowing he was working towards getting back to being the good man he truly was. The man that had swept her off her feet with his kindness, in their youth.

Hurt people may hurt people. But healing people can heal people.

In the church as the first three rows filled up, Emma, dressed in comfortable clothes with her hair tied back, sheepishly took a seat at the back row. She was flanked by her parents, who had flown into town to help with her recovery.

As Kate went to the altar, Richard proudly stood in the first row beside his father. Mickey held the hand of his new girlfriend.

In the row behind were some of Kate and Richard's friends. Anne did not attend. She had told Richard she could not make it, because of an upcoming assignment deadline, which was important to her. Richard completely understood.

Just as Kate composed herself to begin her reading, Richard felt his phone vibrating in his pocket. He ignored it. He wanted to savour the moment, with his twin sister giving a reading on behalf of their family for the first time.

Thirty seconds later, with Kate gracefully reading in front of a pride-filled congregation, his phone began to vibrate again. This time, Richard pulled it out of his pocket and glanced to see who was calling.

As he was looking at his phone, Mickey nudged him in the side.

There was no name saved to the number. That was not unusual as since his post had gone viral, journalists and bloggers had continued to call him.

Just as he was about to reject the call, he recognised it came from overseas. The number of the caller started with +31. It was the international dialling code of the Netherlands. Richard recognised it from his time there.

"Could it be?" he thought to himself.

His phone stopped buzzing.

"No. She is gone. Again.

"Forget it. It is just another journalist," he concluded silently.

As he put the phone back in his pocket, it vibrated once more. An SMS had come through from the same number. He quickly looked at the message. It simply said:

> Hey
> Can we talk?

With a smile, Richard thought: *"Definitely a Dutch journalist. Stereotypically direct and straight to the point."*

Still holding the phone in his hand, it vibrated again as another message came through. Reading the message, he froze.

It was from the same number. It was one word. It had six letters.

Signing off, it simply said:

Finishing her reading with a heavily restrained, contented smile, Kate strode back towards her seat as her father looked on with a sense of pride that lit up the church.

With time slowed down as Richard scanned the scene, a sense of clarity swept across his mind like never before.

His mother was right ...

"Everything is perfect. But not complete."

Continue the Conversation

Email	hello@PatrickHamiltonWalsh.com
Webpage	PatrickHamiltonWalsh.com
Facebook	PatrickHamiltonWalshPage
YouTube	PatrickHamiltonWalsh
Instagram	@PatrickHamiltonWalsh
Twitter	@PatrickHWalsh

Different parts of this book will resonate with different people, depending on where you are on your journey through life.

I would love to know what you take away from this book and what lines or paragraphs have most impacted you. So, if you would dare to share, please take a photo and share with me on Instagram (@PatrickHamiltonWalsh) and/or Twitter (@PatrickHWalsh) where I can easily receive and respond.

From a place of love, it is my sincere hope that this book inspired you, upset you, encouraged you, triggered you, empowered you, guided you and made you go through the entire spectrum of positive and negative emotions, as a reflection of life in our world.

Ultimately, as you read through *Forgive Me, Sister*, I hope that this book caused you to stop and think.

To think about who you really are. Your place in our world today and your place in our world in the coming years.

Wherever you are on your journey and whatever your current conclusions, I send you my love and support.

Patrick

Some of the inspiration for the multi-continental nature of *Forgive Me, Sister* came from my time traveling across the seven continents of our world and meeting weird, wonderful, kind, challenged and loving people every day.

For those interested in my path and how, despite growing up in "the unemployment blackspot of Europe," I managed to design and achieve my dream life, please consider reading either of the books listed below.

Available in paperback or for download from all online bookstores. Also available from Google Play Store and the App Store.

All profits from these books are donated to helping the homeless and the most vulnerable people in society.

Life is

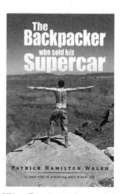

The Backpacker who
sold his Supercar

*"Awarded the Gold Seal of
Literary Excellence."*

If I could have or do any three things in the world what would they be?

This is the simple question that Patrick Hamilton Walsh asked himself at the age of 16. The answer to this question would lead him to living the life of his dreams.

'Life is' (full colour coffee table version) and *'The Backpacker who sold his Supercar'* (black and white version) detail, in an open and honest manner, the goals that Patrick set for himself as a sixteen-year-old and the mindset that he had to develop in order to achieve these goals. Upon the fulfilment of those early goals, Patrick set his sights on ever-greater goals, such as:

- *Travelling overland from London to Sydney*
- *Breaking a Guinness World Record for a good cause*
- *Owning a Porsche before age 30*
- *Swimming off the coast of every continent*
- *Attending dinner with the President*

In these books, Patrick reveals how he achieved his goals, gives an insight into each experience and details what he plans to do in the future. The final section of these books contains a surprising twist that everyone in this rat-race world will relate to.

These are books for anyone that carries unfulfilled potential or has a dream yet to be fulfilled. Ultimately, these are books for anyone that has the desire to do more.

> *"The book tends to be the most informative as far as giving insight into bettering one's life … it is Walsh's positivity and* enthusiasm *for life that makes this format work."*
> –The US Review of Books